COLD KEEP REPRISAL

James Lurid

Copyright © 2023 by Mitchel Wagar

Cover Design by Kayla Campbell
Author Photograph by Chelsea Blyth
Edited by Danny Raye

Harry McClintock's lyrics from *In The Big Rock Candy Mountains* used: Public domain.

First-ish edition: April 2024

Names: James Lurid, Mitchel Wagar, 1993 – Author
Title: Cold Keep Reprisal / James Lurid
Identifiers: ISBN 978-1-7390296-1-6 (Paperback) | ISBN 978-1-7390296-0-9 (Hardcover) | ISBN 978-1-7390296-3-0 (Audiobook) | ISBN 978-1-7390296-2-3 (E-book)

Dedicated to the children lost in
Indigenous schools across
North America

TABLE OF CONTENTS

Reprisal:

An act or instance of retaliation

PROLOGUE

1965

"It's back," Archie whispers into the receiver, his trembling finger forgetting to hold the button down. He grabs his Enfield and peers through its scope, eyes adjusting to the fresh blanket of snow beyond the rows of jagged barbed wire. Across the clearing, the sea of trees sway in the frigid breeze, playing tricks as their shadows dance across dirt and bush, waving to the stone goliath that is Cold Keep Penitentiary.

Archie turns and glances over the frozen complex, fixing on A- and C-Towers' dim glow in the darkness. The radio kicks on, jolting him upright as his finger squeezes the trigger, almost letting off a round.

Click. "Bravo, did you hear that?"

Archie lowers his rifle and shifts the receiver with a sweaty palm. "Yeah, Alpha. It's closer tonight." He jots down a note in his logbook and turns the lantern up, keeping the impending darkness beyond the glass walls at bay.

Click. "I've never seen two full-grown men

1

so goddamn scared of an animal in all my life. It's pitiful," Charlie spouts over the crackling static.

Click. "An animal? Listen to it. It's talking out there! You let any parrots out of their cages lately, Charlie? How about you, Bravo?"

The distant plea for help calls out from the woods, barely audible at first, then builds. "Please! Please!"

Click. "That! Does that sound like a damn animal to you? There's a woman out there!"

Click. "Do you know how many miles we are from the nearest town? There ain't no damsels in distress stumbling through the woods this far out. Especially in the middle of winter at night."

Archie picks the rifle back up and scans the tree line, listening to the men argue.

Click. "I haven't seen a real live woman for over two months now, not counting the lunch lady. I think I would know a dame calling out when I hear one."

Click. "Then why doesn't she call back, huh?"

Archie watches the lantern in C-Tower jostle and gleam off the opening window.

"Hello! Is anyone out there?" he yells, his voice distant, but firm,

Silence hangs in Archie's stale watchtower as he sweeps the perimeter with his scope, seeing nothing but snow-covered pines and the darkness between them.

Click. "See? Just a horny cougar searching for a mate. It's fine. There—"

"Please, yes! Help me, please!"

Click. "I told you!"

Click. "Shut the fuck up... Do either of you have eyes on her?"

The spruces waver and bend in Archie's crosshairs, shifting as something paces back and forth just beyond them. "Wait, I think I see her." He reaches up, flipping the spotlight on as the bulb flickers to life with an unhealthy hum, its light barely reaching the tree line. "Hello? Miss?" Another flash crosses his sights and he does a double take, narrowing in on bare, pale skin.

Click. "Where is she, Bravo?"

"Three hundred thirty degrees northwest, Charlie." Archie fidgets with the deteriorated box of ammunition on his desk, its crumbling paper flaking off between his busy fingernails.

Click. "Oh, yeah. I—Wait… is she naked?"

"I think so." Archie pushes his window open and yells, "Hello! Miss, do you need help?" but only his own voice echoes back.

Click. "Fuck it, I'm going down."

Click. "Are you out of your mind, Charlie? We should call it in."

Click. "You wanna wake the warden up, be my guest."

Static hums over the silent airwaves.

Click. "That's what I thought. I got my rifle, it's fine. Just keep your eyes on me."

The lantern passes through C-Tower's hatch and descends the ladder.

Click. "Bastard's lost his mind."

"Better than waking the warden," Archie admits, swinging the spotlight and focusing the beam on the guard, now on the ground and unlocking the gate leading to the field.

"Hello? Miss?" he calls out, shuffling through the snow, into the empty clearing.

"Here! Please!" she calls back, her voice bled of all emotion.

Archie presses the receiver. "Lost hunter, maybe?"

Click. "That's my guess."

"Why won't she come out?"

Click. "Bear trap?"

"I can see her pacing. She's not stuck in no trap." The spotlight flickers, and Archie jostles it as the beam straightens out on Charlie, now halfway across the field.

"Which way?" he calls out.

Archie swings the light, trailing the glow to the now empty section of trees. "I've… I've lost sight of her."

Click. "Me too."

The spotlight pops with one final flash and plunges the clearing into darkness. "Shit!" Archie smacks the metal housing and clicks the receiver. "Alpha, she finally bit the dust. Can you get your light on him?"

Click. "Mine won't reach."

The lantern creeps across the dark void, bobbing up and down with each trot as Charlie kicks through the heavy snow. "Hey, where's my fucking sunshine?"

"It's coming, sit tight!" Archie assures him, digging through the clutter of spare parts in the chest next to him, searching for the spare bulb.

Click. "Let's move, Bravo. It's dark out

there."

The lantern comes up on the line of trees and hovers there as Charlie's mumbled words call out to the girl somewhere in the wild.

Click. "What's the holdup, Bravo?"

"I said sit tight!" Archie snaps. He spares a glance out the window and pauses, ensnared by the two reflective eyes watching Charlie from the cover of trees.

Archie carefully lifts the receiver, afraid any sudden move will set the whole thing off, and whispers, "You see that, Alpha?" The wind falls from the sky and the vacuum of silence sucks the breath from his lungs as he watches Charlie raise his rifle, aiming it between the shimmering spots.

Click. "Yeah… a woman's peepers don't catch the light like that."

The two luminous points of light shift, then rise, climbing higher, then higher still from the forest floor, looming over the man.

"Jesus, that's not—"

The gun flashes as a crack of thunder lets off, and all at once the lantern blinks out, leaving the night to swallow Charlie whole.

Click. "Jesus! Bravo, get your goddamn light on!"

Archie turns from the scene and finds the bulb. He leans out the window, burning his fingers and almost dropping both sets as he twists the old one out and puts the new one in. It comes to life with a flicker, flooding the field with its brilliant glow, and he centers it, revealing nothing but empty tracks in the snow.

"Where is he, Alpha? Do you have eyes on him?" Archie doesn't wait for a response and turns the knob on the radio. "Emergency. Emergency. We need Boys-in-Blue on the perimeter. Now!"

The broadband hisses over the speaker, filling the night with an uneasy drawl, and Charlie's wavering voice calls out from the trees, cutting the silence, "H-hello?"

Archie breathes a sigh of relief, sweeping the tree line with light. "Are you okay? We've called for help!" No response comes and he turns the dial back. "Alpha, do you have eyes on him?"

More static crackles over the steady airwaves, and Archie checks the knobs. "Alpha, come in."

He turns to the darkness over the complex, no glow from either of the empty watchtowers, no points of light to tether him to the stone prison and lonely valley below.

"Alpha?"

Click. "…"

POINT AND SQUEEZE
1968

The smell of pine and tar shifts from Walter's nose deep into his throat as the twisted mass comes into focus and curdles into his tangled-up son. A crack rings out and a bullet tears through his shoulder, sending him splashing down into the pool of his own boy's blood.

"Walter!" A hand jostles him, sending sharp spasms through the scar tissue beneath his uniform. The tar and pine evaporate, revealing the musk of the parked patrol car's upholstery. Walter opens his eyes, hands already scrambling for the steering wheel in front of him, honking at the passing traffic on the interstate. "You were dreaming!" George says, palm gripping tight over his partner's hip.

Walter's eyelids flutter and he loosens off the wheel, cheeks flushed. "I'm—I'm fine. Got myself lost for a moment is—" The words catch in his throat as he spots George's hand laying over his holster. He throws it back, panic shifting to anger. "Get the hell off me! What are you doing touching another officer's shooter?"

"Sorry. You looked flustered, I thought—"

"You thought what? You thought I was just gonna pull my gun and start shooting at the Sandman. Was that it?"

"No, I was—"

"You weren't doing shit. Keep your hands to yourself, or next time I'll drag you out of this car and throw you in the middle of the interstate." He points to the automobiles barreling down the highway.

George drops his head, saying nothing as he reaches for the floor and picks up the large metallic box from between his feet.

Walter exhales, shaking off the last of the panic. "Just pass it by, kid; I shouldn't have dozed off." He slaps the dash and runs a hand through his graying hair. "I've asked the broad at the front counter a dozen times for a new mattress, but I'll be damned if I could even get a new pillow, for God's sake. I just woke up with a start is all, but you don't touch another man's pistol. You know that." He grabs the box from George and leans his good shoulder out the window, pointing it towards a passing Newport.

Click, hum. The roof vibrates and the screen blinks *54.*

George relaxes and adjusts his seatbelt.

"Why do you wear that thing all day?" Walter asks. "Most of these vehicles are more rust than rubber, and we get about as many speeders as homicides around here. But there you are, day after day pinned to your seat for hours on end."

Click, hum. The screen blinks *61.*

George tugs at his belt. "Duty calls at a

moment's notice. Gotta be ready for it."

Walter rolls his eyes. "In the three years I've been in Drywell, you know how many times I've pulled my gun, George? Once. I've pulled it once for that fox screaming out in those woods by Jack's farm, remember?"

"I do." George nods with a smirk.

"Three in the morning and that thing came running out from those woods sounding like a damsel being torn from the inside out. Still gives me the willies thinking about it today."

"You sure did scream, boss-man." George's smirk turns to a laugh.

Click, hum, 60.

Walter mutters to the ceiling, looking at the bolts used to secure the radar to the roof. "That thing up there is just beaming cancer into our skulls. Come thirty years the doctors are gonna find grapefruit-sized tumors right behind our eyeballs, I guarantee it. And don't call me that. I'm not anybody's boss out here."

"You don't miss it, being in charge?" George asks. "Nothing but lumpy mattresses and screaming foxes in Drywell."

Walter grips the handle with more purpose and closes one eye, staring down the radar's non-existent sights at a passing station wagon. "Not a bit."

Click, hum, 83.

"Got one." He tosses the gun on George's lap and struggles for his seatbelt, his shoulder screaming out in pain as another half smirk flashes across his partner's face. "Yeah, yeah, duty calls at a moment's notice," Walter mocks with a childish tone and throws an exaggerated salute to the steering wheel, popping the car into gear.

The sirens wail and the cruiser fast approaches the speeding car. Walter grinds his teeth, watching the orange hue of the shaking vehicle reflect the early morning sun while its rear tire spews a cloud of putrid tar smelling smoke with each rotation.

"Have you ever seen a vehicle go that fast with a bunked rim?" George asks. "It's too nice to be a reserve ride, so probably not a savage behind the wheel—"

"You best be careful throwing that word around. They are getting real tired of being called anything but Indians or Natives these days." Walter flicks his lights and pulls in closer, the smoke stinging his eyes as he tries to ignore the *click-clack* in the back of his mind. "I had a Native fellow pulled over for expired plates years back. He was a pleasant son-of-a-bitch, too. 'Yes, officer; no, officer,' and all that. He told me it was his fault, that he forgot to renew them with no other excuse than that." The driver ahead flashes a look at Walter's weathered frown in his rear-view mirror and signals, pulling to the shoulder of the road. "Good man."

"The Indian?"

"Right. Pleasant as can be. Nicer than a brunette with her tits hanging out, I swear. But the moron I was on patrol with told him to 'be a good little savage and sit tight.' Well, shit, I never saw eyes lose their color so fast. One second brown, the next gray and filled with burning hatred. I wasn't even the one who said it and the guy had me on the ground knocking my teeth in."

The station wagon creeps to a stop, its spent tire sinking into the soft dirt as a hand waves out the open window. The two unbuckle their belts and step out into the brisk air. "Snow's holding out," George comments, but Walter ignores him and continues.

"I'm just saying, the Natives are growing less tolerant, restless even. So don't be pushing any buttons with those kinds of names. You always show civilians respect, no matter their situation, race, or shit-box they're driving, you got that? The last thing we need is another damn rally."

They approach the vehicle and the young man inside digging through his glove box.

"S-sorry officers. License and insurance, yeah?" he calls to them before they have a chance to speak.

"License and registration. Not insurance," George corrects, but Walter holds a finger up.

"Let's put a pin in that. Sir, can you just stop for a moment and address my partner and I?"

The young man pulls away from the glove box with a curt smile and reaches out to shake Walter's hand.

"I don't shake, son. Not while I'm working," Walter says with an apologetic nod. "Now, let's just start with a simple question. Are you aware of the tire you've been dragging?" A shudder rolls down his spine as the smell of the forest entangles the smoking tar and he buries a tooth into his lip, trying to distract himself from his growing agitation.

"Oh shit! I had no idea." The driver adjusts

his side mirror and laughs at the black cloud rising in the reflection.

"And the speed?"

"Golly, I know even less, officer." His wavering gaze looks to George's name tag, his eyes straining to make sense of the letters. "Officer... George Laundry, huh? That's an odd name. Officer Laundry, how-how fast do you think I was going?"

"Cut the bullshit—" Walter pauses, his cheeks flushing red as the driver stares up at him with bloodshot eyes. "You uh... you been drinking this morning, mister... what was it again?"

The man's coy smile fades and he pulls his visor down, covering his face with shade. "Close to seventy if the old speedometer is telling the truth. She's pretty honest."

"Try eighty-three," George says.

The burnt orange finish glimmers in Walter's eye and the tar and pine works away at something inside him. He looks down at the puddle of black oil pooling between his feet and the uneasy *click-clack* calls to him from below.

"My partner here asked you if you had been drinking. You seem to be a question or two behind," George says, looking to Walter for confirmation, but he stares, enamored with the spreading darkness on the pavement. George waits a moment longer, then peers back at the driver. "There's the ticket." He gives Walter a nudge. "Bottle of hooch, right there."

The dark spot grows, consuming Walter as it spreads, redirecting around his shoe as the driver argues. "Oh, come on, Laundry. The roads ain't busy today. Only one in danger is me. A nip here and there ain't gonna hurt nobody."

The oil snaps out of focus and Walter looks up. "Did you really think you wouldn't hurt anybody? Or maybe you just didn't care if you did, Marvin."

The man looks around his empty car. "You talking to me? I don't know any Marvin, officer." He reaches for his wallet and pulls out a brown square for him to take. "Haven't hurt nobody today."

Walter snaps the license from his outstretched hand. "Not sure you are in the best shape to be climbing back behind that wheel." The paper slips from between his trembling fingers and floats down into the sticky pool below.

George breaks his assured stance, and his concern shifts to his partner. "Now, Walt, you okay?" He puts a hand on his arm, but Walter jerks it away.

"Right as rain. This piece of shit says he slammed on the brakes for a stray cat. Probably belongs to one of the neighbors down the way."

"What the hell is he talking about?" the man asks George.

Walter drops to his knee, reaching for the driver's license, his eyes following the black puddle under the chassis. "Jesus Christ!" He pushes George back and throws himself through the driver's window, grabbing the young man by the neck. "Somebody call an ambulance!" His fist rises and comes down hard into his brow. "You fucker. I'll put you in the ground for this! Somebody call 911. My boy needs help!" He pounds the roof. "Back this piece of shit up, you idiot. Put it in reverse!"

The young man complies, and he reverses the car, revealing nothing but the lonely oil stain in the center of the road.

"He's making a run for it, George. Call it in!" Walter dives back through the window and sinks another fist into his cheek.

"What the hell is going on?" George attempts to pull him back, but an elbow catches him on a backswing and his nose lets out a crack as he fumbles backwards with a tug of Walter's belt on the way down.

Walter's fists rise and fall, each striking harder than the last as the *click-clack* calls out from under the vehicle and something tugs at the cuff of his pants. His eyes roll to the back of his skull in a trance and with one thoughtless, uncalculated motion, he draws for his gun, points between the innocent man's eyes, and squeezes.

FROZEN CARROTS

"Officer Edwards, we have calmed down, I see."

Walter jolts in his seat, eyes fluttering open and adjusting to the interrogation room's fluorescent light as Sergeant Blyth enters. Behind him, George follows with a bag of frozen carrots held between his two swollen eyes, and the two sit on the other side of the table. "Tell me, Walter. How the hell does somebody go from the fit you were in, to sleeping in a chair thirty minutes later?"

Walter cracks his dry lips and groans. "Guess you're just working me too hard, sarge." A forced smile turns to a cough and Walter narrows in on George's face. "Jesus. What the hell happened to you?"

George jerks himself upright, his chair letting out a squeal as Walter reaches out for the carrots. "What the hell happened to me? Maybe that radar really is eating away at that brain of yours. You! You happened to me, you idiot!"

"Just calm down, George." Blyth stands from his seat, looking down at Walter with more concern than anger.

Walter drops an arm on the table, propping himself up, but his caked bloody hands take him off guard and he swallows, grasping at the situation unfolding before him. "George, I—" he stutters, looking for the words. "You don't... I don't—"

"Do you know why you are here, Walt?" Blyth asks.

"Of course, I do!" He closes his eyes, taking a deep breath and sees his fists rain down on a young man's bloodied face in the darkness.

"So, then you are aware of what happened only half an hour ago between you and Mr. Laidlow? And why George here is icing his nose?"

"Laidlow? Who the hell is—"

"The goddamn kid, Walter! Look at your hands for Christ's sake!" Blyth yells. "Tell me what you did. I need to hear it from you right this second, because the story as I know it is going to put this entire department in a load of shit and you behind bars!"

Walter rubs his eyes and stars fill his vision as he wracks his brain, piecing the morning together. "Officer Laundry and I were patrolling Highway 27 this morning when we clocked an orange suburban going over the designated speed limit."

"Station wagon," George corrects.

"Right, station wagon. It was at that time we pulled over the driver who refused to give us his name and appeared to be under the influence of alcohol, though I saw no evidence of said liquor for certain."

"Except for the half empty bottle of hooch

sitting between his legs, but you were checked out long before that, weren't you, Walt? Miles away, all froze up and staring into nothing."

Blyth holds a finger out and silences George. "What next?"

Walter looks hard at Blyth and the warmth drains from his body as the recollection of drawing for his gun comes rushing back. *Jesus, I killed him,* he thinks. "I... I got angry, the smell of those tires and the—"

"You got angry?" Blyth's eyes droop, watching Walter less like a criminal now, and more like a confused old man.

"He—he handed me the license and it dropped. I went to pick it up, but under the chassis I saw..." His voice trails off before returning as a silent quiver. "I stood up straight, and I...I pulled my gun."

George lets out an abrupt grunt. "No, Walt, you thought Mr. Laidlow was reaching for your gun. He went to grab for his license as it was falling, and it set you off." He glares at Walter. "You remember that, don't you? Mr. Laidlow reaching for the license you dropped?"

Walter stares at George, mind reeling, desperate to make sense of the situation, and he nods. "That—that's right. I thought he was reaching for my pistol. In all that mess I suppose I must have struck George. I'm sorry, I didn't—"

Blyth holds another finger up and cocks his head. "Thank you, George. Leave Walter and I to speak privately. I want your full statement before your shift is over."

"Yes, sir." George stands, giving Walter one last look before pointing to the pistol on his hip and holding a finger to his lips as he slips out the door.

Walter stiffens in his chair and readies himself for the arrest as Blyth reaches into his pocket and pulls out his confiscated badge. "What the hell is going on with you, Edwards?"

Jesus. My girls. Will I see them before they haul me away? Walter stares at his badge and speaks. "Like George said, I thought he was reaching—"

Blyth's palm comes down hard on the table between them, anger soaking up his concern. "For fuck's sake! I can't put in my report that an officer with decades of experience did what he did because of a drunk twit reaching for his driver's license wrong!"

The badge leaves a small dent in the table as Blyth retracts his hand and Walter tries to think of a defense. "I didn't mean to do the kid in like that. There's gotta be something we can do here, something that—"

"Half a dozen people saw me dragging that bloodied boy into the hospital, Walt. Now if it was just you and me, we could get a fix on this whole thing, but George was with you, an officer so green he wouldn't even let his own mother off the hook for jaywalking. You think he's gonna be able to hold his word against an angry mob? Half our men ain't seen action bigger than when that mutt went feral and bit that little girl a few years back. And in all those years, you know how many of 'em massacred a civilian for driving sauced-up? None! Now I know damn well you didn't think he was reaching for your hip, and don't tell me any different. So, what the hell happened out there? Have you finally snapped?"

A silent moment of contemplation goes by, and Walter picks the blood from under his nails. "I'd rather be a murderer locked up in a prison than some loony in one of those sanitariums." He juts up from his chair, waiting for Blyth to reach for his cuffs. "I don't have anything more to say." He clenches his jaw, but his pride bubbles up and forces his mouth to run on. "These wannabes don't know jack. They treat their pistols like damn party poppers. None of them could handle that shit out there—"

Blyth throws himself up from his chair, joining Walter on his feet. "And neither can you, apparently!"

"That's not the point. The point is—"

"The point is, I got an entire town that's gonna want your ass on a pike by dinner. And if the only thing you can tell me is you thought he was reaching for your gun, then there is nothing, *nothing* I can do for you because a decorated officer like yourself should either know better or has forgotten what he knew in the first place! Now look me in the eyes and tell me the truth, because what I put in my report is going to determine what the hell I, and the boys upstairs, do with you. I can't help you if you don't help me, Walter. So tell me… Why?"

Walter grinds his teeth, tasting copper. "Do what you gotta do." He pivots on his heels, waiting for the cold metal to lock around his wrists.

Blyth sighs. "Don't be so damn dramatic. Now get the hell out of here until I can figure out what to do with your sorry ass."

Walter pauses, not sure if he heard correctly and turns back, seeing no sign of humor on his superior's face. "I—I don't—"

"Save it. Just get to Dr. Colp's. And I mean directly."

Anger washes over Walter at the mention of the name. "You can't be serious! Now?"

Blyth shoves the badge in his pocket and massages his brow. "At this point, Walter, you're a walking liability. We need a psychological evaluation done after an incident that involves a physical altercation. You know that. Even if you were the stupid son of a bitch that caused it."

"I'm fine, I just—"

Blyth grabs him by the collar and pins him against the cold bricks. "This isn't about you no more! You've put my job, George's job, John, Ron, Micky, Geoff's, all our fucking livelihoods at risk, you unhinged prick! Don't insult me by telling me you're fine when we both sure as shit know you are anything but. Now, I'm not asking. Get your ass in that shrink's office within the hour, or I really will slap your ass in a cell. Do you understand me?" He lets off Walter's shirt and ushers him to the door. "And clean yourself off for God's sake."

Without another word, Walter takes a wide step around Blyth and drifts towards the exit, preparing for the cruel joke to end with a team of men on the other side of the door. He opens it and walks through, his confusion doubling as he steps into the empty hall. As if in a dream, he makes for his locker, stripping his bloodied clothes and avoiding eye contact with the stains. A new pressed shirt covers a layer of his immediate guilt, but he still feels the filth just beneath the rough cotton as he scrubs his hands in the sink and paints the porcelain red. He hurries through the lobby, kicking the front door open to the late morning glow and steps outside, spotting George leaning against his truck. "What more is there to say, George? I'm sorry about the nose."

"I don't give a darn about the nose, Walter. What I care about is you."

"Well, don't." Walter fingers his keys and blows past him, swinging his truck door open. "I don't have time to talk, please—"

George slams it shut, nearly crushing Walter's hand. "Shut the hell up! The way I see it, you got nothing but time to talk now." George's serious nature catches Walter off guard as he steps in closer, demanding his compliance. "You know darn well I stuck my neck out for you back there, so how about you do me the courtesy of listening to me talk for a minute."

Walter gives in and allows George a meek nod.

"Good. You lost your grip on that highway back there, we both know it. Fine one minute and the next you're standing there like a vegetable. I saw under that car; there was nothing there, but you were sure screaming like there was. You don't think we know what happened to you and your family back on the coast? It's a small town; people talk. Been talking for years. It was an accident, what happened to Kevin—"

Walter pushes George and readies a fist. "You keep his name out of your mouth, you hear me?" He drops his hand and climbs into his truck, slamming the door as George yells after him.

"If it weren't for me, you would have killed that kid today, Walter! If I hadn't drawn that gun out of your holster before you pulled for it, you would have murdered that boy. I saw you pull the trigger you thought was there. Now I can't tell if you have come unglued or if you've been off your rocker since we met, but you—"

A gasp of air sucks into Walter's lungs and he collapses into his steering wheel, sobbing. "He's okay? The Laidlow kid?"

"No, he's not okay, Walter. Jesus! Kids got a fractured cheekbone, a broken nose, and most definitely a serious concussion. Nothing about him is okay."

"Oh, thank you! Thank you, God!" Walter weeps, wiping tears from his face.

"Wait… You didn't think you killed him… did you?"

Walter sits up and composes himself. "No, just forget it." With a shift of his key, he pops the clutch and the wheels spin, sending a cloud of tar into the air that mixes with the forest's pine. He speeds away and his feeling of relief shifts to terror as the stench sends a wave of panic through him and toys with his vision. *That fucking smell.* Beside him the passenger seat shifts with the red and blue outlines of twisted limbs, all contorting in his peripherals as the *click-clack* of splintered bones whisper, gnawing at his already fried nerves. "Fuck this." He glances at his watch and pulls the steering wheel hard, turning down a side street. "Dr. Colp can wait."

MR. SNICKLEFRITZ AND
THE PRINCESS

Walter stands on the front porch of his house, listening to the clack of Angie's heels shuffle from somewhere inside when the door swings open. "Hello, dearest," he says, trying to pull his eyes from the stoop.

Angie stifles a smile behind curling lips and forces it into a frown. "I thought we agreed you would call ahead, Walt."

"I know. I'm sorry. I had the day off, and I thought I'd walk Lorrie to school."

Angie stares with protest, but her face softens when his eyes meet hers. "You having the day off wouldn't have anything to do with you pummeling the Laidlow boy this morning, would it?"

Walter takes a step back. "News travels fast."

"The new neighbor said she saw you in the back of your own cruiser. That you were swearing up a storm, throwing elbows and knees, screaming bloody murder."

Nosy cow. "Just a misunderstanding between me and the boy is all, dear."

Angie's brow furrows behind her thick glasses, and she meets his gaze. "You know you don't get to call me that, Walter. No 'dear,' 'dearest,' or 'darling' either. Are the bedbugs in that seedy motel keeping you as warm at night as I would, *dear*?"

Walter bites his lip. "Old habits I suppose. You are still my wife, after all." Silence hangs between the two, and he takes another step back, feeling his heels hang over the step behind him. "How have things been?"

She scoffs, as if baffled by the question. "Oh, you know…living the dream. I met a nice guy the other day."

The blood drains from Walter's cheeks and Angie lets out a small self-amused laugh. "Relax." She pushes the door open and reveals a sleeping dog sprawled out in the hallway. "It's nice having a boy around. We almost forgot what it was like, and he's even better trained than you are." She giggles now, and Walter breathes easy.

He stares at the animal and considers asking why she hadn't consulted him first, but he doesn't, knowing better. "Not as handsome, though." He gives her a coy smile, and Angie flashes him a look that makes his heart yearn for her.

"That's up for debate." She toys with the doorknob. "How's Dr. Colp?"

Walter pauses. "Off for a visit with him after this, actually."

"Oh?" She looks hopeful for a moment, then

it fades. "Because of your incident with the kid?"

Walter nods. "I—I haven't been seeing him as of late, if I'm being truthful."

"I know."

"It's not like the sessions are costing us a fortune. With my union benefits and all that I—"

"What's costing us a fortune is a damn—" Angie lowers her voice and glances into the house. "It's having no daddy home every night to read bedtime stories, to pack lunches, and get his wife's rocks off every once in a while, that's costing us a fortune, Walt. Now I commend you for keeping good on the cheques. The pantry is always stocked, and you haven't missed a single birthday, dance recital, or school meeting between the two of us since you left."

"Since you kicked me out."

Angie takes a step, palms wringing the air. "You've always been welcome back, husband. You know that."

"Yeah, as long as I go and see Colp."

"As long as you work on yourself! Which you clearly haven't been doing. It's been three years, Walter. Three years since Kevin—"

Walter winces, and Angie points a finger.

"See? Right there. That right there is why you should be going to Colp's every single week. You can't even hear our son's name without physically reacting."

Walter bites his cheek, melting a small piece of guilt and bides himself enough time for a defense. "It's hard Angie. How can a man like Colp possibly understand what we have gone through? What we have dealt with?"

"There is no 'we', Walter. No 'gone through' with you." She takes another step and her lonely eyes meet his. "You've never dealt with or gone through any of it. You're still there lying in that street with the bullet in your shoulder." She closes the distance between them, and Walter's chest falls as the uncomfortable words spill from her lips. "The only difference is… I got up."

"Stop." He takes a step back and his foot falls through the air. His arms flail and Angie grabs his belt, pulling him in as he grabs hold of her, making his heart flutter as they lock eyes, but she pulls away and they both collect themselves.

"I—I never said you had to get better, Walt." Her voice takes on sadness and she retreats back to the doorway. "You just had to try, but instead you shack up in that motel, keep yourself busy every second of the day in order to avoid dealing with the mistake nobody has ever blamed you for."

Walter shudders and tries to control his breathing. "I would give anything to sleep in my own bed again, to eat dinner every night with my girls, Angie." He drops his head. "I don't need forgiveness… I need justice."

"Dammit, Walter!" Angie throws her hands up. "We've been having this same conversation for the last three years! I can't keep doing this. Whoever the man was that ran Kevin down is gone and he won't be found. Get yourself in that shrink's chair and start making strides, dammit. I'm not giving my love to a man who refuses to get better, who spends all his time chasing a ghost and is seen running around town kicking the piss out of the townsfolk that he swore to protect!"

The thump of small boots trickle down the stairs and the adults bite their tongues. Walter peers over Angie's shoulder, into the house, but his daughter looks up to him from behind Angie's legs. "Hi, Daddy," her meek voice calls out, both warming and shattering Walter's heart.

He drops and the small stones that dig into his knees go unnoticed as he smiles at her and puts on his best English accent. "Excuse me, miss, I am sorry to bother you, but is Lady Edwards on the grounds this fine morning?" Lorrie giggles and buries her face into her mother's leg. "Perhaps in the gardens, or maybe in the stables? If you could—" He pauses and puts his thumb to her chin, turning her face. "Could this be? Could it… Are you the long-lost Princess Lorrie?"

"It's me! You know it's me, Daddy!"

Angie covers her mouth trying to hide a smile but fails.

"Oh, pardon me, Princess. I hardly recognized you without your gowns. What is royalty such as yourself doing without her crown in public? How are the townspeople to know we are amongst an angel?" Lorrie's giggles grow to bouts of laughter, and Walter allows himself a smile, if only briefly.

"I don't know, Daddy. I don't have a crown."

Walter gasps. "A princess without a crown? Surely you must be mistaken. Come to think of it… on the way here I found something shiny, and I thought it must belong to someone as beautiful as you." He stretches his arm behind him and ignores the pain in his shoulder, refusing to let it take away from the moment with his daughter.

Lorrie steps out from behind her mother with curious, wandering eyes as Walter thrusts his arm back and forth, as if digging through an invisible sack and pulls out a dazzling aluminum tiara inlaid with glass jewels.

"It's beautiful!"

"Might it be yours, my Lady?"

Lorrie looks around the empty street. "Why yes, it is. Thank you, Mr. Snicklefritz."

Walter laughs and places it on her curly head. "Snicklefritz, eh? I like that."

Lorrie spins around and looks up at her mother. "Can I wear my crown to school, Mommy?"

Angie smiles. "Of course you can, darling. But that's no crown; Mr. Snicklefritz is mistaken, I'm afraid." She shakes her head at him with humorous pity. "Princesses do not wear crowns; they wear tiaras."

Walter throws his hands up in defeat. "Forgive me, Queen Sourpuss. I am but a lowly stable boy who does not know any better."

Lorrie bursts with another fit of laughter and repeats the words, clapping. "Queen Sourpuss, Queen Sourpuss!"

Walter laughs some more and takes in the moment as Angie waves him away. "It would be my honor to walk you to school this fine morning, if the Lady would be so inclined?" he asks.

Lorrie scoops up her bundle of books sitting next to the door and steps outside, grabbing hold of Walter's hand. "I would like that very much, Mr.

Snicklefritz."

Angie's laugh fades and her eyes sharpen, shooting him a playful glare. "I don't need a stable boy," she whispers as the pair turn and descend the stairs. "I need my King back. Now get in that chair and sort your head out, Mr. Snicklefritz. It's been long enough."

He smiles at her, and she smiles back, and even though Walter and his daughter talk only about dragons, ball gowns, and handsome princes the entire way to school with their hands wrapped tight, his heart pounds for every moment of it.

***

"You have a good day, my Lady." He bows to her as they stand at the front doors of her school, and she curtsies back, wrapping her arms around his leg with a tight squeeze.

"You too, Daddy." She lets go and Walter takes in her smile one more time as she steps through the doorway and disappears inside.

For a moment longer he stands there, holding onto the small moment of fleeting happiness, then lets the door close on his finger, ridding him of the undeserved joy and replacing it with the familiar comfort of pain.

SHRINKING FEELING

"It's been a while..."

"Not that long." Walter jostles, unable to get comfortable in his seat as Dr. Colp adjusts his glasses and flips through the manila folder in his lap.

"A little over a year is a while, Walt."

"Walter," he corrects him.

Colp clears his throat. "Right, Walter. Well, it's been a year, Walter. I was surprised when you stopped coming; I thought we made real progress last time we saw each other."

Walter rolls his eyes at the cliche line. "That's why. We made real progress like you said, and I didn't need you anymore."

"Really?"

"Really." A bubble of frustration builds in his gut.

"I don't mean to diminish the steps we have taken together, Walter, but you are sitting here today by no choice of your own. Your sergeant filled me in, and from the sound of it, you need some stability in your life now more than ever. Tell me, what exactly made you feel you no longer needed counseling?

"I'd rather not, Doc."

Colp sighs and closes the folder. "I'm going to put this as gently as possible, and please don't hold this against me, but this is not one of our regular sessions. This is a mandatory psychological evaluation that you are required to take part in if you are to have a chance at keeping your position within the Drywell County Police Department. Do you understand that, Walter?"

Walter bites his lip, drawing blood that masks the pine air for a moment and gives him time to take a breath. "Yes," he mumbles through clenched teeth.

"Then like I was saying." Colp opens the folder back up. "Last session we made some big strides. I felt you opened up and helped me understand your frustrations. Have you still been self-harming?" He looks down at Walter's sleeves.

"I don't see how that's relevant to what happened this morning," he says and pulls at his left cuff.

Colp closes the file again.

"Alright, alright," Walter stops him and rolls up his sleeves. "Yeah, I've still been doing it." His arms reveal tracks of scars, some fresh and dozens healed over, permanently discolored.

"And doing this still relieves your stress?"

"Something like that." Walter drops his arms on his lap. "I know you're just doing your job, Doc, but I don't think I have it in me to talk about where this is going."

Colp removes his glasses. "I know it's hard,

Walter, and we're going to approach these topics as gently as we can, but there are no other days, no months between sessions to ease our way into this. What I put in my report today will end up on your superior's desk, and he will use that to determine if you are fit to protect this community or not. So, let's just proceed slowly."

Walter takes another breath and pushes his tooth deeper into his tattered lip. "Fine."

Colp nods and flips a page. "Last session we talked of your self-harm and how it seems to bring you great relief, then of the distance growing between you and Angie."

"Lorrie, too."

"Right. How has that progressed? Do you still feel emotionally distanced from them?"

"Yes."

"And what about the guilt you harbor for what happened to Kevin?"

Walter jolts upright. "Please don't."

"Right, forgive me. What happened to your son, I mean. You are clearly still dealing with those emotions. Do they continue to keep you from feeling like you deserve your family's companionship, their love?"

Walter scans the room, spotting a box of children's toys in the corner and pushes himself up with his good arm, then saunters over, sifting through the items with purpose, happy for the distraction. "I thought you were going to approach gently." He picks out a red View-Master and holds it up to his face, seeing a dozen dwarfs lighting sticks of TNT embedded in a coal mine wall as Colp waits patiently.

"Believe it or not, Walter, this is the gentle approach."

The pine and tar sticks in his throat, working its way past the taste of blood and the slight *click-clack* rings in his ears from the corner of the room as he walks back, dropping himself into the chair. "What do you want me to say, Doc? I couldn't protect him. I've said it before, and I'll say it again. What kind of father wouldn't have guilt about letting his son wander out into the street while he was snoozing away in his recliner? I was the one who should have checked the latch on that screen door, so I'm the one who let that son-of-a-bitch run his boy down like a stray cat. So don't go asking me if I still feel undeserving of my family's companionship because there is no debating that. Nothing's changed; not unless you have seen my son walking around town, risen from the grave like Jesus Christ himself." His trembling hands flip the toy's lever and a dark-skinned man with flames rising from his palms replace the image of the coal mine.

Colp stands, walks over to the cabinet behind his seat, and opens it. A dozen bottles shine in the afternoon glow, pouring in from the window, and Walter admires the selection.

"How about a drink? It may be unorthodox, but we have established this is no ordinary session. It might loosen you up a bit."

"Do I seem uptight to you?" Walter asks.

"Drop the act. You've been honest with me before."

"A lot of things change in a year, Doc. I've

had time to ferment."

Colp raises the glass, offering once more, but Walter sulks and lets out a long exhale. "I'm more of a smoker." He pulls a pack from his pocket and lights a cigarette from the book of matches in the center of the spotless ashtray sitting between them.

"We all have our vices, Walter. You smoke; I drink." Colp pours a glass of dark liquid and sits back down, pushing the ashtray forward as Walter abandons the View-Master to the cushion next to him. The smoke furls deep into his lungs and the nicotine goes to work.

"Alright, so what was it then?" Colp asks.

"What was what?"

"The breakthrough. The one that made you feel like our visits were no longer necessary."

Walter's eyes gloss over for a moment and his mind drifts inwards.

"Well?" Colp insists, leaning in.

Walter blinks the distant thought away and brings himself back. "I uh… realized I had found a better way to get my"—he pauses, trying to think of a word other than revenge—"family back."

Colp jots something in his folder and Walter watches the pen scribble, wondering about the words, but chooses to take another drag of his cigarette instead of inquiring.

"That's great, but I'm not convinced your alternative method is quite working for you. What was it? Your better way?"

"Yoga," Walter blurts out, wishing he took a moment longer to think.

"Yoga?"

"Yeah, it's stretching mostly, but—"

"I know what yoga is."

"It's good for the heart; gets me sweating real good."

Colp slaps the folder on the table and finishes his drink with one swallow. "You realize I have a doctorate in psychology, yeah? *Human psychology.*"

"Yeah, that's why I'm here," Walter answers.

"Then why is it you think you can bullshit me?"

The smoke catches in Walter's throat and he fights back a cough. "I'm—I'm not bullshitting anybody, Doc."

"So, you, Walter Edwards, discovered the violent aftermath of your child's manslaughter—"

"Murder," Walter insists.

"Fine. Murder. Your child's murder at the hands of a drunk driver, then nearly bled out and died yourself after being shot by the same man. Then, after a long recovery you relocate your failing marriage to Drywell, hoping to ease your shellshock, only to live in a motel for months on end by yourself. And yoga fixed all of that? Stretching?" Colp fishes inside the table's drawer, pulls out a large stamp, and hovers it over the file without blinking.

Walter eyes the papers inside and wracks his mind for something more convincing to say. "Yeah... it's good for your—" The stamp comes down and Walters hands lunge out in defense. "Wait, no!"

Colp pauses.

"Okay. Just wait, Doc. Wait..."

"Why did you stop coming, Walt?"

"Walter."

"Why did you stop coming, Walter?"

"Fuck, fine! I found him!" He throws his hands on the folder, swiping it off the table, sending papers and hand-written notes raining down. "I found the bastard, alright?"

"Who?"

"Who do you think? His ugly mug was right next to the Sunday funnies. Page twenty-seven one morning when I was reading my paper. A footnote, an afterthought. The man who killed my boy and tried to do me in was on page twenty-fucking-seven, right after an article about goddamn geese. Geese, Doc! I turn the page after reading about migration patterns, and there's the son-of-a-bitch's face staring back at me with his two greasy eyes set between two even greasier sideburns. All for a crime that wasn't even related to my boy. He got pinched for murdering some poor schmuck in a mugging gone wrong. Nobody the wiser to what he did to my boy, my wife, me! Marvin! Marvin-fucking-Wilmore is the reason I stopped coming. So there, jot it down quick!"

Walter takes another puff of his cigarette and sighs the smoke out, his anger now sadness. "The man is behind bars. Locked up on the other side of the country in some prison called Cold Keep."

Colp straightens up, interested. "Well, you know where he is then. This is a good thing, Walter. Go see him. Confront him and get some closure."

"I've tried. You don't think I've tried? I made it most of the way once. Told Angie I was going to some lock and key convention and hightailed it out there only to make it halfway before I lost my nerve and turned back."

"You haven't told her you found him?"

"I haven't told a soul, Doc. Just you."

"Why wouldn't you tell your own wife?"

"What would I wanna set her back like that for? She's moved on."

"We both know that's not true."

"No… I know, I know."

"Maybe you were afraid she would push you into confronting him. Could that be it?"

Walter pauses and picks up the View-Master once more.

"Put that damn thing down and answer my question."

He squeezes the toy and its plastic groans as the pine and tar dig deeper, the *click-clack* growing louder. "Could be that," he lies and pictures his confiscated pistol blowing a hole between Marvin's sideburns.

"Or maybe you don't trust what you would do if you did meet with him," Colp says.

Walter takes another drag of smoke, holding it in with the flood of tears building behind his eyelids. "Neither here nor there, Doc. What's the difference? The bastard's locked up and that's that. There's no proof of what he did that day anyway. No making him responsible for my wife and daughter discovering me out there on the street in a pool of mixed blood. He's locked up for life with no chance of parole. It's done. It's over. It's page twenty-seven news."

"But he's been locked up for good," Colp

argues. "Sure, it wasn't because of what he did to your boy, but he's never going to see the light of day. Can't you take some solace in that? Can't you move on?"

Walter's tears break free, and he drops his head, hiding his brow from Colp as he fights for breath between sobs. "It's never going to stop being my fault. It's etched in stone until the day the devil drags me down to his pits of hell." He lifts the View-Master and peers through, putting another layer of defense between him and the world. The image of a gnarled hand holding out a loaf of bread from between two dead trees sends a shiver down his spine, and he looks away. "So I occasionally put a cigarette out on my arm, run my straight razor across my thigh here and there. Not because I like it; not at first, but to remind myself that I don't get off easy. I don't get to smile and laugh because I know I'm always only one small trigger away from seeing him again."

"Marvin?"

"My boy. There, right in the corner of my eye. When I get to feeling too tired, angry, or overwhelmed, the smell of that day comes rushing back; those burning skid marks from the tires that didn't stop in time fill my nose, and Marvin's pine breath reeking of gin creeps across my tongue. That tar and pine, they're a warning. And when I can't swallow them down, when they overwhelm me, there he is, Kevin's blue jean jacket soaked with his red blood, his bones *clicking* and *clacking* as he crawls his way into view on broken arms and twisted legs. I've never worked up the nerve to look, but I know it's him, choking on his mouth full of broken teeth, waiting, just waiting for me to put a bullet in my skull so the devil can wrap himself around my soul and take me down to where I belong. This very second, even, my boy's in the corner by the shelf, beckoning me to look over and face what I did to him, face what I turned him into."

"Jesus," Colp whispers.

Walter wipes his tears away. "I can't even remember how he used to be. Every time I picture his face I just see a tangled mess, and in the center of it that bastard Marvin is staring back. His greasy eyes shining over his toothy grin like he's happy about what he did. It makes me sick to think about my boy now. I couldn't even show my face at his funeral. My pathetic ass left my confused daughter and mourning wife to weep in arms that weren't my own, all while I stood not eighty feet away on the curb, smoking a cigarette, unable to open that chapel door. How sick is that?"

Colp thumbs his glass. "It's certainly not healthy, but we all deal with grief differently, Walter."

Walter drops the View-Master and melts in his seat. "Stamp what you gotta stamp, Doc. Just send me home, please... I'm tired."

Colp rises from his seat and herds the papers back into Walter's file. "I can't pretend to know the pain you are in, Walter, but it's clear you desperately need peace in your life. You did not kill your boy."

"Yes, I did."

"No, you did not! This Marvin person did. I know that and so do you. It's time to start with the healing, with the forgiving."

"Forgiving? I'm not forgiving that asshole."

"Not him; you, dammit. Yourself."

Walter extinguishes his cigarette and lights another, letting the smoke escape through his nose. "I send him letters, you know."

"You do?"

"Two a week since he landed himself in Cold Keep."

"What kind of letters?"

The crackling tobacco fills the silence, and Walter pulls another long drag, but doesn't bother to inhale. "Mean ones, mostly."

Colp picks up the last of the papers and taps the folder into order. "And does he write back?"

"Just once."

"And?"

Walter shakes his head. "Said he would remember running down some gutter punk kid." The smoke floats up, burning his eyes as he blinks, thankful for the pain. "He doesn't even remember killing him."

"Well, he wouldn't admit it even if he did."

"No, but I could tell. It's my business reading folks. Not as much as you, of course, but part of the job all the same. He really doesn't remember a thing."

"Maybe it wasn't him. Maybe you got the wrong guy and convinced yourself it was him out of desperation for some kind of resolution to your anger. A face to blame."

Walter pulls the cigarette from his lips and points it at Colp. "See, I thought that, too. But I checked his name against the registries. Burnt orange, 1957 GMC. The very one he used to snuff my kid out."

"Shit…"

"Yeah… shit." Walter stamps the smoke out next to his last, giving up on it. "I've tried it all, Doc. No matter which way you swing it, I should have checked the latch, so let's just get on with the stamping. Like I said, I'm tired, and I've got an especially mean letter to write before going to sleep on the shitty motel mattress that I plan to die on. If I'm lucky it will be sooner rather than later."

Colp flashes a look of concern.

"Oh, relax," Walter huffs. "I'm not going anywhere as long as my girls are around."

Colp goes to speak but refrains and places the stamp back in the drawer, then slides the folder to the center of the table. "Do you know how much I charge an hour, Walter?"

"Not a clue," he answers.

"I know you don't. I know because the government you work for, our government, signs my cheques. You don't pay me a dime. Suppose you lose your job over this. I can say with the utmost certainty that you and I wouldn't be making any further progress together, good or bad. Now, I want to see you get better; I ache seeing you blame yourself for something nobody else blames you for. So, I'm going to tell your sergeant that you are going to commit to weekly sessions with me. And I mean weekly. None of the six months here, a full year there hiatus bullshit either. You hear me? And I'm going to leave what happens concerning your job up to your boss. I'm not deciding your fate; that's for you to do. No red stamps as long as you come see me week after week until I say otherwise. Can you do that?"

Walter nods, feeling his tired brain wobble inside his skull. "What choice do I have?"

"Very little by the sounds of it." Colp smiles and reaches a hand out, pulling Walter from his chair. "Now go home and get some rest. Are you okay to drive?"

"Yeah." Walter turns, avoiding eye contact with the blue and red corner.

Colp opens the door, pushing Walter through with an encouraging but painful squeeze of his shoulder, and he winces, feeling the small rush of endorphins calm his nerves as he steps out.

"We will see you next week," Colp says, unconvinced.

"Here's to hoping." Walter nods and glides out into the hall, the door closing and leaving him on his own.

***

Walter pulls into the motel parking lot after the short drive home and spots George leaning against their cruiser in his spot. He cringes at his partners swollen face and steps out of his truck with a nod. "George." He points awkwardly at his nose. "Looks like that's… swelling up nicely."

George stares, unamused. "I really think the purple brings out the color in my uniform. What do you think?" he asks. "There's been chatter non-stop about you on the radios since you left." He pulls out a stack of papers from his back pocket. "I need you to sign my statement."

Walter snatches the papers and signs them with the pen plucked from George's breast pocket, wanting nothing more than to just be left alone.

"Don't you want to read it?" George asks.

Walter clicks the pen and returns it. "No need. Like you said, I was checked out for the big show. As far as I'm concerned, it's you with the story to tell, not me."

George nods, shoving the papers back into his pocket. "Blyth has been locked up in his office all afternoon. Damage control would be my guess. You got a lot of folks talking up a storm around town, that's for sure."

"Is that all, George?"

"No. Blyth wants you out at the Heslup farm first thing in the morning."

"Heslup's? Why?"

"I don't have the details, but I'm supposed to deliver you myself. Blyth thinks it would be good for the healing process between you and I, but I think we can both agree it's best you find your own way there, yeah?"

Walter climbs the steps to the second-floor walkway and turns, looking down at his partner. "George?"

"What is it, Walter?"

"I pulled for my gun... I know it, and you know it. If it weren't for you, I would be sitting in a cell and there would be a hell of a lot more than just townsfolk talking right now. If you hadn't snatched that gun from my holster, I—" He swallows hard. "Well, we know what you did. What you stopped me from doing, and I didn't thank you for it. Not to mention the courtesy you did me by keeping it to yourself." Walter stands silent and George's face hardens, looking up at him.

"I know why you did what you did, Walter. You pretend you're fine and we pretend you're fine, that everything is business as usual. Until one day a civilian takes a bullet for jaywalking, and you land this town on every newsstand in the country. I pulled your gun to save that kid's life. I didn't do it for you. And the only reason I didn't report what you did is because of that little girl you got at home. Now I don't know what Blyth intends to do with you, but I sure as hell advocated that he keeps that gun away from you, and you away from me. So, get yourself together and get to Heslup's first thing in the morning." He turns without another word and climbs into the cruiser, leaving Walter standing with his apology in his hand.

Walter turns and steps into the dark, musky room where the beer-stained lampshade lights his home. Without wasting a moment, he slides into the flimsy chair, fishes a blank sheet of paper from the dwindling stack in one of the desk drawers, and feeds it into his typewriter, clacking away at the keys.

Dear Fucker:

CONSTABLE SHOVE-AND-STUFF

Happy to be out of city limits, Walter pulls up to the Heslup farm and steps out of his truck to Phyllis's shrill voice as she strides over with Blyth trailing close behind.

"Well, if it isn't Officer Shove-and-Stuff. Hey, Officer Shove-and-Stuff, I got a few overdue parking tickets. Would you like to loosen my pearly whites now, or later?"

"That's enough, Phyllis," Blyth says. "Do you want those traps cleared or not? I got words with Walt here, and I don't need your nagging cluttering up my morning air."

Phyllis looks Walter up and down, then storms up the porch and into the house. "Do any of you want something to drink?" she calls from inside.

"No, thank you, Phyllis. We will be out of your hair soon enough," Blyth calls back, untying a burlap sack from his belt and turning to Walter. "How're the hands?"

"Drying up. They hurt to squeeze," Walter answers, flexing his fingers open and closed.

"Good." Blyth eyes the dried over scabs as they wind between the trees, pushing further into the property.

"I was thinking, Sarge, if I can still call you that. I don't—"

"I've got people in town calling for your resignation, Walter. Demanding I do something about the loose cannon I got on my squad."

Walter's mouth dries. "I don't have an excuse for what I did to that kid, Blyth." He steps over a log, spotting a metal trap fifty paces ahead, and within, a dark mass shuffles back and forth. "The wife is telling me that if she doesn't see me making strides in the shrink's office, I can kiss my daughter goodbye."

"She said that?"

"Well… no. But it's coming, I can tell. Do you know what a doctor like Colp charges just to listen to someone flap their gums for an hour? It's a hell of a lot more than I can afford, that's for sure. Listen, I'll do what it takes to make things right. I can't lose this job. The pension alone —"

"Nobody's losing their job, Walter. Relax. Colp gave you the all-clear. Reluctantly, of course, but he said you both came to an agreement. If that is the case then there may still be hope for you yet."

Walter blinks, hardly believing the words as he repeats them back. "Nobody's losing their job? Y-you mean. I'm not—"

"That's the beauty of the Union, Walt." Blyth lifts the sack and pulls out a pair of thick leather gloves from inside. "But repercussions are being called for, you bet your ass. I spent the better part of yesterday evening in Laidlow's hospital room striking a deal with him to keep this incident off the books, and he agreed to not press charges in exchange for all the money we had in the picnic fund, which was well over eighty dollars. And you be sure as shit I ain't gonna be the one to tell the boys there's not gonna be any frankfurters come June. That one is on you."

"That's all?" Walter asks.

"That, and the kid's got diplomatic immunity within Drywell from now until his balls drag on the ground from old age. Any and all incidents regarding him will be handled by me and me alone from here on out. And you are to stay the hell away from him at all costs, you hear me? Him and his entire family." He slips the gloves on and pulls them up to his elbows. "You know this town, Walter. People talk and whisper and talk some more. Everyone up to Stillheart County knows what you did to that kid's face."

They come up on the steel cage and a black ball of fur jumps at the sound of them approaching, rearing its masked face upwards. Its small fingers spread, it bares its teeth, and its striped tail puffs out like a willow. Blyth holds the bag out, stepping on the trap's release, and the hatch swings open. In an instant the confident raccoon's facade withers away and its growls fade to a whimper. Blyth reaches his arm deep into the box, clambering at the creature huddled against the back as he pinches at tufts of fur within, giving them a sharp tug and gaining himself a better grip. Its scared whimpers turn back to bared fangs as its teeth sink deep into the glove, its back legs scratching frantically, trying to do as much damage as possible. Blyth shoves it into the sack as it screams and he swings the bag through the air in a wide arc, silencing the creature within.

Walter stares and his superior speaks, as if reading his mind. "Makes the buggers dizzy, forces 'em to be docile for a bit."

They wind between a few more trees, and Walter spots another box ahead as the leaves crunch beneath their feet.

"There ain't no explaining away why you did what you did, Walt. Now you won't say why, but we both know you've got your demons." Blyth stops and stares hard at Walter. "You've come unhinged. Maybe not all the way but you are coming loose at the seams."

Walter wants to argue, but he knows the words are true. "Sergeant, I—"

"I know never finding that bastard stopped you and the Missus from getting any closure, and that must be damn hard. When you came over from the coast, your recommendation letter followed with a few words of warning, but I looked past it. And considering the biggest criminals we get out in these parts are nipping dogs who we can't arrest and the town drunk who needs driving home three times a week, I figured you'd be able to handle your own. But I've been watching the cracks form for some time now and nobody's blaming you, son. How could they? But I got a mob on my hands, and just like you, they want closure on an injustice that has been done to one of their own."

Walter takes the sack from Blyth and slips the glove on as they approach the trap. Inside another even larger raccoon raises its hackles and bares its teeth. "So, what then? A public flogging in the town square? A stoning perhaps?" He steps on the release and the raised hackles drop; its bared teeth turn to belly up as he pinches its foot and tugs. A scream comes again, and a tooth finds its way through the glove. It sinks into his finger, sending a jolt up his arm and he winces, pushing his flesh against it, sinking it deeper as the pain calms his nerves. He pulls the animal out and gently lowers it into the bag next to the other. The sack explodes into another fit and Blyth grabs it with another swing, instantly calming the creatures within.

"We're not gonna stone ya. Nothing so barbaric." Blyth purses his lips and drops his head. "A transfer."

"A transfer?" Walter stares through him. "Have you lost your mind? I—I can't fucking transfer! I got a marriage on the rocks, Sarge. I could barely convince Angie to move out here when we were still doing the dirty. We're barely talking these days, and you think I got a chance of getting her and Lorrie to follow me anywhere now?"

Blyth holds his hands up, trying to put a pause on Walter's downward spiral. "Relax, Walter. Hold up now! Transfer isn't the right word. A leave of absence is more like it. Some time to let things cool down."

Walter turns to the trap near a clearing in the trees and he heads towards it, Blyth following close behind.

"Hear me out, Walt. It's a complicated situation we're in, but nobody's relocating. Just calm your ass down and let's start over." He rests a hand on Walter's bad shoulder and a moment of silence brings down the tension. "A while back there was a call sent out for a volunteer to help with something out east."

"How far east?" Walter asks, feeling a trickle of blood run down his finger inside the glove.

"Far. Just listen."

They come up on the trap, and inside, a kit shows its belly, pleading for its life, causing Walter to feel a pang of guilt for making the innocent thing fear him. "I'm listening." He takes the sack back from Blyth and tips the cage, pouring the baby directly inside before swinging them in another large arch.

"There's a min-max prison with a problem." Blyth continues. "Well, more of a problem prison if you want to get poetic about it. In the Missinaibi. A real stone mortar mother of a stronghold. I was there myself once, overseeing a transfer years back when I was just starting out. The place is something to see. Solid iron walkways; none of this cheap aluminum bullshit they got out here, and the—"

"I'm no prison guard, Blyth." Walter hands him the bag of chattering mammals and they head back towards the driveway.

"It's no guard job, let me finish. The problem is the Warden. Nobody can seem to get any answers out of him. Can't get any answers out of anyone out in those parts, really."

"What sort of answers?" Walter Asks.

Blyth's expression darkens. "The mortality rates... Nobody has an exact number because the boys running the joint won't send any statistics, but in the year before last, multiple men who were set to walk free didn't do any walking at all. It was only after the families came asking questions did they pronounce 'em dead. Same the next year, too. Deaths are six, maybe even seven times the normal rate of lockups. The violence is off the charts and that's saying something about a place like that."

"Nothing strange about a prison with violence, Blyth."

"Not this much. I thought it was a joke, that the numbers couldn't be right until a while back the commissioner of the district called me up asking if I had anyone that could help with the situation. They tried sending in auditors but only came away with reports of malnutrition picking off the poor bastards and violent outbursts resulting in inmate-on-inmate fatalities. But the food shipments leave no reason for there to be mouths unfed and when offered extra guards, the warden himself turned them down. Needless to say, heads are starting to turn."

A cold breeze works its way through the trees and cools Walter's flushed neck. "I can interrogate just as well as the rest of them, Sarge, but I don't see why they would ask for one of us to get involved. Why would a commissioner be looking for an interrogator this far from home?"

"He wasn't looking for someone to ask questions; he was looking for an unfamiliar face. For someone who has zero ties with the criminals locked in there, someone who can hold their own in a pinch. You're not gonna find a single law officer out in those parts that hasn't put away at least one of those men behind its bars. They're not calling for an interrogator, they're calling for someone to go in themselves, unrecognized."

"Undercover or not, I told you I'm no guard."

Blyth shakes his head and stops Walter by the arm. "Not a guard. An inmate. You go in as one of 'em, get a good look at the cogs spinning around inside, and then we file for a transfer and get you out with none the wiser."

Walter waves Blyth away. "Hell no, Sarge. Are you kidding me?"

"It's a win-win, Walter. We tell the pissed off townsfolk that you're on suspension, anger management, rehabilitation, or some shit like that. It eases their nerves showing 'em you aren't getting off easy, and in the meantime, we help our brothers in arms. We will have you back before you know it and we can all get back to being normal. Tickety-boo. Plus, maybe you could let some of those demons of yours out on the goons inside while you're at it." Blyth lets out a laugh but swallows it down. "No, no, forget I said that. You'll wanna keep a low profile in a place like that."

Walter looks over the harvested fields and shakes his head. "Listen, Blyth... that's a fine offer, and a unique one at that, but I just can't leave my girls right now. Things are fragile. A week could be enough to push what little I got left of this marriage over the edge. There's got to be some other way, some other option. Isn't seeing Colp enough? I'll carry a baton, forfeit my gun for a bit. How about that?"

Blyth turns, closing in on his cruiser as he digs his keys from his pocket. "There is another option," he calls back. "It's kicking your ass to the curb. Now, I've put my neck out seven inches farther than I would for anyone else on the force, Walter. So you got two options and two options only: Pack your suitcase or pack your desk because I've already told the big wigs that I'm sending a man tomorrow, and that man better be you."

Walter catches up and imagines shoving Blyth into the sack with the three raccoons, then giving it a shake. "I put men in jail, I don't join them." The *click-clack* calls out from the woods but Walter pushes it down. "You give George a call and tell him he better get his prison stripes pressed because it's not gonna be me going in." He shoves the sack into Blyth's hand and storms past the cruiser, swinging his truck door open with a pained squeal.

"You know as well as I do those boys in Cold Keep would eat George alive. Don't be a fool!" Blyth shouts.

"I've made my choice!" Walter drops himself into the driver's seat and pulls on the door, but the words echo in his mind. "Wait… What did you say?"

"I said he wouldn't make it a day in there. The kid reeks like Rookie of the Year. The inmates would find him out in a second."

"Not that. The name. The name of the place."

Blyth smiles, sensing Walter's interest. "Cold Keep. Just north of Kasabonika… Why?"

The name bounces around Walter's skull and the world spins around him as he sits frozen in place.

"What's the problem?" Blyth takes a step closer, raising an eyebrow.

Walter shakes his paralysis and clears his throat. "N-nothing. I'll do it. A few days, that's all."

"Eight," Blyth says.

"Three," Walter rebuttals.

"Five."

"Fine."

Blyth straightens up and shakes Walter's hand. "Five days, you have my word. It will be good for you." He bends over and picks up a fist sized rock, dropping it in the sack with a softened thud. "I would say go home and pack a bag, but all you are gonna need in there are your striped pajamas, so maybe just go tell the missus." He ties a knot in the burlap and lowers the sack into the bed of Walter's truck.

"Best she doesn't know. I'll just tell her I'm going to another seminar in the city, and you will back me up if she comes asking. That's gotta be part of the deal."

"Whatever you want, big city cop." Blyth winks. "Oh, and drop the rodents off the bridge on your way back into town. I'm gonna swallow down a glass of Phyllis's iced tea before hitting the road. I'll arrange for the transfer first thing tomorrow morning. You just be sure you shit, shower, and shave before you get on the bus."

The sack shifts in Walter's rearview mirror as he tries to collect his thoughts. "Aye-aye, captain." He flashes a half convincing smile and pulls out of the driveway, hardly believing the last thirty seconds, sure it must be some kind of mistake.

Cold Keep, he thinks, throwing the truck into gear and pulling to the edge of the driveway. He sits at the crossroads for another moment, and instead of turning right towards town, he pulls the wheel left, following the forestry road for the better part of an hour. On the way he repeats the name in disbelief until he is sure he has traveled far enough out of town and pulls to the side of the road, killing the engine.

Cold Keep.

He steps out and reaches into the flatbed, untying the knot in the burlap sack. The three bandits stare up at him with fearful eyes from inside as he gently lowers them to the ground. One by one they creep out of the bag, smelling the wild forest air that makes him sick, and skitter off into the trees. Walter watches as their thick tails wobble left and right, lurching into their new home as he pulls out the rock from the bottom of the sack. He holds it up, visualizing Marvin's smug face in the center and wraps his hands around the neck of it, twisting with one violent jerk, hearing the snap in his mind. The stone tumbles to the ground and he whispers under his breath, afraid the words will call the whole thing off.

"Cold Keep."

SMOKE?

The bus winds through the unkempt roads as rolling forest and pockets of countless lakes pass by Walter's window. He shifts, ignoring the ache in his lower back and the driver comments from the other side of the metal partition.

"It's nice not having to drive on slick roads."

"What's that?" he asks, wishing for silence.

"The snow, it's holding out. Roads become a nightmare when there's ice. Name's Gloria by the way; thought you would have asked ten or so hours back, but it seems you got other things on your mind."

Walter sighs and nervously rubs his legs. "I'm sorry. Not much good at making new friends these days." He gives a wave and Gloria flashes him a smile in her rearview mirror. "I can't imagine a prison being way out in the middle of nowhere like this," he says, giving in to his boredom.

"Yup." Gloria cracks her neck and rolls her shoulders. "There was a big rush out here in the early 1900s. At least four active mining towns were in this valley at one point. A few smaller ones, too."

"Doesn't seem like enough to warrant a penitentiary."

"Bored men with jingle in their pockets breed crime. Not enough to justify a place like Cold Keep, true, but the tycoons in the surrounding areas at the time were convinced this valley was gonna be the home to the next big metropolis. Oh yes, they commissioned the big house to be built in a hurry, at that. Enough cells for hundreds of the best, worst, and most evil men you've ever met. The whole kit and caboodle was complete in three years and built from the stones dug up from the mines all around."

The bus sways from left to right and makes Walter sick as Gloria watches him from the mirror more than the road.

"I don't see any metropolis," he says, growing anxious as he flails around his seat.

"Yeah, well… like all good things, the rush ended and the ore dried up faster than my coochie after '50. Thousands of folks from all around had to pack up their pickaxes and join the rest of society in the real world. Only problem was they just finished Cold Keep and the taxpayers would have had a riot if they knew their dollars went to waste. So, they kept the place running way out here in east-Jesus-nowhere. It worked out alright; it keeps the delinquents—" She clears her throat and glances at Walter. "The inmates, I mean, away from the public eye." The bus skids towards the ditch, sliding on loose gravel, and Gloria spins the wheel, bringing the rig back to the center of the road as Walter's head slams into the window.

"Dammit, lady! Keep this thing on the road!"

Her cheeks flush and she falls silent, bringing the bus to a steady crawl.

Walter takes a breath and leans forward. "I'm sorry, my first day of school has got me a little on edge, and I haven't had a smoke all day."

A raspy laugh ruptures from the driver and the entire bus shifts back and forth again. "It's okay, sweetheart," she says. "Not your finest day, I'm guessing."

"You got any kids?" Walter asks, trying to steer the conversation elsewhere.

"Nope. I could hardly take care of myself most my life. You'd have thrown some pumpkin eaters in the mix and we all would've gone up in flames." She clears her throat and reaches into her pocket, pulling out a cigarette. "You won't rat on me if I give you one of these, will ya? It's bad enough I didn't put you in any chains."

Walter's eyes light up at the stick held between her manicured fingers. "You have my word," he promises, trying not to sound like a man deprived of tobacco. "Not sure the next chance I'll get."

She lights the cigarette and reaches back, dropping it through the holes in the partition. "Ya ready?" She stomps her foot on the accelerator and the cigarette rolls down the dirty aisle towards him, the momentum propelling it forward as he reaches down and snatches it before it passes by. The engine settles to its normal drone and Walter puts it to his lips, then inhales deeply. The relief is almost instant, and he blows out a cloud with a satisfied 'thank you'.

"I wouldn't be too worried about finding

smokes in Cold Keep. They're pretty loose on the puffing regulations. Only place in the world you'll find an Indian richer than a white man." Another laugh escapes her tobacco-stained lips, and Walter bites his tongue, but despite his composure Gloria spots the look on his stoic face and her amusement cuts short. "You got some red in ya?" she asks.

Walter takes another drag and blows it out his nose. "No. Just seen too many bad things done to undeserving people. I once arrested a man—" His throat closes around the words and she glances up at him. "Seen a man get arrested, I mean, for planting his steel toes right into a Native's side while he was sleeping on a bench. The guy was just minding his own business, dozed off when he got himself three broken ribs just for the color of his skin." Gloria's eyes fix back on the road and her shoulders sink as Walter continues. "Anyway, I still eat the pigs they raise and fill my truck with diesel from their stolen land, so who the hell am I to advocate on their behalf? Just don't think it's right belittling any man is all."

"Fair enough," she says, perking up as they round the bend. "Home sweet home."

The narrow road opens, revealing the vast clearing shaved out from the woods, and Walter's window fills with the giant stone behemoth that is Cold Keep. The world around him shrinks as he takes in the stretching walls, the sharp barbed wire draped over giant stones that cobble together and make up the monstrous spans and clusters of buildings within. Towers spew from the corners, looming high into the heavy silver sky and look down on the prison with judging spotlight eyes.

"What the hell…?" Walter furrows his brow, trying to make sense of the shining glass dome bubbling out from the center of the ancient-looking decay, its multicolored glass like a beautiful cyst ready to pop.

"Makes you wanna puke, doesn't it? In a good way," Gloria says.

Walter nods, unable to find the words as the wonder and menace of the entire thing fills his mind with terrible awe and makes him both glad and somehow disappointed that he will only be there for a short while.

"How long you book yourself in for?"

He blinks the view from his watering eyes and recalls the words typed in his forged file. "They tell me I'll be out in three to five years, depending on how well I behave." He drops the cigarette butt to the floor and stomps it out as the last of the nicotine puts him further on edge.

The bus peels away from the safe embrace of the forest and sputters up the road into the barren field. Smoke pours from a large stacks sprouting out from behind the walls and the entire penitentiary grows, threatening to swallow them whole with each inch carried closer.

Two pale-faced guards pull the chain-link gates open, letting the vehicle creep through the twisted fence and seal Walter's fate as they close behind. Further up, the bus lurches to a stop outside the towering stone wall that hosts its monstrous gates, and Gloria lets out a sigh. "There's the boss."

Outside, a man cloaked head to toe in a tan

three-piece suit stands with his hands behind his back, speaking to a short guard with a miserable frown. Gloria stands from her seat with a palpable stretch and exits the bus with a moan. A moment passes and Walter sits in silence, taking in the last morsel of solitude, enjoying the soft hum of the idling engine.

The lock clatters and the door swings open, filling the bus with the valley's rancid pine stench. Gloria steps inside and looks at Walter with a smile, and for a moment his nerves settle in the warmth of her kindness. "Can I leave you with a little piece of parting wisdom, mister?"

Walter nods and he rises from his seat.

"You see that man out there?" She turns and points out the window.

"Yes."

"Do not step on that man's toes." Her smile fades and Walter's nerves fall back in line.

"Will do. With a man that dapper, I bet his shoes cost a pretty penny."

"No, dummy. The short-stack behind him."

Walter looks again, surveying the stout guard with the bulbous nose standing beyond.

"You keep that man in your good books, stay out of his radar, and you just might have a pleasant enough stay. And don't forget, if they ask, tell them I had your legs chained up the entire ride, will ya?"

Walter nods once more and gives Gloria a wink. "You got it."

"Good." She smiles and winks back, giving him a shove. "Now move, you filthy inmate!"

CASA DE COLD KEEP

"Well, well, well, let me take a look at Cold Keep's newest cog," the man in tan calls out with a southern-soaked voice. He strides with a long casual saunter towards Walter, arms extended and stretching wide as if greeting a long-lost brother. "You must be…" He snaps his fingers at the guard following close behind, prompting him to remove his hand from the club on his hip and use it to rifle through the clipboard.

"Edwards," he whispers.

"Mr. Edwards! Welcome to your new abode." His outstretched arms motion up to the monstrous doors behind them.

Walter looks down the length of the wall, its jagged interlocking stones giving him the impression of a medieval castle that changed careers at some point.

"Thank you, I—"

"So, Mr. Edwards, what brings you to our little inn? Business… or pleasure?" He grabs Walter by the hand and shakes it with vigor, prompting the guard to rest his hand back over his club. "Oh, relax, Archie-boy. Our friend here is only going to be with us for a brief spell. Aren't you, Mr. Edwards?"

"That's right. Three to—"

"You see, Archie, Mr. Edwards here only stole from me. It's not as if he murdered an elderly with a firearm."

Walter shakes his head. "I beg your pardon?"

"That's right. Hell, he stole from you, too, Archie. He thieved from your mama and my daddy, furthermore." He laughs, still pumping Walter's hand up and down.

"He did?" Archie asks.

"You are the one with Mr. Edward's file clutched in those mitts of yours. Says right there." He releases Walter's grip and snatches the clipboard from Archie, rifling through the pages. "Yes, right here." He pulls a pair of glasses from inside his suit and slips them over his large ears. "Tax fraud, it seems. Mr. Edwards has claimed to have had five children for the last seven-odd years when in fact, he has had zero the entire duration of his dubious deceit. Therefore, he has been reaping the generous government kickbacks for single guardians this fine country of ours doles out. Sucking off the proverbial teat of us fine, law-abiding citizens, to put it in layman's terms."

Archie frowns. "That don't seem very fair, Warden."

"No. It does not seem fair at all!" His voice rings out and gets lost in the forest all around. "But that's okay." Both of his arms sprout out and wrap themselves around Walter, pulling him into an unexpected embrace. "Shhhh, it's okay because you, Mr. Edwards, are here to pay your nickel. You are here to cleanse yourself of all your wrongdoings, and all in as little as three to five years, so says your file."

Three to five days more like it, Walter thinks.

They sway left and right like two friends on a small boat. "But knowing you, it's only going to be three, isn't that right? I just know it."

He lets go and Walter pulls back, face flushed from such a strange welcome to the equally strange and intimidating place. "That's—that's right, Mr...." Walter takes his turn to pause.

"Oh, I beg your pardon! Here I stand flapping my gums while you don't even know who you are rightfully addressing!" The man in tan laughs into the heavy sky like a boy fed too much gas at the dentist. "I, Mr. Edwards, am Uncle Bill, and the Boys-in-Blue call me Warden Willy on the account of me being their boss, but I am not your boss; Archie here is. Now come along, we've got your presidential suite all set up inside and your cellmate is eager as a spring beaver to meet you, I'm sure." He wraps his arm around Walter's and they turn. "Oh, do wait a moment, will you?" He holds a finger up and looks over his shoulder at Gloria, still loitering outside her bus.

"My dearest Gloria," he yells, "will you be joining us, or will you be fearing those dark, lonesome roads this frightful evening?"

She mumbles something then follows from a distance as Uncle Bill turns with a pleased smile. "I'll admit, I've got quite the shine for that woman. Don't tell the missus, though. Just a schoolyard crush is all."

They approach the set of impending doors, once deep red, but now brown and rusted with years of weather.

"Are you normally so involved with each prisoner's arrival, Bill?"

"That's Uncle Bill to you, my boy. My father calls me Bill, my mama Billy, and you Uncle Bill. I believe we just went over this, but seeing as we have yet to adorn you in your proper milky attire, I will let this one discrepancy slip. Are we on the same page now, Mr. Edwards?"

"Yes… Uncle Bill." Walter grimaces, his ears flushing red as he bites his tongue and swallows his pride. *Low profile*, he reminds himself of Blyth's advice.

They reach the gate and Uncle Bill lets off Walter's arm. He pulls out a large brass key from his jacket and breathes on it, then sinks it into a hole between two steel plates, turning it with large, exaggerated flails, making the gears grind and argue within.

"Good. And moreover, I dislike the word 'prisoners.' It implies you have no choice in being here, when the choice was entirely"—he grunts with another turn— "and completely yours to make in the first place. Archie here calls you 'prisoners' and that's his obligation, but I prefer to call you a 'visitor.' And to answer your question, yes, I do greet each and every one of my visitors with the same gusto as you have been welcomed with today."

A final and resounding clink thuds and Uncle Bill retracts the key with a deep bow. "Welcome to

Cold Keep, Mr. Edwards." He makes a sudden sharp turn from the giant gates and reaches for the handle of an entirely different, average-sized door beside them. With one swift pull, it opens, and Uncle Bill gushes with another fit of laughter. "We only use the gates for numerous and simultaneous arrivals. But I'll promise you this, my good man, if you do me right and get yourself out of here in those three years instead of five, I'll personally escort you out of those pearly gates myself. And boy do they squeal something awful when they open. It drives Archie here absolutely batty, doesn't it, Archie?"

"Sure does, Warden Willy," Archie sighs.

A cool breeze kicks up from the south all at once and a single snowflake drifts down from the foreboding sky above, landing on Archie's padded shoulder and melting out of existence as if never there at all. Walter looks up nonchalantly and pauses at Archie's face, suddenly cold and stiff, as if the single flake had drained all the warmth from his body.

Gloria stops in her tracks. "On second thought, Willy, I best get home. You understand."

"Of course, of course, my dear." Uncle Bill steps to Gloria's side and nods at Walter with a smirk pulling at the corner of his lips, his demeanor seemingly aroused by the negative shift in season. "I fear this is where we part ways, Mr. Edwards. Archie here will see you are suited in your proper dress and get you situated in *casa de Cold Keep*." He turns to Gloria. "Let me escort you back to your chariot, my dear."

Gloria smiles and affords Walter one last

discrete wink as Archie pushes him through the small door and pulls it shut in his face.

Walter turns to the complex, swallowed by the giant stone walls and the barbed wire nests sat atop them. Small, medium, and large buildings pepper the expanse, all surrounding the octagonal fortress in its center with its festering body and brilliant glass dome topping it off. "A glass roof on a prison seems like an interesting choice," Walter notes.

"Keep your mouth shut, inmate. Warden Willy just showed you the last kindness you're gonna see for the next five years. Now move your ass." Archie shoves Walter towards the main building and through an even less impressive door marked *Processing.*

***

The evening hours crawl by as the guards check Walter in, meticulously filling out paperwork, never once asking what the 'W' in 'W. Edwards' stands for in his file. And when the time comes for Walter to strip down, his face blushes rose pink as Archie tells him to bend over and cough. After the assault, he hands Walter his eggshell-colored denim jacket, pants, and t-shirt, all one size too large with the promise that no others are in stock. One quick change later and the reinforced doors open and the haze inside the lobby catches Walter by the throat, its pungent tobacco aroma mercifully clearing his head of the pine stench outside.

The eight-sided cavern sprawls out and sends

a shiver up his spine. The stones all around climb from the ornate tile floor and twist into a jigsaw of carved out intention, shaking hands with the giant glass dome far overhead, tangled in a mess of pulleys and chains. In the center of it all, a set of green French doors sit atop the giant iron staircase. Walter tries to take it all in at once, the task feeling futile as he reads each of the stenciled words above the octagon's branching corridors: *A-Block, B-Block, Workshop, Cafeteria, Library, Offices, Processing.*

"Move your ass, Edwards. You've wasted enough of my time today." Archie takes up the lead and Walter follows, noticing the inmates staring at them with glazed eyes. He lowers his gaze in turn, trying to help himself from scanning their faces. *Low profile.*

"You're a Bastard," Archie says.

Walter acknowledges the insult and swallows another mouthful of pride. "Alright then."

"We got the B-Block for the Bastards in the east hall, and we got the A-Block for the Assholes in the west."

A middle-aged man with a childish grin and drooping eyes approaches, tipping an invisible hat to Archie as he passes by. "Morning, Boss-boy."

"Fuck off, Eddie!" The man half laughs, skittering away as Archie kicks at the air after him and turns back to Walter without missing a beat. "Cold Keep is what we call a min-max lock-up. We got minimum Bastards, being you shit-birds who steal cars or God forbid cheat on their fucking taxes. And we got maximum Assholes who are prone to stabbing their daddies in their sleep and putting their peckers where they ain't got permission, if you catch my drift."

The words echo in Walter's mind as he stares at A-Block's door and visualizes Marvin on the other side.

Archie points across the lobby. "There's the commissary where you get your treats, newspapers, and smokes. You have me to thank for those. Are you listening? I don't like repeating myself." He snaps a finger in Walter's face and he nods. "Good. Warden Willy wanted to get rid of the smokes altogether, but they are good for morale, and good luck preventing a riot when you got just shy of five hundred criminals all going cold turkey at once."

"Morning, Boss-boy." Eddie tips his invisible hat and passes Archie once more.

Archie shouts and makes Walter—but seemingly no one else around him jump. "I thought I told you to fuck off, Eddie!"

Eddie hunches over, reaching into his pockets. "Eddie got some Chicklets, Boss-boy." He pulls out a piece of gum and holds it out, but Archie brings his hand down and smacks it to the floor.

"I don't give a shit what you got, you simpleton. Now pick that up before I shove it so deep in your ass you'll be farting bubbles for the rest of your days. Get out of here!"

Archie jolts his boot upwards, threatening to kick, and Eddie takes off, adjusting the phantom hat on his head. "And it's evening, you thick son-of-a-bitch. No 'good mornings' here!" Archie turns back to Walter and shakes his head. "No lighters, though. Or matches. Causes too many issues, but that don't seem to stop you cretins from getting the damn things lit." He points through the grand staircase into the large room littered with tables and benches beyond. "If you ain't in a cell, shower, or workshop, you are there. You eat, pray, and soak in the courtyard's light through those arches, but tough titties if you like fresh air cause no one's allowed in the rec yard in the winter, so don't you dare come asking. Also, I don't give a fuck how often you and the Big Guy speak, you only do it in the chapel on Sundays. Hell, if I were God, I would have forgotten this shit-hole and the scumbags inside it long ago. But if you think your soul is worth saving, so be it."

Eddie stops in the middle of the lobby and pivots back, walking straight towards them with his naïve smile, and Walter takes a step away, distancing himself while Archie points to the French doors on the landing. "Infirmary and solitary are up there," he says. "If you're walking through those doors, you better be bleeding from the fucking eyes or else Warden Willy's got a dress shoe to shove up your ass. Either way, you better be limping in or limping out." He rounds back, turning towards B-Block's sliding door and opens his arms wide when Eddie's voice calls out from behind.

"Morning, Boss-boy. You want some gum?"

Archie pivots on one foot, face turning red as he steps forward and closes the gap between them, hand coming to rest on his club. "What flavor do you got there, Eddie?" he asks with a forced smile.

Eddie laughs, as if finding the question ridiculous. "Purple, Boss-boy. Grape. Wet raisins."

"I bet it tastes real good. Do you think I could

have a piece of that grape gum? Could you reach deep into those pockets of yours and pull me out a stick of the good stuff?"

Eddie's face lights up. "Oh sure, Boss-boy. I got lots!" He digs into his jacket and pulls out a purple Chicklet, eagerly pushing it into Archie's palm.

Archie plops the gum into his mouth and chews with a smile as they both chuckle, staring at each other while the surrounding dopey-eyed inmates glance at the pair, no set lingering for too long. "Oh yeah, that's real good, Eddie. It tastes just like grapes, don't it? Do you know how to blow bubbles?"

Eddie jitters, barely able to contain his excitement, and nods, kneading the gum with his tongue as he prepares to fill his piece with breath.

"Well, let's see then! Let's see."

Walter takes another step back and Archie's knuckles turn white around his club.

A large purple balloon grows from Eddie's pursed lips, and in one fell swoop the club comes dislodged and sails straight through it, stopping hard against his mouth. The bubble pops, echoing the sound of wood colliding with enamel, and Eddie drops to his knees, letting out a pained wail. The sudden shift of the innocent man's joy to pain jars Walter into pulling away completely as the blood spills onto the tiles below.

"I didn't do nothing, Boss-boy. I'm sorry!" Eddie cries with more apology than pain.

Archie turns to the onlookers and shouts. "You boys have been getting a bit too comfortable around here. Now, it is my duty to keep you shit-birds in line. It is not my job to greet you with a fucking smile or a how-do-you-do every time we cross paths! Eddie's mistake here was thinking I am a man to be addressed." His voice attracts more curious men, and they shuffle out from the cafeteria. "Let me make something perfectly clear. I, nor any other Boy-in-Blue are your complaint department. We are not your welcoming committee and we sure as shit are not someone to greet with a smile! Do you cretins understand me?" He spits his gum at Eddie and the French doors swing open, dispatching two guards who drop to the injured man's side with little urgency and drag him up the stairs.

"See?" Archie asks. "Limping in or limping out." He looks back out at the slack-jawed inmates. "I asked if you understand me!" His booming voice reverbs around the lobby, and the men mumble in agreement as one. "Good. Now thank Eddie for the early bedtime and get back to your cells." He looks at Walter with a satisfied sneer, then turns to the large metal door faceted on its rails by two sturdy wheels. "Here we are. B-Block."

"Home sweet home," Walter whispers to himself, staring in and scanning more of the men's faces inside.

"Am I boring you Edwards?"

Walter blinks and shakes his head. "What? No, Archie. I just—"

The club comes loose even quicker than moments before and rises. "Using a guard's name is an outside luxury you lost when you stole from my mama. It's 'sir,' or 'Boss-man' to you. And if I hear you call me anything but, I'll give you the Eddie Special. Say yes if you understand me."

The muscles in Walter's arm flex and he glares down into the stout man's face. *Low profile.* "Yes, sir."

"Good. Now, after you."

Walter steps into the jungle of stone and metal and he gawks at the blackened steel walkways sprawling out from the north wall, nearly disappearing down the block. Cell after cell clamber four levels high, their thick bars staring across the hall and out the barred windows that stretch from floor to ceiling, flooding the block with moonlight. "Jesus..."

"Not here, I'm afraid. Now move," Archie barks.

Walter starts forward and looks to the feet clanging above as more men shuffle across the catwalks up high.

"Turn," Archie demands. Walter looks to the corkscrew staircase and climbs the dizzying loops upward, ignoring his vertigo with each step higher. They turn onto the third level and Archie stops, knocking his baton against one of the cells. "Looks like the redskin's got your mattress for the night."

Walter peers into the dim room, spotting a stack of bedding wedged between the sink and toilet against the back wall. On it, a brown-skinned man with tattered and uneven hair lays asleep, his face pushed into the impromptu bed.

"I'd tell you to take what's yours, but it's not safe to wake a sleeping savage." Archie laughs to himself and shoves Walter inside. "Welcome to Cold

Keep, shit-head." He slams the door and trots off with a whistle.

Walter drops onto his mattress-less cot, listening to the inmates shuffle into their cells, doors rattling in their frames as the guards make their rounds. Finally, the breaker pops with an electric crackle, plunging the block into darkness, leaving him with only a mind full of tiaras, greasy sideburns, and a lingering feeling he can no longer ignore.

The feeling that he is finally where he belongs.

WAKE UP, JAMESTOWN

"Wake up, Jamestown!"

A sudden jolt awakens Walter, and he sits up to the mob of inmates crowded on the catwalk beyond his cell. *Not even a full day.* His fists instinctively rise, readying for a fight, and he jumps to his feet, pulling up his sleeves. "What's the fucking problem here?"

The men back away and look to his cellmate sitting at the bars for some kind of explanation. "Easy there, fella," he says, smiling up at Walter. "I need your help, yeah?"

Walter stares at his chopped-up hair and the three smoking cigarettes hanging from his lips and takes a breath.

"Name's Dakota." He pulls Walter down with a hand so warm it dampens his skin, then yells, pointing to the inmates outside. "You know the game: one at a time. Make it quick!" He puffs on the three cigarettes, lending large plumes of smoke that fill the cell with a thick fog, then grabs Walter by the face, heating his already flushed cheeks, and plants a smoke between his puckered lips.

Walter slaps him away and considers raising a fist, but the inhale of tobacco calms him instantly. "Th-thanks, kid."

"Suck on that while you count. It's a fast-paced gig, so let's keep it simple. These fine Bastards need their morning smokes lit and I'm the only one with the means to do so. Now, the smoke sends me for a loop, so I'm gonna need you to be my cashier. It's two dry sticks in exchange for a wet one. A stick of—"

"Wet?" Walter cuts in.

"Unlit and lit. Keep up. Or one dry stick and chips for a wet. I'll even accept three bags of chips or a candy bar with gum. I don't take Juicy Fruit, only Chicklets and Big Red. The Tribesmen smoke free; one-for-one, a clean exchange."

"Tribesmen?"

"Natives. Indians. My people. But I'm no Tribesman." Dakota reaches into his pocket and pulls out two more cigarettes, lighting them off the ones left dangling in his mouth, then hands them to the passing inmates before starting the process over again. "Smokes, chips, candy, and gum. Simple exchange of funds for services. You got it?"

Walter nods. "Y-yeah, I got it." He pulls another drag off his smoke and furiously grabs at the dry cigarettes clutched in the inmate's palms, others holding chips and packets of gum. He nods with each transaction and tosses their payment on Dakota's cot behind him, scanning the faces shuffling by as his head spins from the onslaught of smoke swirling around.

The line moves forward, each man waiting as Dakota continues to produce stick after stick, lighting each off the last like a magician pulling scarves from his mouth, and before long the entire block is filled with the morning haze.

"Darcy, I see you down there," Dakota yells to the landing below. "Nobody quits in Cold Keep. If I see you with a lit smoke, I'll send the Tribesmen after your ass."

"So, you provide the cigarettes for Cold Keep?" Walter asks.

"Me? No. I just light 'em. Commissary sells 'em."

"And they don't sell matches?"

"If they sold matches, would we be lighting these right now? Think, Jamestown. No prison's gonna be giving its inmates fire. Not since the riot back in '61."

"Hey, out of the way!" a voice cuts through the crowd of men.

"Running late, Wayne?" Dakota asks the man working his way to the front of the line with a kind smile. "Wayne don't pay neither."

"Damn right I don't pay." He laughs and, with tobacco-stained fingers, hands a pillowcase to Dakota.

Walter looks through the thin material as it passes by, spotting more cigarettes and gum inside. "Thought you said he doesn't pay."

"He don't. Wayne here runs the show in A-Block. Only inmate in Cold Keep who's got a foot in both doors. He's in charge of taking the first lit cigarette to the other side each morning. Takes the goods over there, lights their smokes, and brings a share of the profits back to me."

Wayne turns with a proud smile and points to the *Sanitation* patch sewed into the back of his coveralls. "Yup, filth has its rewards." He holds out a hand to Walter.

"Right, sorry. This is Jamestown," Dakota says.

"Edwards, actually. Walter Edwards," he corrects and shakes Wayne's palm.

Dakota rolls his eyes. "Isn't that the whitest white man's name you ever heard?"

"Can't be any worse than Wayne O'Neill."

"Good point," Dakota laughs.

"What's the holdup?" someone calls from the line.

"Hey, you're lucky I'm not charging you double on a day like today, asshole!" Dakota shrugs. "They're right, though, better keep it moving. Snow's got everyone anxious for their morning dart and coffee." He plucks a smoke from the corner of his lip and puts it between Wayne's fingers.

Walter flashes a look to the rooftops across the hall, all blanketed in a thick layer of snow, the powder still coming down hard.

Wayne closes his eyes and sucks deep on the cigarette, then opens them dreamily. "Be seeing you around, Edwards." Walter nods and Wayne turns, disappearing amongst the agitated men.

"Alright, alright, who's next?" Dakota shouts to the outstretched hands as packs of gum fly, cigarettes exchange, and the occasional trade for unsavory magazine clippings meet their approval with a nod until the line eventually thins and Walter snatches the final two smokes from the last man.

"You're a good count, Jamestown." Dakota lunges for the toilet, wrenching so hard a stream of vomit splashes into the water below.

"Thanks, kid. You alright?"

"Yeah." Dakota gets up and wipes his mouth on his sleeve. "Just can't stand the stuff."

"What? Tobacco?"

"Come one, come all, the only Indian in the land who doesn't like a Peace Pipe." He waves his hands above his chopped-up hair and drops himself onto his cot, sorting the profits into piles.

Walter feels the tobacco loosen his nerves further and he chuckles. "Doesn't bother me, none. You wake me with one of those sticks each morning, and I'll count the stones of this cell if you tell me to."

"Three hundred twenty-three." Dakota shakes his head, shuffling through the pile and pulls out a pack of Juicy Fruit. "Missed one." He separates a portion of the stash and tosses it onto Walter's cot. "Your cut."

"Not much for chewing gum. Can't stand the stuff if I'm being honest."

"Don't care what ya do with it. Darcy down there would snag just about anyone for three stacks of Big Red. Everything's got value in Cold Keep." He sandwiches a handful of smokes between two packs of gum and gently shoves them into his breast pocket. "Was hoping no one would show up; it was nice having the extra cushion." He grabs the mattress from between the toilet and sink and tosses it onto Walter's cot, then turns for the door. "I got some drops to make, I'll give you the grand tour."

Walter shakes his head, following onto the catwalk. "I've got some catching up to do with an old friend." The lie burns on his tongue.

"No friends in here," Dakota huffs. "First day and you already got a breakfast date with Darcy? His moist lips can wait, we got an hour before the Assholes across the way move in for their grits, and trust me, you don't wanna miss the grits. Who you got the hard-on for, anyway?"

Walter grinds his teeth at the thought of Marvin's greasy sideburns, and he comes up with something quick. "Old work pal. Got himself locked up years back for putting a bullet in his cheating wife's bonnet."

Dakota puts a cool, steady hand on Walter's shoulder for balance and they descend the spiraling staircase, joining the men pouring into the lobby. "Not too sure about your man, Jamestown. Murder lands you a room with the Assholes in A-Block. If he's killed someone, I guarantee you he's over there." He points across the lobby to the large door mirroring their own.

"Thanks, kid." Walter picks up his pace and strides across the giant expanse, stopping as Dakota laughs. "What?"

"You don't look like no killer to me, Old-timer. Cold Keep is as good as two different lockups altogether. When the bell rings, the Assholes and the Bastards swap out."

Walter stares at the door, then Dakota. "You're telling me the A's and B's never cross paths?"

"Here and there, but mostly no. They keep us pretty segregated."

"For fuck's sake!"

"You got unfinished business with this friend of yours, Jamestown?"

Walter steps closer. "How old are you, kid?"

Dakota's brow furrows and he takes a step back. "Old enough to know that's an odd question to ask."

"Well, by the way you carry yourself, I reckon you're not even thirty, so my guess is you've been in here for a couple years, max."

"Bit longer than that."

"Well, kid, I've been in here not even a full day, and I already got it figured out that it's looking for trouble asking another man's unfinished business. If you haven't figured that out by now, how the hell have you make it this long without ending up like Eddie?" Walter leans in, hoping his forward demeanor is enough to change the subject and throw Dakota off.

"Eddie?" Dakota asks, his face shifting to concern.

"Yeah. Archie caved his chompers in last night. Well, nearly. The point is, I got my reasons for seeing an old friend and those reasons are none of yours. So do you wanna pry further or should we get on with your grand tour?"

"Sheesh, forget you then!" Dakota turns away and the two walk into the sprawling cafeteria littered with long benches fixed to even longer tables. "You got a bit of a grit, you know that, Jamestown?"

"So I've been told."

They join the line forming against the wall and Walter grabs one of the metal trays from the stack. He grips it tight, noticing several sets of eyes watching him for only a moment before darting back to their laps, one after another. "Everyone likes a new guy," he mumbles, trying to ease his nerves.

"Something like that," Dakota says. "You got a knack for timing, that's for sure."

"Yeah? And why is that?"

"Snowed something awful last night. First dump of the season. Few guys are even blaming you for it. A bringer of bad omens."

"You got holes in the roof or something?" Walter catches another shifting glimpse from one of the dazed-looking men in the crowd. "What's the deal with you guys in here, anyway?"

"What do you mean?"

"I heard spending three to five would be hell in Cold Keep, that I'd be in with the worst of the worst."

"Yeah, what's your point?" They shuffle ahead with the line.

"As far as I can tell, this place is one step above a hospice. These guys are either walking around with their heads hung low and tails between their legs, or in another world altogether. I thought a place like this was for criminals, not geriatrics and dopers."

"You looking for action, Jamestown?" Dakota peers back at Walter. "Go over to that Boy-in-Blue there. Take my spoon." He pulls the utensil from his pocket and shoves it into his palm, pointing to the guard standing at the front of the line. "Grip it tight and drive the handle into his neck. Guaranteed your ass will be on the other side with the Assholes in an hour. I'm sorry things aren't living up to your expectations here in B-Block." The line shuffles once more and they move along. "Give it some time, the violence always comes, even amongst the Bastards."

Walter huffs. "Relax, kid. Jeez. You got a bit of a grit yourself, you know that?"

"So I've been told," Dakota echoes, and Walter pushes the spoon back into his hand. "If you think it's all rainbows and bo-diddley, you just haven't had enough time to make these animals hate you. Here, watch." He steps out of line and raises his hand, motioning to a passing inmate for his attention. "Do you—"

The man's hand comes down hard on Dakota's empty tray and slaps it to the ground. "Powwow with someone else, Kid-killer." He throws a shoulder and sends him spinning back into the line where Walter catches him, softening the blow.

"Jesus! What the hell did you do to him?"

"Paints don't mix well in Cold Keep." Dakota points across the room and Walter looks out amongst the tables, noticing each row sporting their own demographic. "Blacks on blacks, whites on whites, reds on reds. Then you got my Eddie-boy there, a wild card on the account of the scrambled brain and all. Most everyone just lets him do his own thing most days." Walter watches the childish man pick at his tray and pour dry cereal into his cut-up mouth.

"Hold up a second, Jamestown." A Tribesman strides towards them and Dakota pulls the gum and cigarette sandwich from his pocket, slapping it into his hand with not so much as a glance, then turns back to Walter and continues where he left off. "And every deck of cards has its joker. Not good for much, but it has its uses. That's me."

"You don't play well with the others I take it?" The smell of bland grits fills Walter's nose.

"Don't play well with me, more like." The man with the cigarette sandwich joins the rest of the Natives and flashes Dakota a satisfactory nod. "I give 'em a cut of the morning profits and they ensure those cherries on the ends of the smokes we light don't get passed around too generously. I see a man smoking a jimmy that I didn't get paid to light that day, and I send the Tribesmen to rough 'em up. That's as much as they want to do with me, and me them."

"So, what's stopping me from hiring the other white fellows in here and starting up my own smoke shop?" Walter asks.

Dakota laughs. "You find out how to start a flame in here, you let me know, Jamestown. That way I'll know who to shiv in their sleep. Would be pretty easy with you sleeping right next to me, too." He gives a half-joking smile and steps up to the metal counter where a pile of goo steams behind the glass and pulls at Walter's growling stomach. "Georgina!" Dakota greets the woman serving up the food. "How is my favorite lunch lady today?"

She looks at him and rolls her eyes. "Hello, Dakota."

"Georgina, this is my new cellmate, Jamestown."

"Edwards, ma'am." Walter reaches his hand.

"I don't shake, Freshie. Not while I'm working." She smiles and shovels a spoonful of grits onto his tray.

"Georgina here is probably the only one in this place who treats us criminals like actual people."

"They pay me to cook, not bust the balls of you degenerates." She pours another spoonful into the center of Dakota's tray and he slides two cigarettes across the counter-top as he pulls his breakfast back. Georgina clicks her tongue and grabs them, reaching below the counter. "You are lucky my husband doesn't let me buy my own or your little bribes would dry up quick, I'll tell you that much for a fact." She pulls a small can out and hands it to Dakota who shoves it into his jacket with a quick look around.

The line shifts again and Walter nods a 'thanks' as they step into the maze of tables, towards Eddie who is still gently dropping cereal into his mouth.

"You had a nasty run in with Boss-man, I hear," Dakota says.

They take their seats across from him, and Walter glances across the lobby to A-Block with an anxious leg that bobs up and down.

"Boss-boy don't like bubbles much, Kota. New-boy saw."

"Yeah, I saw alright," Walter says. "Archie didn't seem to like you speaking to him all that much, it seems."

Eddie laughs and eats another handful of cereal, proceeding to talk with a full mouth. "No, no,

New-boy. Boss-boy don't like the bubbles. I just said Boss-boy don't like bubbles. I said it, didn't I, Kota?"

Dakota nods. "Sure did, Eddie. But Jamestown here is old, and the elderly start to lose their hearing when they get that way. Bit slow in the head, too. Doesn't hear so good or think so good, either these days."

Walter flashes Dakota an unamused glare.

"Boss-boy don't like bubbles, New-boy!" Eddie yells and the surrounding breakfast eaters look their way.

"Jesus, Eddie, I was just kidding!" Dakota yells back. "If you got such a bad lip why are you eating corn flakes, anyways? You lick your tray clean on grits day. You love 'em."

Eddie points to the officer with the spoon missing from his neck. "Blue-boy said it's corn flakes to Georgina. No grits for me. I asked him why and he said it's Archie's—I mean, Boss-boy's orders. So I just eat my cereal this morning. They hurt my mouth, though. No milk, neither, they says." Eddie cocks his head, dropping a few more flakes into his mouth and gently chews.

"You best mind yourself for a while, Eddie. You stay away from Boss-boy, and all those Boys-in-Blue, okay?" Dakota plunges his hand into his pocket and pulls out the small cylinder from Georgina. "Here."

Eddie's eyes light up and he snatches it. "Oh, Kota, thank you. Thank you! You know I love my pudding!" He pulls a spoon from his pocket and pries the canister open.

Walter watches the two men dive into their

breakfast, then looks down at his tray. "She didn't give me a spoon."

Eddie laughs. "Georgina don't give spoons. Where you put your spoon, New-boy?"

"I didn't put my damn spoon anywhere, Eddie. In order for me to leave my spoon someplace, I would first have to be in possession of one, wouldn't I?"

Eddie looks at his utensil and smiles, as if to rub it in.

"Everyone gets their own spoon from Archie when they check in," Dakota says, flashing the stamped number on the handle of his utensil.

Walter slaps his hands on the table, exasperated. "Well, I don't know what to tell you, kid. I didn't get a fucking spoon from that moron. How the hell am I supposed to eat this with no spoon?" He lifts his tray and drops it back in place. Dakota chuckles, trying to hold his laughter and Eddie does the same. "You think this is funny?" Walter looks around the hall, feeling his pink face turn red.

"Here," Dakota pulls two smokes from his pocket and pinches them together. "You know how to use chopsticks?" The two burst out with thunderous applause, and Walter rises from his seat, ready to explode as the loud screech from the intercoms stop him in place.

"Good morning, my little blueberries!" Uncle Bill chimes out in a singsong tone. "I require each and every one of you gentlemen from B-Block to convene in the lobby, post-haste. I have some news worth sharing." The speaker cuts out with an abrupt crackle and Walter looks at his comrades' suddenly gray and sickly faces.

"You boys okay?"

From seemingly nowhere, Archie strides into the cafeteria with his billy club swinging high over his head like a pissed off cheer captain. "You heard Warden Willy, shit-birds, everyone in the lobby, now!" He brings it down on one of the tables and clips a tray of grits, sending it in every direction. "You idiot, look what ya did!" He grabs the closest man by the collar and drags him to his feet.

Eddie leans in with a mouth full of pudding and Dakota stands from the table, watching Archie continue to barrage the innocent inmate with insults. "Why's Boss-boy so mad over some spilled grits? That boy ain't blown a single bubble today, I know it."

"I'd be mad, too if I was in charge of giving the Boot," Dakota says, leading them towards the lobby.

"What's the Boot?" Walter asks.

Dakota looks at him with nervous eyes and some of the nearby inmates drift away, as if the question dirtied the already dirty air.

They join the crowd of white denim men, and the morning light spills through the glass dome above, washing them in multicolored tones. Walter looks up at Uncle Bill standing on the summit of the stairs, his grin spreading ear to ear with a worn boot hanging by its laces from his clutched palm. Next to him, Archie leans in a cockeyed stance, his one stained sock planted on the metal platform. The cool room stiffens, and the inmates tense up at the sight, like a doe in its last moments on a freeway.

"You want some action, Jamestown? There it is," Dakota whispers.

Eddie whimpers and removes his invisible hat, lifting his fingers to his mouth. "That's it, New-boy. That's the Boot."

Silence hangs over Cold Keep as the prisoners gawk up at Uncle Bill until finally, he speaks. "Good morning, gentlemen. Thank you for consolidating so quickly. It's always important to be timely, and I, for one, pride myself on being prompt."

Walter rolls his eyes and wonders if Uncle Bill wears the same suit every day.

"Get on with it, Colonel Sanders," Dakota mutters under his breath, tugging a smile at Walter's cheeks.

"Can any of you fine fellows tell me why today, of all days, is so special?" Uncle Bill scans the quiet room. "That's right, class. It's because if you look outside, you'll see the valley that blesses our little slice of paradise has been painted as white as…well, snow, of course."

"This guy has got a real hard-on for theatrics," Walter whispers.

Dakota looks at him and manages a gloomy nod. "You've got no idea."

"And as luck would have it," Uncle Bill continues, "this morning I received the production numbers from the Pocket Protectors upstairs." He gives the green French doors behind him a rap. "That's right, it all comes down to this!" He reaches deep into his jacket and produces a slip of paper along with his glasses. The air leaves the room and the inmates cling to the note, waiting patiently for him to fit the spectacles over his ears.

"I don't understand," Walter says as Uncle Bill drones on about the hard work and determination of the men over the last year.

Dakota leans over. "They put us prisoners to good use in the workshop. Slaving to turn out all the shit anyone could possibly want to waste their nickels on. Flags, shoes, mufflers, you name it. Last while it's been kettles. A while back Uncle Bill got the bright idea to pit the Bastards and the Assholes against each other by mandating the block with the least units produced gets the Boot for the winter. First snowfall of the season is when the clock stops, and the numbers decide if it stays in its current home or moves to the other side. That way we're always working hard and that sleazebag up there gets a bigger slice of the pie."

"Bigger the pie, more whipped cream to lick off the top," Eddie chimes in.

"That doesn't explain why everyone has such an aversion to Archie's foot odor," Walter argues.

"Wouldn't worry about the Boot unless it comes back to B-Block, yeah?" Dakota says. "Just shut up and pray we got better numbers, Old-timer."

"Stop calling me that." Walter locks his jaw and his gaze floats over to A-Block for the third time that minute. *I don't have time for this shit.*

The room holds its collective breath as Uncle Bill unfolds the slip of paper, toying with their emotions.

"Theatrics," Dakota sighs.

"It says here, gentlemen, that the Assholes in

A-Block shipped a total of 11,500 completed units this year!"

"Jesus!" someone gasps.

"Jesus indeed, my fellow visitor." Uncle Bill spares himself time for a chuckle and he adjusts his glasses, only to look clean over them and down at the paper. "Those are impressive numbers to say the least. But what about yours? It says here"—he pauses for more dramatic effect—"just shy, with four hundred behind A-Block, I'm afraid. With a total of 11,100 completed units."

The room breaks into a frenzy, and Walter stumbles into a man who shoves him back. "I chose a bad time to visit," he says in Dakota's direction, but looks to see his cellmate now holding Eddie, fear welling in their eyes.

"That's not fair. They got extra days!" someone calls.

"What about all the lockdowns they stirred up when it was our turn in the shop?" another pleads.

"That's enough, quiet!" Uncle Bill shouts as he pulls the grits-covered club from Archie's hip and slams it against the handrail. The loud gong fills the lobby, but the men ignore it, rattling like a steaming kettle as Uncle Bill shouts again, this time raising the Boot high above his head, silencing the inmates with the shoe like dogs fearing a newspaper.

Walter stares at it in wonder, trying to conjure a reason why they would react in such a way to something so menial.

"I will not have you acting like untrained monkeys!" Uncle Bill screams, a vein bulging in his neck. "You will fall in line or Archie here will make you fall in line. Now, act like the fully trained simians you are!" He drops the Boot and slicks back his thinning gray hair. "I understand this is a tough loss for you boys, and I know how hard you worked, I truly do. But the numbers speak for themselves, and that's just how it is. You are right, however, those miscreants in high max, the Assholes, as it were, did cause quite the ruckus when it came time for your turn at the helms, thus losing you several days to make up ground. Now, I am no fool, and neither are any of you. That was taken into consideration, so let me bestow upon you a glimmer of hope." He takes off his glasses and tucks them back into his jacket. "Archie and I discussed it, and under normal circumstances I would say all is fair in love and war, but since it was such a close race, I say you spit in the face of accounting and forge your own destiny!"

The inmates share glances and Dakota tries to calm Eddie's soft whimpers. "What's he talking about, Kota? I don't want no Boot."

"It's okay, Eddie. Shush."

"That's right, men. I'm giving you a shot at redemption. There's nothing I love more than a good show, so I asked Archie here to get me some lions for an impromptu coliseum royal, but he put his foot down and told me it would be unethical to have the animals fight such beasts." He chuckles to himself again and continues. "So instead, we decided it would be up to you and the Assholes to sort things out yourselves. With my favorite sport as a child, in fact, a friendly game of jacks!" Hushed chatter spills over the crows and Uncle Bill pulls a small pouch from his seemingly endless pocket. "Now, boys, it's not often we convene, but for the sake of a fair fight we will allow you Assholes and Bastards to muddle together for the show. But I expect you to be on your best behavior. If I see a single stray fist fly, I will shut the whole thing down and Archie will level out his limp—one boot for each of you. No second chances."

"What's he talking about?" Walter asks.

"Looks like you might get to see your long-lost pal sooner than you thought, Jamestown."

"Bring them out!" Uncle Bill slams the borrowed club against the railing once more and the sudden squeal of A-Block's rusted door calls out, letting the Assholes from within spill into the already packed lobby.

One after another, the hardened faces of murderers, rapists, and thugs funnel in and mix with the fraudsters, thieves, and petty criminals. Walter's heart pounds in his chest as they enter, too many at a time to get a fix on the only one he cares about, and the ghostly stench of tar and pine that only he can smell begins to flood the room. He shakes his head and the relentless *click-clack* rattles somewhere off in one of the octagon's many corners.

The crowd shifts and sways as the men push closer still.

"So much for a fair game, Uncle Bill. We shipped those units fair and square!"

"Who said that?" Uncle Bill snaps. "Come on now, don't be shy."

He scans the crowd and Archie clears his throat, pointing to the assailant within the sea of riled up men. "That man, Warden Willy. Right there."

"Well then, bring him forward!" He motions

a finger and the few Boys-in-Blue move in, ushering the now frenzied-eyed Tribesman forward by his thick, tattooed arms. "Looks like we have a volunteer for today's festivities. What's your name, boy?"

The man looks around, trying hard to hide his concern behind the dark braids dangling in his face. "Didn't mean nothing by it, Uncle Bill, I just—"

"I said what the hell is your name, short-stack?" Uncle Bill hammers the club and forces Walter's shifting eyes to focus upwards.

"Chicago," the man answers.

"Chicago…" Uncle Bill pauses. "I understand your frustrations, but the Bastards make a fair point to consider. It was not a clean or fair fight when it came to time spent on the clock this past year. In fact, the books told me you lot caused a total of eight lockdowns since last snowfall. All of them during the Bastards turn in the shop. Meanwhile, B-Block only caused one. That's eight to one, if I'm counting correctly. And since the ponies were so tight, I see it only fair the two sides duke it out with a gentleman's game. Wouldn't you agree? Don't all you fine men agree?"

"It's okay, we still got a shot," Dakota tells Eddie.

Walter jitters and scans the men for Marvin as his tooth draws blood from his lip, the pain unable to calm his nerves as the *click-clack* works its way through the crowd.

"Good," Uncle Bill says with a satisfied smile. "Now, how about a volunteer from the home team?" His gaze sweeps across the hundreds of lowered brows. "Who here is good at jacks? Come on now, don't be shy."

"School yard shit." Dakota mumbles, letting go of Eddie and looking at Walter's pale complexion. "Jesus, Jamestown. You alright?"

Walter nods, trying to wave a dismissive hand but his stomach churns and a flash of red and blue skitters past the inmates' feet. A painful knot twists his gut, and his head spins out of control. *Please, no.*

"Oh, come now. If I don't have a volunteer, I'm afraid you will have to forfeit. Be brave gentlemen. Be brave!"

Another flash of the blood-stained jean jacket darts by, buckling Walter's knees as Dakota throws a hand under his shoulder, dodging an arm that flails to regain some balance.

All at once, Uncle Bill zeroes in on the raised hand, his voice ringing out with glee. "Mr. Edwards, it seems you are trying to make a good first impression within your ranks. Good for you!"

The eyes of Cold Keep turn as one, locking onto Walter's dizzy expression and Dakota lets go, no longer concerned if he stands or falls flat on the floor.

Shit.

In less than a moment the Boys-in-Blue spring into action and sweep him forward, plopping him next to Chicago at the base of the stairs.

"Now I want a good, clean game, gentlemen."

Walter shakes his head, catching up to the situation just in time to snatch the bag tossed down by Uncle Bill.

"Seeing as the Assholes in A-Block did technically emerge victorious, cheating or not, I have rewarded them with one less jack. Chicago here will have nine, and Mr. Edwards, ten. First one to clear their lot is the winner; the loser's block gets the Boot, simple as that. Now clear some room, you wonderful guests of mine. Form a circle so we can all cheer our competitors on!"

The sea of once sullen inmates parts, now whooping and hollering as Walter is whisked away by reaching hands and finds himself in the center of the cheering men circling around like a fish avoiding a shark. He looks around and spills the nineteen metal jacks and two rubber balls from the bag, homing in on Chicago. The pair lowers themselves to the jagged tiles and Walter hands his opponent his half of the items.

Bounce the ball, snatch the jacks, catch the ball. Bounce, snatch, catch. Easy, he reassures himself.

"Don't you dare fuck this up, Edwards!" someone calls out.

"Are you ready, gentlemen? This one's for all the marbles."

Walter and Chicago reluctantly nod, and the warden brings the club down, signaling to start.

BOUNCE, SNATCH, CATCH

Bounce, snatch, catch.

One.

Bounce, snatch, catch.

Two.

Walter's hands make simple work of the toys as he grabs the tenth jack, catches the ball, and clears the first round. He tosses them again with a metallic clatter, spreading them less far apart this time and proceeds to bounce, snatch, and catch while trying to block out the screaming inmates all around.

Two.

Bounce, snatch, catch.

Four.

"Come on, Edwards!" someone calls.

"Let's go, Chicago!"

Six.

Eight.

Ten. Another round closes.

Spread, bounce, snatch, catch.

Three.
Six.
Nine.
Ten.

Walter focuses on the metal pieces, spreading them closer in rounds four, five, six, and seven, his mind zeroing in on the win closing nearer. The cartilage in his arm burns with each toss, but the pain keeps his nerves in check. Unable to help himself, he glances up at Chicago as he snatches five jacks in one swoop.

"You're ahead, Jamestown. Don't stop now!" Dakota calls from somewhere in the madness as the ball veers off Walter's finger.

"Fuck!" He grabs it and spreads the ten jacks, starting over.

Bounce, snatch, catch.
Eight.
Bounce, snatch, catch.
Ten.

"Two more rounds, Jamestown. Focus!"

"Shut the hell up, kid. You're making me nervous!" Another glance up shows Chicago still behind as he scoops seven jacks, but Walter's optimism is dashed as he recalls his opponent has one less round to close out than him. Distracted, an uncalculated grab snatches all ten jacks in one go. "Shit, come on!" He spreads them and Chicago claims the last of his seventh round, then begins his eighth.

Frustrated, Walter bounces the ball, scoops the nine jacks, and repeats the process on the remaining one.

"One more. Just grab 'em all and catch the ball!"

"I thought I told you to shut it, kid!" Walter bounces and scoops, only grabbing seven as the other three slip through his fingers. He swallows his frustration, saving it for later and re-spreads them so tightly they look like the barbed wire that holds Cold Keep and its prisoners within captive. The slew of voices call from all over.

"Come on!"

"What the hell are you doing, Chicago?"

"One more!"

"Let's make things interesting, gentlemen."

"Don't stop now!"

"Hurry the fuck up!"

"All rules off the table. The gloves are off!"

"Hit him!"

Walter's ball floats up as Uncle Bill's southern drawl singles itself out in his mind, making him wonder if he heard the words correctly. He shakes his head and reaches for the final jacks as a fist mashes the bridge of his nose, flooding his vision with stars.

"Get up, New-boy!" Eddie begs as Walter's vision returns and he finds himself sprawled out across the cool tiles. He shakes his spinning head and shuffles to his knees, searching, gaining his bearings as Chicago skulks back to his side and closes out his eighth round.

"He's got it!" Dakota shouts.

Walter looks over at his ball lodged under Chicago's foot, and he throws himself across the circle, burying his throbbing shoulder into the

Tribesman's chest. The metal trinkets rain down from his opponents clenched fist as the two tumble, hands grabbing uselessly at the air. Chicago throws his head back, catching Walter in the nose and a loud crack escapes his ears and a gush of blood pours from his face.

"Now it's a show!" Uncle Bill screams with delight.

Blinded by watering eyes, Walter feels around and reclaims his ball, somehow ducking out of the way as Chicago's fist cuts through the air. Walter kicks, and his foot collides with Chicago's gut, sending him to the ground as he climbs to his feet and stands over him, gasping for breath. Instinctively, he reaches for his holster, but is jolted to feel only air and drops his hand, hoping the surrounding eyes don't make the connection.

Chicago's boot sails up, returning the favor. Walter's feet leave the ground, and he falls back, slamming down onto the scattered jacks, the hard metal prongs piercing through his jacket, burying themselves deep into his flesh. The crowd collectively gasps and he screams out in pain.

"Get up!" an unsympathetic inmate calls out.

Walter rolls to his stomach and clambers to his hands and knees, but Chicago stomps on his ribs, pinning him down as a cough paints the tiles with a spatter of blood. Chicago crawls on top of him and raises his fist high, but Walter cocks his head, avoiding a direct blow to his already broken nose.

A stray jack pops into his view as he dodges another attack. He slides it between his knuckles and punches Chicago in the brow, the metal point popping through the man's eyelid like tissue paper, sinking deep into his eye as another collective gasp lets out from the crowd, joining in on Chicago's screams. He stumbles back, grabbing the toy protruding from his face, his moans of pain shifting to terror.

Walter pulls himself across the jagged tiles and bounces the ball high, grabbing all final ten jacks. His eyes lock onto the sphere as it tumbles back to earth, his open hand waiting to receive the win when the set of blurry sideburns loom in the distance and his blood runs cold at the sight of Marvin Willmore standing in the crowd. The pine and tar rips through his skull, and the ball slaps his frozen palm, veering off and meeting the ground.

"What are you doing, you idiot?" Dakota's muffled voice shouts, miles away.

The sickly blue and red creep into Walter's peripherals as he stares into the face of his son's killer, now aged with an oxygen tube strapped under his nose, but with the same sharp eyes he could never forget. The *click-clack* of bones mix with the sound of angry inmates, and he stands there with locked knees, unable to move as Marvin glances over his shoulder for some kind of explanation to the sudden interest.

The son of a bitch doesn't recognize me.

Chicago's rage-induced fist slams him in the gut and he falls, avoiding the jacks protruding from his back as the floor comes up hard, expelling even more air from his lungs. A foot comes down on his spine and he gasps, his eyes fluttering, unsure of the sight beyond the sea of legs. He blinks, trying to make sense of Marvin's burnt orange GMC sitting idle between the rows of tables and their benches in the cafeteria. He wipes the tears from his eyes, but the mangled blood-soaked jean jacket remains under the chassis, sizzling against the hot tailpipe, fluttering beneath the vehicle like a pigeon with a broken wing.

Chicago's rubber ball bounces inches from his nose as a crack of gunpowder sets off in his mind and he feels the bullet rip through his shoulder all over again.

With one final snatch, Chicago tears all nine jacks from Walter's back and catches his ball, igniting half of the crowd into fits of joy, the other half cursing loudly.

"We have a victor!" Uncle Bill yells. The circle floods with inmates and Dakota swoops in, helping Walter to his feet.

"You threw the game, you candy-ass!" a Tribesman shouts, striding over to Walter as Dakota throws a hand into his chest.

"If you could have done better, next time you volunteer, candy-ass." He shoves the man back, and the crowd sways as the men's arguments ramp up. A fist flies and the all-out frenzy begins to take hold of the prison, but settles when the club strikes the railing and the Boot is held high.

"That's enough!" Uncle Bill yells, his face gleaming with a mixture of excitement and anger. "Just because you victors of A-Block have won does not mean any one of you is better than Archie's boot here. Now fall in line and get back to your cages!" He waves to the Boys-in-Blue who herd the celebrating Assholes back into A-Block with a bloodied Chicago high on their shoulders.

Walter looks up from his pool of blood to Marvin funneling out of the lobby with the rest of the hardened criminals and the remaining Bastards stare daggers from all angles.

Low profile my ass.

"Calm, calm now, gentlemen. It was a good fight, and Mr. Edwards fought valiantly. He would have emerged victorious if you hadn't had the disadvantage of ten jacks, may I point out. But *c'est la vie.* It is not all bad news, however." Uncle Bill shifts his voice to that of a game show host. "As a consolation prize, each and every one of you will be going home with not one, but two packs of the good sticks!"

Wayne bursts out from the cafeteria with a mountain of cigarettes, packs piled high in a laundry cart, and emphatic chatter lightens the tension as Walter takes a breath, happy to have at least some anger off him, if only for a moment.

One by one the defeated men line up and grab their smokes as they siphon back into B-Block with heads hung low.

"Better watch your back, Edwards," a man sneers and knocks his blood-soaked shoulder, cutting him in line.

"Hey, New-boy tired hard!" Eddie says and steps behind Dakota. The man turns away and grabs his packs from the warden standing in the doorway, then moves on.

"Truly well fought, Edwards," Uncle Bill says. "I applaud your determination. And fear not these wretched scoundrels, for I have a solitary cell with your name on it. In case some of these jokers get any ideas. A bit lonely, but a couple of months and they will forgive and forget."

Walter wipes another drip of blood from his lip and holds up a finger. "That's awful kind but—"

"Now, now. No need to thank me. We will speak momentarily. In the meantime, have an extra roll on the house." He hands Walter three packs and a clean sock from the bin, then pats him on the back, forgetting about the blood. "Oh, my apologies." He lets out an awkward chuckle and pulls a handkerchief from his breast pocket, wiping his hand.

Dakota shuffles Walter into the block and Eddie takes the lead, waving to the pair. "See you soon, Kota. Take care of that nose, New-boy." He tips his phantom hat and Dakota pulls him close. The pair nod, exchanging mumbled words and after a moment or two, they let go and Eddie turns, taking off down the hall and into one of the cells further down.

The pair climb the stairs, and Walter holds back a moan as he presses the sock to his bloody nose, each step stinging his ribs, face, back, and guts. Finally, they turn into their cell and Dakota gently lowers him onto his cot, then spins, turning back with a lit smoke that he hands to Walter.

"How the fuck did you—" Walter begins but doesn't bother. "All this over a fucking boot? Spit it out, kid. What's—what's so special about the damn thing?"

Dakota stares, face shifting from concern to worry. "It's not about the Boot, Jamestown. It's about what the Boot tracks in."

"Tracks in? Enough with the cryptic bullshit, just tell me!" He edges his aching body to the edge of the cot, and a draw of smoke calms his nerves, numbing the pain.

Dakota grabs the door and heaves it shut with a clang. "L-listen, Jamestown," he stutters. "Cold Keep ain't like the rest of 'em."

"No shit."

"Yeah, no shit, no shit. Listen to me. You don't gotta concern yourself with this crap right now; you got your golden ticket. Uncle Bill gave you your own cell in solitary away from that Boot. Best thing you can do now is cash it in and live in blissful ignorance until you got no other choice."

The adrenaline fades and Marvin's face moves back to its normal spot in Walter's mind. He stands, letting a different problem take hold. "I'm not taking no free pass, kid. I've got better shit to do than sit in solitary for months on end. I got less than four days before—" He bites down, cutting himself off as a set of inmates walk past their cell, throwing insults.

Dakota steps close, hushing his voice. "You don't understand. Jesus, you gotta believe me. You wanna be anywhere but here when... when... Shit, just take your private room and bug out, okay?"

"When what? What's got you so scared?" Walter pushes Dakota onto his cot.

"Alright, you skags, everyone better be in their cells!" Archie calls from the corridor below. The sound of one firm boot, followed by the dampened thud of a sock works its way up the winding stairs, down the catwalk, and stops right above their cell on the fourth level. Walter and Dakota pause, motionless, watching the shadow sway above as Archie's sullen voice floats down. "As you know, Claude—"

Instantly, the man inside his cell breaks into tears. "No, Boss-man, please!"

Archie continues. "I have the burden of giving one cell in this block the Boot tonight. It's with a heavy heart that I do this, but you know as well as I do that I have no choice in the matter."

Walter steps to the bars for a better listen, and Uncle Bill emerges.

"Boo!"

He pushes himself back, nearly falling onto his cot, and the warden laughs.

"My sincerest apologies, good man. I only came to scoop you up from these slums and deliver you to sanctuary. Sanctuary being your private suite in solitary, of course. I do hope my red feathered friend here has filled you in on this horrible little place."

Walter looks to Dakota, then back. "Apparently there is a lot to be said around here, but few mouths are doing any talking. Do you mind telling me what kind of show you're running here, Uncle Bill?" He lets out a puff of smoke that hangs between them, then drops his shoulders, reminding himself to play his part as he takes a step back, attempting to appear docile behind the sock still gently held against his face.

Uncle Bill scoffs. "I do not answer to you, Mr. Edwards. However, I will blame your lack of respect on your current physical afflictions. Now, I suggest you collect your things and come with me before I retract my generous offer." He pulls the lone key from his jacket and extends it to the door, but Walter reaches through the bars, covering the keyhole.

"That was more than a kind offer, Uncle Bill, but I think it's best I stay put for now. I'm still getting settled in and the kid and I have hardly gotten to know each other."

Uncle Bill steps back, processing Walter's rejection as Archie and Claude ramble above.

"Claude, I'm sorry."

"No, Boss-man, please. I only got two years left. Please, I'm begging you!"

The cries spill down on the thinking warden, and finally he speaks. "Trust me son, come with me and we will—"

"I would just as rather take my chances out here with that smelly old Boot than see the inside of the same four walls all winter. With all due respect, of course."

The cries for mercy turn to sobs, and Uncle Bill looks up. "Just tie the damn boot and move on, you idiot. What's done is done, *c'est la vie!*" No response comes and Uncle Bill snaps his attention back to Walter. "Listen here and listen good, Mr. Edwards, there will be no other chances to take me up on this offer; after tonight you will be begging for this opportunity back. I assure you a solitary cell will smell like a spring petunia compared to this room for two with a red-skinned kid-killer."

Walter stares Uncle Bill down. "I have made my decision; give my spot to someone else. Eddie, in fact. Give it to Eddie."

Uncle Bill walks away with an upright glide and yells, "That spot was given to you out of the kindness of my heart, and if your posterior will not be situated in that cell, then nobody's will!" He trots down the stairs and out the block, leaving Archie's hushed whispers above as he embraces Claude through his cell bars.

"I have to go, I'm sorry." Archie pulls a key out from his pocket and places it in the infamous boot, then ties it to the handrail by its laces with a firm double knot. The smell wafts down, filling Walter's crooked nose with enough stink to make him wretch.

"No, please. Don't do this. Please, Boss-man."

Archie turns away, locking eyes with Walter through the perforated walkway.

Walter pushes himself back, this time falling onto his cot with a painful thud as Archie's one boot shuffles down the stairs, takes a sharp right turn and stops outside his cell.

"Come on, one pack," he barks and puts his hand out.

Walter stands, looking at his outstretched palm.

"Did I stutter, chicken-shit? Warden Willy gave you three packs; I saw it. Now hand one over."

Walter holds his ground, but Dakota springs from his cot and gives him a nudge. "Fine…" He fishes a pack from his pocket and Archie snatches it with a smirk.

"A lesson in minding your own business,

Edwards. Now go to sleep." He turns and descends the stairs. "Sweet dreams, you Bastards!"

"Sweet dreams?" Walter looks at Dakota. "It's not even ten in the morning."

Dakota peels the mattress from his cot and lays it between the sink and toilet. "It's a prison, Jamestown, not the Ritz. What did you think we would be doing with our time? Arts and crafts? Get some sleep; you'll wanna be alert for tonight. Come one, come all!" He beats the thin bedding with his fist, trying to work out the lumps.

"Tell me why—"

"Aye-ya, white-man. Give it up! I'd just be wasting my breath." Dakota throws himself down on his mattress. "You might want to consider squeezing in next to me."

Walter huffs. "I don't swing that way, kid."

"Neither do I. Ah, forget you then." He pulls a worn book from under his cot and flips it open in silence.

Claude's begging peters off after an hour, and within two, the chatter amongst the Bastards fades to the occasional hushed exchange as Walter counts the stones that make up the four walls around him, the rocks weighing down his eyelids better than any sheep ever could.

Three hundred twenty-three.

Bounce, Snatch, Catch

WHAT THE BOOT
TRACKS IN

"Wake up, Jamestown!"

Walter cracks his eyes open to the thick cloud of breath hanging between him and his cellmate. "What? What's going—"

Dakota throws a hand over his mouth, but Walter smacks it away.

"Paws off! I told you, I don't fancy boys, kid!" He pauses at his own breath clinging to the air. "Why—why's it so damn cold in here?"

Dakota tosses his hands up and crawls back to his mattress at the back of the cell, motioning for Walter to follow. "It's not like that, you old bigot, please," he begs with a voice barely more than a whisper.

"Paws off, off, off," a broken mumble echoes from somewhere in the block, its words tainted with the distinct tone of Walter's stolen voice. "Fancy boys, fancy, fancy, fancy."

Walter stares out the cell, getting ready to

address the inmate with the sense of humor, when Claude cries from above. "Dear Jesus, please have mercy on me!"

"Jesus. Jesus. The Man who forgives. Be fast, show mercy: the Man who forgives," the crooked voice sings, no longer flavored with Walter's pitch, but now Claude's.

Walter stands from his cot and steps to the door, watching the Boot sway from the handrail above as Claude reaches out for it, unable to bridge the gap from behind his bars.

"Why's he talking to himself like that, kid?"

Dakota stands and carefully steps to Walter. "Please, just come away from there."

"I don't wanna die. Dear God, Jesus, please!" Claude prays.

"Please, please, please. Jesus Gaaaawd," the voice mocks, not from above, but down the hall.

Walter takes a precautionary step back, feeling his shivers turn to chills. "Why—why's he doing that?" He shakes his head and holds his ground. "You alright up there, mister?" His words ring loud, and Dakota throws himself at Walter, but Walter raises a fist, stopping him in his tracks. "You grab at me again and I'll put you to sleep."

Silence hangs in the block for what feels like forever when finally, the vacuum is filled with Walter's faux voice echoing back. "Mister, you okay? Mister? Up, up, up?"

The clatter of hard sounding stones against cement send vibrations through Walter's legs as an inmate further down lets out a terrified scream.

"Mother of God, it's there, over there!"

"Here, there. Can you see me now?" it calls with a self-satisfied moan.

Walter throws himself back, eyes wide as he bumps into Dakota and they topple to the floor, the mattress doing little to soften their landing. Another scream lets out and the steady metallic thrum of footsteps approach. Walter grips his stomach, wincing at the devouring pain deep in his gut as the cold thickens around his breath, the plumes of moisture growing larger with the creeping sense of unease that twists around his chest and forces the breath from his lungs.

Dakota leans closer and whispers in his ear with chattering teeth. "That's it…"

"That's what?" Walter asks.

"That's what the Boot tracks in."

A small tap pulls Walter's gaze, then another. Small white balls fall from the level above and stick to their catwalk. He leans in, squinting at the pieces of gum, their minty scent mixing with the stench of Archie's boot.

"It never works," Dakota says.

"What?"

"The gum. Poor bastard's trying to cover up the smell of the Boot."

Claude's prayers join the crinkling wrappers above, and Walter winces with each small tap as the gum misses its mark and finds its resting place on the cascading catwalks below.

"What the hell is this place?"

Dakota lunges, grabbing the other mattress and sandwiches them like cigarettes between two packs of gum. "Don't look, just leave it be,

Jamestown."

The foundation rattles with each step and the inmate's screams let out, one after another as the shuffle works its way down the line, finally coming to a stop somewhere just beyond their cell. Walter holds his breath, his lungs burning and suddenly craving a smoke as a soft hum calls out, singing a tune he feels he should know. Beyond the cover of bedding something sniffs, searching for its mark between notes of its song.

"Don't look, don't look, don't look," Dakota whispers over and over, his words becoming a mantra as he rocks back and forth.

"Look, look here," the voice beckons to them. "Here, here, here." A faint scratching ripples through the material pressed against Walter's ear and turns to nips, gently tugging at the mattress as it lifts.

They bury their fingers into the foam, holding it tight as the scent of decay fills the small cell and burrows itself next to the tar and pine in Walter's mind. Terror rolls through his bruised body, and against his better judgment, he pulls the mattress back, fist ready to strike as Dakota screams out in desperate protest.

His eyes adjust to the pale moonlight and his throat cinches tight at the sight of the festering palm and its flesh that falls short of its fingers, leaving only bone at its five tips. The thought of stones clattering against cement now feels like an optimist's dream as each digit *click's* and *clack's* against one another and pinch the mattress, trying to gain hold of their only line of defense. Walter's fist falls to his side as his eyes lock onto its palm, etched with an image he can't quite make out, then a wrist, draped with translucent, tattered skin. It rises—its elbow bent where any normal arm would end—and stretches up towards the ceiling, disappearing into the darkness between the bars.

A scream catches in Walter's throat and he cowers, feeling like one of the raccoons stuck in its trap, huddled against the back of its cage while hands reach in, nipping to drag him out. He stares past the unnatural appendage, unable to look away from the two eyes reflecting back at him, their sheen glowing green like a deer caught in headlights. It lets out a deep, chilling breath, and the smell folds his stomach, forcing out nothing but bile across the mattress.

"Thank you...," it whispers with rotten breath that gasses the cell. It trails a finger through the run of vomit and pulls it back with an audible slurp. The two shimmering spots stare through him, and they lean in closer, observing Walter's frozen demeanor. "Interesting..." The eyes break away, freeing him from their hold and blink, locking with the Boot overhead. "There you are..." The faint outline of hands reach to the platform above and grab hold. Another wave of nausea threatens Walter's stomach as its foot—robbed of all toes—steps onto the railing like the rung of a ladder and the black, frostbitten holes rise, then vanish.

"What- what am I seeing, kid?" Walter asks without even realizing it, but Claude's terrified scream leaves no room for an answer.

"Jesus. Dear God, Jesus, no. Stay back!"

The Boot sways from its laces as Walter

watches the faint silhouette of the thing reach inside and pluck the key from within. With little say in the matter, he leans in for a closer look, desperately wishing to turn away.

The key finds its hole and sends Claude into a flurry. "I said get back. Help me, somebody help me, please!" The lock *clinks* as Walter and Dakota shake violently against one another, helplessly listening to the thing mock its next victim with his own voice.

"Help him, help him!" Its laughter mixes with the squealing cell door. "They gave you to me. No God to help you here."

"Get away. Get the fuck back! God of heaven's army, rescue us from this perilous time. Deflect these arrows that are aimed at me and—no, no, please. Somebody, please!"

A sound like no other belts out, filling the ears of every last man in B-Block with a violent explosion of animalistic screams and tearing meat. Walter pulls the mattress back over and Dakota buries his head into his arm as a slow trickle of blood spills down onto their catwalk, building into a steady stream.

With one final whiff of the thing's rot, Walter's mind finally gives in and he tumbles into unconsciousness, leaving only a moment for one last thought: *This is where Cold Keep's missing men are going.*

TWISTED AND BROKEN ANGLES

Arms, legs, and frozen faces jut out from the drifts of snow at twisted and broken angles, rising from the piles like once living saplings, now succumbed to the outlasting winter. Across the village, all but one wigwam lay in crumbled heaps, the last trickling smoke and struggling to stand upright against the wind.

Walter wakes and sits up, focusing on what's left of the family within the angled walls:

A young woman stares at the horrors outside through the slit in the hide flap and pulls it closed, turning to the warmth of her home and her brother across the dying fire with the bubbling kettle nestled amongst its coals.

"Why us, Tahki? Have you eaten anything

it's offered?" he asks.

Tahki looks at him with disgust. "Do you think I'm a fool?"

"It whispers to me, too. It's okay."

"I haven't, Hosa!" She throws a mitten over her mouth as the shout bounces around the small refuge, and her babe stirs next to the fire, letting out a gentle coo while the siblings sit, listening to the embers crackle.

From beyond the thin walls, the quiet, hollow imitation of her voice whispers back, growing and taking on her husky tone. "Haven't, haven't at all. Not once."

Tahki holds her breath and the rambling fades away as she looks to the dwindling flames, feeling its heat fade by the second. "There is nothing left to burn. We have to do it now."

Hosa reluctantly nods and drags himself to the far side of their home. He pulls out a knife and works the sharpened bone into the wall with gentle hands, rocking it back and forth, tearing a slit that leaks the darkness and falling snow inside.

Tahki turns to the flap that was once their door and confirms. "Are you ready?"

"What choice do we have?" Hosa says.

"Now." She forces their last piece of kindling through the slit, whooping and hollering as it pivots in her palm, twisting in the cold winter air. The snow crunches under the thing's bounding feet, and its cheap imitation of her voice mixes with something more ancient and animalistic. The thing bats at the wood, and Tahki looks to her brother, plunging his arm through the slit, then retracting it with a split log clutched in his mitten.

"Quickly," she whispers as he reaches for another. The kindling tugs in her grasp and she squeezes tighter, ignoring the mad ramblings on the other side, its whispers telling her things it has no right knowing. Her daughter's gentle coo builds into a whine, and she winces, unable to calm her worries from the job at hand.

The pile of wood grows with each draw, and Hosa breathlessly complains, "Why didn't we store the meats with the timber?"

The thing's guttural call mingles with the gentle cry, growing louder and more distorted as it struggles to hold on to one single voice at a time.

Tahki whips her head around, wishing she had another set of hands to cover her ears. "It's how we have always done," she says." Never have you suggested otherwise in all the winters before this spirit came to devour our people, Brother."

"I'm suggesting it now!"

"It's a little too late, now!"

"Farrrr too late now. Mmmmmmhhhmm." It laughs, unable to help itself.

"We never should have let the others go after it!"

"And instead do nothing?" Tahki argues, no longer trying to be quiet. "Continue to let it snatch the children while they slept in their beds? They did all they could!"

"At least you have your daughter. I have no one!"

"Your father, your mother, cousins, and elders were mine, too; ours, if you have forgotten the blood we share, you selfish doe. Am I no one to you? Is your own niece nobody as well?" Tahki points to her child. They stare at each other in the flickering light as the kindling waves free in her hand and she pauses, realizing the loss of interest from the other side. "Hosa!"

"Mmmmmhhhmhmh."

The air fills with another deep, twisted laugh and large bounding steps wrap around the wigwam towards Hosa as he yanks his arm back. The tear catches on his mitten, snaring his hand in place, and a small yelp escapes his lips.

"Brother, now!"

"*Hunta*, Brother. I'm coming, Brother-boy!" It laughs with delight.

Tahki watches in disbelief, unable to do anything as her sibling pulls, trying to free himself as the dark shadow glides across the walls with steady precision and drops fast.

Hosa comes loose, falling backwards into their sanctuary and sits up, allowing himself a nervous, but relieved laugh. "Nearly got me." He raises an arm, brushing back his dark, wild hair, painting his face with a stroke of thick crimson blood. His eyes cross, landing on the jagged bones protruding from his wrist and the strands of flesh dangling from the thing's quick work. "What is— What? T-Tahki…help!"

"Stay still!" Tahki pleads. She throws her mittens off and drags her gaunt legs behind her, clawing towards Hosa as he tries to back away from his own missing appendage.

She stops, eyes rising from her brother and

glimpsing into the dark tear above. From the night, two eyes reflect back, their sheen glowing green like a wolf caught in torchlight. "Brother…" she utters with breathless lungs, her voice lost in the chaos. She waves her arms frantically, trying to grab his attention, but they fall to her side and give way as the nightmare before her unfolds.

Fingers—long and even longer devoid of warmth—stretch out from its thick sleeve of stitched furs and crawl in from the wild nothingness, its palm uncoiling as Tahki tries to call to her oblivious brother one last time.

"Please, Tahki!" he begs, unable to take his eyes off his gushing stump.

It strikes, grabbing him with one sickening twist, and drains the hope from his face, filling his eyes with fear as Tahki drags herself like a wounded coyote, desperate to reach him. Its fingers weave through his matted locks and lift him from the ground, his cries of horror curdling to ones of pain as his feet dangle, wrist dripping like an elk hung to drain.

The ancient thing laughs with delight as its arm rises higher, ripping the seam towards the peak of their home and letting the stiff wind threaten the already weak flames.

Tahki throws herself around the smoldering pit, desperate to save the last of the dying warmth and the iron kettle within scalds her ribs as she prays to the Great Spirit.

"No," it whispers. "You worship me now." It flicks its wrist, snapping Hosa's neck, and drags him through the hole.

"Hosa!" Tahki turns away, desperate for the sight of anything else, but only finds more horror as her daughter stares at the scene and smiles.

All at once a stillness blankets the chaos and the wind dies down. Tahki rolls from the fire, reaching for one of the lesser blood-covered logs and pulls smoke into her lungs as she blows on the coals between panic-induced gasps, desperate to revive the flames.

"S-Sister…" Hosa calls out from the night.

Tahki jolts upright, staring into the darkness. "Brother?"

"Help me, please…"

She scrambles to her knees once more and drags herself towards his voice. "I'm coming, Brother, hold on."

"Please, Sister. I want you…"

Tahki pauses at the empty plea and throws herself from the path of the palm that swipes through the air, snapping her exhausted mind in two as she collapses next to the smoldering pit and weeps.

"So close, *nuntanuhs*…"

"What more is there to take?" she screams. "Do not say you still hunger when you leave the waste of my family outside to spoil. A foul creature such as yourself would not mind chewing through frozen flesh, of that I'm sure."

The unblinking eyes hover in the night. "Why eat from the reserves when you keep so fresh on your own? Why chew and gnaw when warm, soft bites are just a pinch away?"

"Then do it! If your appetite is never-ending, have your way with us already." She scoops a handful of burning coals and heaves them into the darkness, lighting its fur hood as they trickle down, giving way to its true massive size.

"No. No meal left here. The babe would be a single swallow, its fat flavorless and unseasoned with fear." It disappears with a flurry of snapping wood, and branches rain down, patching the hole in the wigwam leading out. The cold breeze ceases as the pine arms wrap themselves around the home and the thing's foul breath blows between them, giving life to the fire inside. Tahki stokes the flames with traumatized relief and throws another log into the pit, unable to deny any longer that her once comforting home has now become a terrible prison.

"I can care for you. I can provide for my kind, *nuntanuhs*," it whispers only to her.

"I am not your kind, wretched spirit," she spits, tears rolling down her cheeks.

"But you could be." The long sleeve enters uninvited once more, dropping her brother's stolen hand next to her. "Eat… feast… gorge."

The scene fades around Walter as Tahki sobs, then stops, her expression growing distant as she looks up at him. She reaches deep into her robes, suddenly aware of his presence, and pulls out a piece of bannock from within, extending it for him to take.

Walter turns away, but the bread's warm scent fills his stomach and he can't help but look back at the offering, unable to deny that it would rid him of his growing hunger. He reaches out and the last of the ravaged village fades away, leaving Cold Keep in its place.

LAUNDRY DAY

The inmates go about their morning in silence, sucking on cigarette after cigarette as they eat their grits with trembling spoons that chatter against metal trays, filling the prison with an anxious rattle.

"Come on. Come on." Walter digs his fingernails into the back of his neck and repeats the Drywell Police Department phone number over and over, glancing back and forth from A-Block to the scuffed receiver hanging from its metal box. *What would you even say?*

"Hi-ho, hi-ho, Jamestown."

Walter jumps and turns to Dakota, trying to make sense of where the morning went as his stomach growls, realizing it missed another meal.

"Buggered off real quick after counting smokes this morning. I left your cut under your mattress."

Walter nods 'thanks' and reluctantly follows Dakota down one of the corridors with the rest of the shaken-up inmates. "What was that thing last night, kid?"

"Would be in poor taste to say its name. Like I told you this morning, it's best not to invoke such things by droning on about 'em. Ya know?"

"No!" Walter snaps, his nerves fried. "I don't know. Why don't you fill me in?"

Eddie catches up and holds his invisible hat to his head, smiling with chocolate pudding smeared across his face. "Nasty morning to be a Sock-monkey, New-boy."

"Oh? And what is a Sock-monkey, exactly?" Walter asks, not really wanting an answer.

Dakota lifts Eddie's shirt and wipes his face, answering for him. "Newbies who don't know the first thing about pouring iron in the workshop get to scrub the sheets."

"You got me scrubbing shit stains?"

"Me, no. Cold Keep, yes. Can't have the rookies bringing down the numbers. Don't think you need telling why. And there are piss stains, too; don't forget those." Dakota points ahead at the sign marked *Clean-Line,* now scribbled over with *Sock-monkeys* in thick black letters.

"It's okay, New-boy. We will make Kota do most of the work."

"You're a Sock-monkey, too?" Walter asks Dakota, and Wayne pipes in, pushing a cart of yellow stained sheets in his trolley.

"Dakota's a Sock-monkey for life. Tell him why, go on."

Dakota sticks a tongue out as Wayne and Eddie share a laugh, throwing elbows into each other's sides. "Let loose a couple pounds of slag was all. One time," he admits.

"A couple pounds?" Wayne blurts out. "Try a whole damn vat of glowing hellfire. The entire shop looked like the *Divine Comedy*! It took us a week to grind it all up and haul it out of there once it cooled."

"You're never gonna live that one down, Kota. No, no," Eddie says, continuing his chuckle.

***

For the rest of the afternoon, they take turns reaching into the barrel of detergent with watering eyes, the fresh smell a welcome relief as it washes away the stench left in Walter's nose from the night before. They sprinkle the pungent powder over the yellow and brown stains on almost every sheet, working the suds into the spots before sending them off in their trolleys for Dakota to load into one of the many oversized washers.

Eddie points at Walter's swollen eyes. "What happened to your face, New-boy?"

"Dammit, Eddie, you've asked him that four times this afternoon!" Dakota shouts from the platform above.

"Got punched by one of the Assholes when I was playing jacks," Walter answers while working on a particularly deep stain.

"Who did, New-boy?"

Dakota throws his hands up in defeat and storms away. "I'm taking ten! I can't listen to this shit for one more second."

"Just forget it, it's not—" Walter bites his tongue, spotting Eddie's smirk as he watches Dakota trot away.

"It's funny watching Kota get mad, New-boy. It's too easy some days." Walter tries to hold back a laugh, but it breaks free as Eddie's mischievous smirk turns into a full-blown grin.

"So... Eddie," Walter composes himself, trying to sound casual. "What's the story of that thing in our block last night?"

Eddie drops his brush with shifting eyes, his grin fading like it was never there at all. "I don't know what you're talking about, New-boy."

"Oh, come now. You know, that thing crawling around the catwalks. The thing that snatched up—"

Eddie raises his voice, panic setting in. "I said I don't know what you're talking about, New-boy! We don't talk about it!"

"So you do know!" Walter points a finger, and Eddie smacks it away.

"Talking about it only makes it come back sooner, dumdum."

"How could—"

"So, how's he do it?" a hushed inmate asks, approaching them with a dirty fingernail pushed between his crooked teeth.

Eddie backs away, suddenly put off by the new company. "Go away, Darcy. Nobody asked you nothin'!"

"How's who do what?" Walter asks, excusing the interruption as he continues to work the detergent in.

"You know, big chief in your cell." Darcy looks down the line at Dakota arguing with another man about the proper way to load the spinning drums. "How's he get those fucking things lit? The cigarettes?" He stares at Walter, flashing a fake cordial smile.

"He just lights 'em off one another as far as I can tell."

"Yeah, I know that, dipshit. I'm talking about the first one of the day."

Walter lowers his sheet and turns to the man. "Haven't got a clue. One second he's sitting there, the next he's got a cherried dart hanging from his lips. Whatever his secret is, he's not indulging me."

"Oh, bullshit!"

Darcy closes the gap between them, but Walter stands his ground, slowly sinking his hand into the barrel beside him and feeling the grains of detergent dance between his fingers as he clutches a tight pile. "You mind backing yourself up there, mister?"

Darcy pauses at Walter's handful of detergent and lets out a defiant laugh. "And what if I'm happy right where I am?" He pulls his gaze from the grains draining between Walter's fingers and stares into his swollen eyes. "How about I buy the answer off ya? I'll pay you my two good packs from Uncle Bill for the trick. How's that?"

"How's my whiskers?" Walter asks, catching Wayne's eye across the shop and signaling to his full bin of sheets.

"Your what?"

"I asked how my whiskers are. Are they straight? Cause it sounds to me like you think I'm some sort of rat willing to sell out my business partner for chicken scratch." He squirrels the detergent away, letting it drain into his jeans as Wayne strides over and goes to exchange his trolley. "Hold up a second there, Wayne. I got room for one more." He drives his fist into Darcy's nose and pulls his jacket over his head, giving him one more punch for good measure before flipping him over and discarding him into the cart.

"Holy cow!" Eddie shouts.

Walter spreads his sheet, draping the urine stain over the unconscious man's face and gives Wayne a wink, handing him a few sticks of gum.

"Always a pleasure, Edwards." Wayne returns the wink, and rolls the trolley away as Walter brushes himself off and looks down at the dried blood spattered across his shirt from the day before.

"Where they keep the clean shirts around here, anyway?"

"Just sheets today, New-boy. Uniforms are done Tuesdays."

"Alright, shit-birds!" Archie hollers out over the whirl of machines and strolls in with a Boy-in-Blue following close behind, pushing a cart filled with cans of beans. "Come and get it."

Walter feels his stomach pull towards the food as he watches the inmates take their lunch, one by one, prying the lids with their spoons. He clears his throat and approaches Archie. "I haven't been given a spoon."

Archie sneers up at him and rests his hand on his club. "You sure as shit have, inmate."

An awkward pause lingers between the two and Walter tries to keep his ears from flushing red. "I was told I was to get one when you gave me my uniform, but I didn't." He glances at Dakota and Eddie spooning at their cans in silence, and a wave of envy runs through his gut.

"What do you think is more likely, Edwards? A trained correctional officer forgetting to issue a godforsaken spoon, or a petty criminal—a leech on society's underbelly—not remembering where he left his one and only slop stick?"

Walter goes to argue but drops his head, noticing Archie's boots impatiently tapping as the faint smell of mint wafts off them. He looks up with disgust and turns to the end of the line, deciding to drink the beans from his can rather than argue any longer. "Nice boots," he calls back.

"You like 'em? How about a closer look?" Archie slips the club from his side and presses it against one of the bloodstained holes in Walter's jacket. "I'll even let you stare at 'em outside your cell if you like. I've got you all figured out, Edwards."

Walter grins as the pain sends a satisfying sting through his body, calming his nerves. "Is that right?" He turns back to the short man.

"That's right. You losers are all the same. A disappointed wife that you stuck a kid or two on back at home. Hell, maybe four or five little shits if you're the farming type, but you got city written all over ya."

The tar and pine works its way across Walter's tongue, and frustration bubbles up inside him for letting a man like Archie get under his skin so easily.

"Am I close?" Archie continues. "Three to five years in here, my ass. I can see the fire in those eyes. Men like you come in for some petty crime and land themselves an extra two years for assault. Then another eight after that for stabbing some poor schmuck because their big egos got bruised."

Walter slides his hand into his pants, pinching his thigh as the taunting words take hold of his emotions and the grains of detergent trickle around his fingers.

"Next thing you know, you've got yourself stuck in here for decades. All while your wife has another man's johnson wrapped around her lips, and a daughter forgetting what her daddy's face looks like while mommy moans the night away in the room over."

Dakota's words play in Walter's mind as the red and blue tumble in his peripherals, the mess of color folding over and over in one of the washers beside him. *Take my spoon. Grip it tight and drive the handle into his neck. Guaranteed your ass will be on the other side with the Assholes in an hour.* He squeezes the detergent and pulls it from his pocket, his aim locked onto Archie's eyes as he revels the thought of him rolling on the floor, clawing at his face while it burns out his retinas. His fist loosens, but his arm stops dead against Dakota's beefy hand as it wraps around his wrist and holds it in place. Walter lunges again to even less result and drops his arm in defeat, feeling a wave of relief wash over him as he regains control.

Archie jumps back, club lifted high and eyes wide. "What the hell do you think—"

Dakota spins and holds up a steady hand. "Leave poor Jamestown alone, Boss-man. Stupid bastard passed up Uncle Bill's offer for his own private cell yesterday. Man was white as a ghost after the night us men in B-Block had. Got a front-row seat thanks to you hanging that boot of yours over our heads last night; he's just a little shook up is all." Dakota plucks a smoke from his pocket, its tip already smoking between his pinched fingers as he puts it in Walter's mouth, giving his arm a shake and dislodging the fist full of poison back into his pocket.

The tobacco replaces the tar and pine with a different flavor altogether, and the blood drains from Walter's hot cheeks as the blue and red wash away with the rinse cycle.

Archie smirks, pushes Dakota back, and looks at Walter. "That's right. You should be in solitary, shouldn't you? You really must be the stupidest son-of-a-bitch in here. This is your one and only warning, Edwards. Stay out of my sight." He whistles a tune and struts away, snapping his fingers at the Boy-in-Blue. "No beans for Edwards today."

The inmates stand frozen in place as the guards clear out and another meal goes by.

Dakota turns, wrapping his hand around Walter's neck and pins him against one of the hot dryers in half a second.

"Whoa, hey now!" He pushes back, but Dakota shakes him, and his head bounces off the vibrating machine, sending him into a daze.

"You wanna get yourself killed, go right ahead, Jamestown! But I'm not dying because of you!" He reaches into his pocket and pulls a pinch of the detergent out. "What were you gonna do? Blind the son-of-a-bitch? Shove it down his throat and poison him?" He throws the powder down.

Walter pulls at Dakota's hot fingers, his spent muscles useless against the built physique of the Native man as the dryer's hot shell bites into his cut up back.

"You saw what happened to Claude. If you wanna end up like him, that's your choice, but if you get yourself the Boot, you drag my ass down with you." He lets go and Walter drops to the floor, coughing, fighting to catch his breath as he gets to his feet.

"I'm sorry, kid, I just—"

"Just nothing." Dakota's voice drains of anger and adopts a remorseful sadness. "You're gonna march up to Uncle Bill the second you see him next and you're gonna beg for that spot in solitary back. Do you understand?"

Walter raises a desperate hand. "I'm not going in there, kid. I won't. I got business that can't wait." He looks towards the exit and Dakota follows his gaze.

"Is that what that was? You thought that stunt was gonna get you the honeymoon suite with your pal in A-Block? It's not like that when we got the Boot, idiot. Any other time sure, maybe, but the only thing blinding Archie would have done is put your ass on the menu. And that ain't happening as long as we're sharing a damn cell!" Dakota looks away, disappointed. "Why you gotta go and ruin a good thing, Jamestown? We were getting on." He forces his anger back and glares. "Well, I'm sure as hell not living with no loose cannon." He storms over to a shelf littered with dozens of boxes and rifles through them, producing a large sponge. "I got enough targets on my back around here as is, I'm sorry. I can't be babysitting on top of it all." He slaps the sponge into Walter's hand, forcing his fist around it. "You wanna get in with the Assholes? The only way to do it now is by striking a deal with the Shit-talker himself."

Laundry Day

ONE HUNDRED METERS

"Relax, it never comes back two nights in a row," Dakota whispers.

Walter peels his eyes from the darkness beyond the cell and looks down into the stained toilet bowl. The rough cement digs into his knees, and he squeezes the sponge. "You just want someone to scrub your shit stains, is that it, kid?"

Dakota rises from his cot. "Look." He snatches the sponge with burning hands and plunges it into the toilet, pores filling with the stale liquid, then wrings it out in the sink with a slosh. "Now you."

Walter turns his nose up and dips it in, the cold washing over his hands, numbing his fingers as the water in the bowl lowers with each dip. "I'm not sure how—" He stops as the last of the liquid drains and the faint whistle seeps into their cell from the pipes below.

"That's him," Dakota whispers, looking down into the corroded bowl. "You wanna make it to A-Block, he's your man."

"Who?"

"I told you: the Shit-talker. An inmate with strings, that much I know. Now talk; he's a busy man."

Walter looks down, avoiding eye contact with one of the stains, and calls out. "Hello?"

***

Wayne snaps his fingers in Walter's face. "Is this guy toasted or what?"

Walter blinks the previous night away, seeing both Eddie and Dakota sharing a concerned glance.

"New-boy is just nervous is all. Leave him alone," Eddie says, giving the custodian a nudge.

"Gah, just give us a minute." Dakota pulls Walter under the large *Rec Yard* sign as the others turn and mumble to each other. "You with me, Old-timer?"

"Yes, stop calling me that."

"Then quit acting like one. You remember what the Shit-talker told you last night?"

"Yeah, yeah." Walter shuffles towards the double doors, outfitted in too many layers of jumpsuits, gloves, and earmuffs to count, all scavenged from the rec yard supply closet. He pulls at the scarf around his neck and the wool unravels. "You got anything… less tattered?"

"You get what you get, and you don't get upset. Now, as soon as you're outside you'll see the utility garage against the far fence, can't miss it." Dakota turns, grabs the key from Wayne, and places it in Walter's breast pocket with a pat. "This will get you inside. Get there, grab the duffle bag, get back, and drop it off with Wayne. Do that and you got your one-way ticket to that star-crossed lover of yours in A-Block."

"I told you, I know the plan, kid. You got a hearing problem?"

"Alright, alright! Garage is a hundred meters out or so. A quick sprint there, a little longer with the duffel on your way back. Ten minutes tops."

Wayne heaves the metal bar off the door and the others scan their surroundings for any Boys-in-Blue.

"You ready?"

Walter takes a few deep breaths and leans like an Olympian ready at his mark. "Let's just do this already."

Dakota swings the door open with a burdened grunt, and Walter throws himself forward, stopping as the flurry of white powder blasts inwards, cutting through them all. The wind slams the door shut, and Eddie moans.

"Ah, shoot, New-boy! You're gonna need a few more coats."

Walter sighs. "I think you're right, Eddie…"

Dakota shakes his head and steps between the two. "Nu-uh, plans off, Jamestown. That's suicide."

Walter stares through the cafeteria and its cluster of tables at A-Block. *Less than two days*. "A hundred yards isn't that far," he reasons, trying to convince himself it's true.

"In knee-deep snow and with hips as old as yours?" Dakota argues.

"I don't see any other choice, do you? Quit

telling me what's good for *me*!" Walter yells, letting his nerves get the better of him.

Dakota steps out of his way and throws his hands up. "Gah, either way you're out of my cell, go on then!"

"Just tell me which way I'm going."

"Should be that way." Dakota points.

"No, more that way," Wayne says and adjusts the direction of Dakota's arm.

"No, dumdum. It's way over there." Eddie jabs a finger nowhere near the other two's direction.

"Dammit! Which fucking way is it?"

Dakota takes a step back, looking Walter up and down. "Do I look like a mapmaker to you, Jamestown?"

"I thought you Natives were supposed to be good trackers," Wayne says as more inmates wander over, curious to the gathering.

"And I thought you white men were supposed to be smart." Dakota averages out the directions and points. "Go that way, and you'll eventually see it through the storm. This crowd's gonna catch an eye any second. *Hunta,* hurry."

Walter takes a deep breath and kicks the door open, stepping into the wall of snow and sinking to his knees.

The door slams behind him and he lifts his legs, pushing his foot through the white nothingness as snow spills over the lip of his boot, chilling his toes instantly. He squints, following his pointed glove and counts to himself aloud with each step. "Thirty-seven, thirty-eight." His stomach twists and growls, angry for not having the nerve to force down any of the morning grits before heading out. "Eleven, twelve." *What are you doing out here?* "Twenty-one, twenty-two." *Just go home, Walter.* The cold permeates his outer layers, and a chill settles into his legs, making each step burn his rubbing thighs. The wind howls in all directions and the feeling of floating creeps up as he stares into the empty void.

A hollow metal clang rings out as his boot catches something hard below the surface and he topples into the snow, vision plunging into darkness. A deep, panicked breath fills his mouth with ice, and his teeth scream out in pain as the cold wraps around them. *Stand up!* His knees skim the ground, and he gets to his feet, feeling both relieved and foolish at the same time.

All at once the wind kicks up from the north, carrying the smell of rot that replaces the pine-tainted air. Walter stiffens with dread and throws a glove over his nose, resisting the urge to vomit more bile. He turns and visualizes the garage, proceeding with newfound panic. "Thirty. Don't stop," he tells himself.

A guttural shriek gushes out from all around and curdles into an otherworldly cackle. Walter covers his ears, sacrificing his nose as the smell carves into his skull, and another call spews forth, closer than the last. He looks all around and takes off, unable to determine the direction of the horror.

Snapping branches call out between the muted flakes of falling snow and Walter's feet plow through the drifts, no longer lifting at the knees, but sending plumes flying in all directions. "Sixty-three, sixty-four!" he screams to himself now. The smell carries on the wind, growing stronger as the screams draw nearer. "Where are you?" he calls to the fabled garage. "Sixty-six, sixty-seven. Come on!"

Triangles bleed through the storm ahead, and Walter's throat cinches shut seeing the knitted metal fence instead of a solid building. The thick forest beyond the transparent wall sways and pulls at his stomach as the thing's hollow voice calls from somewhere between the trees, counting down, undoing his progress.

"Seventy-seven, seventy-six, seventy-fiiive." It wheezes with cruel joy in between numbers, and the snapping quickens as the lines between the trunk waver and bend, making room for more of the thing's growing malice.

Walter peers to the east, then west, seeing nothing but outstretched fence. "Dammit!" He pivots, trusting his gut. "Left because I'm never right!" His burning legs pump, and the giant mass bleeds through the dense thicket in his peripherals, striding alongside the fence with the blue and red twisted mass clinging to its back, along for the ride.

"Come baaaack! Back, back, back."

Dread grips Walter as the wind gusts and pulls him off course, closer to the fence and the thing on the other side. *I went the wrong way.* He considers turning back, but the forgiving silhouette breaks through the storm and the garage grows more defined with each count closer.

"Twelve, eleven, tennnn," the thing calls after him.

Walter rushes to the front of the structure, passes the large garage door and comes up hard against the man-door next to it. He throws himself against the reinforced entryway and reaches into his pocket, clawing for the key as it fumbles from his shaking fingers and vanishes into the snow below. "No, no, no!" He grasps at the padlock and heaves on the unrelenting steel as the words slip from his lips, "Should have checked the latch."

The chain link chatters like a rattlesnake readying to strike, and rotten fingers poke through, grabbing hold of the permeable wall.

Walter strips his gloves and drops to his knees, sifting through the powder with desperate wide sweeps. Unable to help himself, he looks up at the thing's naked, tattered chest pressed against the fence, spots completely devoid of flesh and revealing its rotted innards. Its ribs rattle and skip off the metal supports like an otherworldly washboard as it climbs with eyes that cut through the whipping storm and stare over the barbed wire. Walter turns away, unable to hold the thing's gaze any longer, and his numb fingers squeeze something rigid in the shifting snow.

"Just a taste," it calls, pulling itself through the jagged metal, the razor-sharp steel ripping through its skin, causing strips of foul-smelling flesh to peel away in streamers of rot and rain down on Walter.

Walter pinches the key, fishes it from the snow and grips it so hard it stings. He gets to his feet and pushes it into the padlock, coming up hard against the thick layer of ice coating the hole. "Fuck! Come on!" He rattles the lock against the door and the thing topples over the fence, its feet now tangled in the barbwire mess as it hangs, stretching down with ungodly hands.

Walter slams the lock over again and glances up, ensnared by the image of a buffalo seared into the outstretched palm reaching for him. The ice dislodges from the hole, and he plunges the key into the slot as the screaming thing comes loose and tumbles to the roof above, its frantic bones and frozen flesh scraping against the tin as it rushes towards the edge. The lock pops and Walter spills through the doorway as the thing swipes at the empty air, grabbing hold of the frame. Its cateraxed eyes dip, peering into the garage at its prey. Walter stumbles to his feet and heaves the door shut with a slide of the merciful deadbolt.

A scream shakes the building from the other side as the thing's lifeless fingers crack and splinter in the sealed door frame. It rips them out and more loose pieces of flesh come free and rain down on Walter's shoulders. He brushes them off with another sickening gag and stumbles backwards, desperate to make room between himself and the only exit. A brief moment of silence passes and the heavy footsteps begin to circle outside, heavy knocks searching for weak spots that send deafening booms throughout the flimsy garage.

Walter clambers to his feet and looks around the dark space. Worn out hoses, field tools, and three lawnmowers worth of parts cluttered the area, all piled around a long-neglected snowmobile. He shuffles towards the back with burning lungs and his eyes meet the giant duffle bag, cutting his odds of getting back to Cold Keep with it in half. Jagged points stretch the material from every angle inside, straining the bag's zipper as though a porcupine had been shoved inside. He stumbles over a jungle of paint cans, and to his relief the bag lifts with ease from its hook. A deafening knock dents a nearby wall and jolts him as the zipper gives way, raining wicker shoes down into a clattering heap. Walter pieces together the shapes, at first unable to make out the items. "Snowshoes! All this way for fucking snowshoes?"

"Aren't you cold?" the thing whispers to him from outside. "I can wait, wait, wait. I don't mind the colllld."

Every word draws from Walter's quickly fading courage, but he shakes his head, severing the thing's hold on him as he shoves the snowshoes back into the bag. *I'm fucked. I'm fucked!*

Another knock dents in the large overhead door and the whole thing shifts on its rails, settling into a cockeyed slant. "A soft spot? So tender…," it says, and another tap caves in the bottom panel further.

Walter darts around the room, knocking over piles of junk as he skitters like a frightened cat without a plan, and another tap spreads the crack further.

"I won't hurt you…"

Walter arms himself with a stray screwdriver as the two decayed nostrils stare in and exhale, filling the room with the stench of lonely death. He strides over and lunges the tool through the gap, jamming it against the thing's hard flesh as it pulls away with little urgency and lets out a howling laugh. The knocking starts up again and the metal rails twist, beginning to give way.

Walter looks towards the door, calculating. *Wouldn't even be a chase.* He shakes the thought, but the word bounces around his skull. "Chase.... *Chase?... Chase!*" he shouts, turning to the dust-slathered snowmobile with a flicker of hope. His heart skips a beat at the key sitting in its ignition, and he sweeps the collection of junk away from the machine, then turns it as the motor sputters. "Come on..." It coughs, bellowing thick black smoke. "Please!" The mechanical steed clears its exhaust with one final wheeze and sucks in a gulp of fresh air, then roars to life. "Yes! Thank you, God!"

The entire building shifts and moans and the bottom panel bursts free from its track, coming to rest at Walter's feet. He slings the duffel bag over his shoulder and strips a scarf from around his neck, wrapping it around the throttle with a knot. The engine screams, filling the room with a cloud of gasoline as the second panel tumbles to the floor. The thing's disheveled legs sprout up from the snow and vanish behind what's left of the crooked door, and Walter closes one eye, heaving the vehicle a couple inches to the left, lining it up with the yard. The putrid fingers reach in, gripping the rails, and with one last jerk, the entire door comes loose and crumbles to the ground.

Walter knocks the gear into drive and the snowmobile skids wildly, chewing up old newspapers beneath it as it takes off, threading between the towering legs. The thing whips towards the roaring vehicle and screams, glossing over Walter completely as it takes off in pursuit, bounding on all fours like a wild animal into the void.

Walter stands in the empty doorway, shocked, then sprints without another second of hesitation. "Ninety-nine, ninety-eight." The motors hum fades over his shoulder and the sound of the pelting snow takes back its rightful place. Walter keeps his eyes fixated on the ground and meets up with his old path carved in the snow. "Seventy-three, seventy-two." Another clang of chain-link ripples out in the distance as the snowmobile meets its final end and an infuriated shriek rattles his nerves. "Forty-four, forty-three. Keep going," he tells himself, trying his best to suppress the breathless wheeze building in his lungs.

The smell of rot worms its way back into his nose and signals the end of his distraction. "Thirty, twenty-nine." The bag slides from his shoulder, throwing his balance off, but with a desperate heave he sets his path straight as the ground shakes and the thing's footsteps fast approach. "Ten, nine, come on, come on!"

The storm gives way to Dakota standing in the open frame of the mess hall, reaching out. "Go, Jamestown! *Hunta, hunta!*"

A blood vessel gives way in Walter's eye as the thing grabs hold of his scarf and tears it free, leaving his neck vulnerable to the freezing breath that sears his exposed skin.

"Just a taste!"

The white world around him fades to black and he dives for Cold Keep's protective stone embrace, away from the wretched thing's *clacking* jaws and bone-laced fingers inches from his heels.

POWDER KEG

Walter bursts through the door and Wayne slams it shut behind him, stopping the thing on the other side with a thud and fit of screams. The inmates jump back, clearing the path as Walter slides across the jagged tiles and comes to a stop.

"Just shy of five minutes!" Dakota yells, and the men erupt—some cheering, others cursing loudly—as he waves a handful of cigarettes. "Richard, that's three to one! You owe me nine sticks, you prick! Don't think I forgot about you, Darcy! Pay up or I'll match that black eye of yours and give you a set!"

Walter convulses with the mixture of cold fear, and Wayne yanks the duffel bag from his shoulder, shoving it into the garbage trolley by his side.

"I'll tell the Shit-talker you came through twice over, Edwards." He turns and vanishes into the crowd, giving Archie a cordial nod as he and the Boys-in-Blue close in on the commotion, dispersing the inmates as if he were a live grenade.

"What the fuck is all this?" Archie stops and shakes his head at the thick layer of frost covering Walter's makeshift snowsuit, then squats by his side. "Went out for a stroll, did ya, Edwards?"

Walter stumbles to his feet, snow sloughing off him as he tries to find an excuse, but only offers breathless gasps for air.

Dakota steps in. "Had a running bet, Boss-man. Said the Old-timer didn't have the grapes to spend at least two full minutes out in the yard; he said otherwise."

Archie looks Dakota up and down, then Walter. "You really are the stupidest son-of-a—"

"What's the harm?" Dakota asks. "Not like there's anything out there but the cold. Isn't that right, Boss-man?"

Archie frowns and reluctantly nods. "Why is it you always seem to be the center of attention around here, Edwards?" He leans in, clicking his boot on the floor. "I'm getting real tired of dealing with your blood-covered ass." He spits between Walter's feet and turns away with three long strides. "How long he make it?" he calls back with a side eye.

"Four minutes fifty-seven seconds," Dakota answers.

Archie's jaw drops just an inch, then closes quick. "You would have made a better Eskimo than a thief, Edwards… Shame." He turns away with a whistling tune and joins Uncle Bill in the lobby, giving the group a dismissive wave.

A lit smoke appears from Dakota's breast pocket, and he hands it over, joining Eddie across the table with a matching look of wonderment. Walter nods a thanks and lifts it to his lips, taking a drag as it calms his nerves.

"So, what was in that sack?" Dakota asks.

Walter hesitates for a moment, working his frozen lips open and closed. "Snow—snowshoes. Sack stuffed full of them."

"Snowshoes? What in the hell does the Shit-talker want with snowshoes?"

Eddie laughs. "Why didn't you wear some, New-boy?"

Walter cocks his head. "What?"

"Snowshoes for walking on snow, New-boy. Why didn't you wear a pair on your way back? Woulda been faster."

The eavesdropping inmates laugh at Walter's expense, and he drops his head in shame. "Good question, Eddie. Guess I didn't think of that."

"No point wondering about some asshole wanting a new pair of shoes," Dakota pipes in. "Not when our days are numbered, anyways."

Walter narrows in on Dakota. "What are you going on about now?"

"Ah, forget it. No need to concern yourself, Jamestown. Ignorance is bliss and all that."

"Quit dicking me around!" Walter shouts and straightens Dakota out. "I'm a big boy, so do me a favor and quit acting like my damn babysitter. Now, I came face to face with that thing all you sad-saps are afraid to even acknowledge, so the least you can do is let me in on your damn secrets!"

"Howah! Fine! Just cool it, Old-timer." Dakota drops his shoulders. "I'm only gonna tell you once, so listen good."

A handful of inmates stand, fleeing from the scene as Dakota's eyes darken and he starts with a nervous stutter. "Y-you know that key Archie hangs in that Boot of his?"

Walter nods.

"The key that thing used to unlock Claude's cell the other night before tearing him to shreds?"

"Yeah…"

"Well… there's nothing special about that key, Jamestown. It's the same one every other guard carries on 'em."

Walter sighs, trying to remain patient. "Okay, so?"

"*So* that God-forsaken, everyday key opens each and every damn cell in both blocks. And the day's coming, Jamestown, the day when that demon finishes its latest meal and wonders for the first time if that key it just used can also open the cell door next to it. And when it does, and that devil makes the connection… there's gonna be a goddamn feeding frenzy even the Boys-in-Blue won't be able to stop."

"Don't be so macabre, Mr. Landrite, please!" Uncle Bill chimes in and the remaining inmates turn away as one, minding their trays in front of them. "Don't listen to him, Mr. Edwards. He's only serving to scare you with his Navajo tales!"

Dakota stands for the approaching warden, but he waves him back down into his seat. "Sit down, son, sit down. It's alright, Mr. Edwards here is a smart man; he knows a ghost story when he hears one, don't you Mr. Edwards?" He produces a handkerchief from his pocket and wipes off the section of bench next to Walter, then sits.

"That's—that's right. Just a ghost story," Walter agrees, trying to mask his shaken nerves.

"Good. Mr. Landrite here has a knack for selling stories. Don't you, son? Telling lies is second nature to the redskins. Growing up without radios or televisions, surely, they had no choice but to weave yarns as thick as sheep's wool at the ass-end of winter."

Eddie leans back on his bench, but Uncle Bill reaches across the table and pulls him in by the collar with one smooth tug. "Don't worry, my simple visitor. I know my friendly demeanor can be displaced, and dare I say otherworldly amongst you mean, unruly men. But I assure you I will be quick about my little expedition into your homely underbelly." Eddie stares, his face twisting, trying to make sense of the words as Uncle Bill lets out another chuckle. "Oh, I'm sorry. I sometimes forget we are amongst the feeble minded as of late. Fear not, Edward, I am not here for you. I have business with the other Edward, Mr. Edwards as it were." Eddie nods with a blank, nervous smile and slides further down the bench, out of reach.

Uncle Bill looks at Walter. "A little birdie has brought to my attention that you would like a transfer to A-Block. Is that right?"

Walter sheepishly looks around as hushed whispers spill out amongst the Bastards, and he nods. "That's—that's right."

Uncle Bill frowns, resting a finger on his chin. "You will have to excuse me, for I've found myself a bit bewildered by it all." He digs his glasses from his jacket and places them over his large ears.

"Not two days ago I bestowed upon you your very own cell. A private room, some would say. I thought it fair considering you had yet to forge a single kettle in our workshop, and in turn, did not deserve Archie's boot yourself. But you rejected my humble offering and are now, out of the blue, requesting to be moved into a whole other block altogether. One filled with men far more crooked than these good samaritans upon us now, may I add." Uncle Bill looks around, lowering his gaze and switching to a hushed whisper. "I understand that Archie's boots have a fierce odor to them, if you catch my drift. But that's no reason to shack up with those truly horrible derelicts in high-max. You mind your own and keep that nose clean, and there will be nothing to fear, my good man."

"That's not it, Uncle Bill. I'm just interested in—"

"Now, I am a gracious man, Mr. Edwards. You could have simply come and persuaded me to undo your silly lapse in judgment you made by passing up your luxury suite. I am having a good day, so go on, ask me for a second chance and I may be so inclined to put my offer back on the table." He stares patiently and Walter shifts in his seat.

"That's kind of you, Uncle Bill, but..." His mind races, gripping for anything convincing to say, but only the truth spills out. "I've got some unfinished business with a man in A-Block, you see." *Just a simple throat I need to cut so I can get on with living my life and fucking my wife is all.*

His mouth runs on, building a narrative even he doesn't believe. "You see, I've g-got an old war pal on the other side, in A-Block, I mean." The lie burns on his tongue. "One that I've kept ties with through letters back and forth, even when he landed himself in Cold Keep. And I'll admit, I'm eager to see him again, even if that means I will have to rough it with the Assholes on the other side." He holds his breath, trying to read Uncle Bill's face as the spent cigarette burns his fingers and he drops it.

A moment of silent contemplation goes by and finally Uncle Bill smiles. "Well, who am I to stand in the way of a man and his… proclivities." He laughs with a mischievous wink. "If I were to concern myself with all the intimacies, physical or intellectual, going on within these walls, the government would have to double, no, *triple* my salary!" Another fit of laughter belches from the man and Eddie joins in, getting wrapped up in the moment as Dakota rests a steady hand on his shoulder, silencing him while Uncle Bill continues. "That's no problem at all, Mr. Edwards. One of the guards will escort you over and I'll have Archie consolidate your belongings post-haste. I warn you, though, this will be a one-way trip. You can surely understand there are far fewer complexity in moving a good boy to a bad boy's room, and not the other way around."

Walter swallows hard. "I understand."

Dakota reaches into his pocket and pulls out his spoon. "Nice bunking with ya, Jamestown. Here." He places it in Walter's palm with a firm clasp on his shoulder. "I can always get another."

"Thanks, kid."

"Did I not… Oh lord, Willy!" Uncle Bill slaps his thinning hairline. "You, my red-feathered friend, are going with him!"

Dakota stands, confoundment taking hold of his smile as he backs away from the table. "That— that ain't right. It was just Jamestown here set to move, not me, Uncle Bill."

"I certainly am not mistaken, Mr. Landrite. Your presence has been specifically requested alongside Mr. Edwards it seems."

A high-pitched whine builds in Eddie's throat as he watches the men from his seat, fingers hanging from his mouth. "Kota?"

Dakota holds a hand out, trying to pin the rising situation down. "No, Uncle Bill. There's some kind of mistake here. There is—"

"No mistake, redskin!" Uncle Bill slaps the table and rises from his seat. "Archie, get over here and take off your Boot!"

Within seconds the small man slinks in from the side-lines and joins Uncle Bill, shoe already off and being handed over.

"Now listen to me, you goddamn kid-killing savage. I run this show, so how would it be possible that I am mistaken in a place where I call the shots?" Eddie's whimpers build and tears well up in his eyes. "Shut that retard up!"

Archie pulls his club from his hip and raises it high as Eddie cowers, shaking his head wildly.

Uncle Bill adjusts his crooked glasses and smiles. "Now, this Boot is going to be hung outside your cell in B-Block tonight, Kid-killer. That leaves you with two choices: Stay there with it, or move on over with Mr. Edwards back to A-Block where you belong. And if I hear another word about it, I'll throw you out in the rec yard myself. Right here. Right now."

Dakota drops his head, allowing himself a moment of thought. "C-can Eddie come with me, Uncle Bill? He's got no one else."

Eddie nods, looking up with pleading eyes, and Uncle Bill signals the Boys-in-Blue. "Does this look like a fucking bed and breakfast to you? Dammit, I'm done. Get these jokers to their new block and go collect their shit, now!"

Archie clubs Eddie on the back and he screams, severing his hold on Dakota across the table as he's swept away.

"You be good, Eddie! It's okay!" Dakota yells. He looks to the inmates watching all around. "A carton of sticks. No! Two! Two cartons for any man who takes care of Eddie while I'm gone! I'll be back, Eddie, it's okay! I'll be back!"

Dakota yanks the spoon from Walter's grasp and throws a fist into his temple, bursting his vision with reds and blues as his angry words ring out in his fading mind.

"Give me my fucking spoon back!"

RUN DRY

Walter sits up, eyes adjusting to the flickering amber glow cast on the wigwam's angled walls. Beside him Tahki massages her drained breast next to the fire, begging her own flesh and ignoring her daughter's cries. She grabs a split log from the pile, picking at the emeralds of congealed sap, melting them between her fingers as she slathers the goo across her nipple and raises her daughter to the sticky tip of her breast, latching her on. "There you go," she whispers, kissing her on the forehead, flashing an uneasy glance to the flames and the steaming kettle burrowed amidst the hot coals.

All at once the forest holds its breath and the wind abandons the air, making room for the distant steps that crawl in from the night and twist Tahki's gut with another wave of starvation. Her hands tremble, building into a nervous tremor as the footsteps come to a stop outside, and the thing's deep breath beats against the walls, tainting her air with each patient huff.

"Hello, spirit," Tahki utters, finding the nerve to speak.

"Hello, *nuntanuhs*," it whispers back from beyond the tattered veil. "You look hungry."

"We are."

"Why? I have smelled your broth simmering for days." An impossibly deep breath sucks the remaining warmth from the wigwam and dims the flames.

"We do not have the taste for your broth," Tahki spits. "You bring us wood that we can burn all winter long, but not one rabbit. Surely you can pluck a fish from the river like you did my family from our home."

"No need. Your broth… it simmers," it repeats.

"Or maybe you have never had a taste for anything other than the innocent, so you have never learned to hunt," Tahki continues.

The thing trails off and the wind picks back up as it screams like a child throwing a tantrum, snapping branches and stomping around. Tahki squeezes her daughter tight, and the forest falls back into its silent routine as it returns. The branches rip away from the patched wall and two rabbits, a trout, and a balled-up owl appear, clutched in the thing's frozen fist. Tahki's heart skips a hopeful beat, and she crawls to her knees, dragging herself over as she balances her daughter in her arms and reaches for the dangling meat.

"I have lived in these woods long before your ancestors, girl." The thing's words waft down and choke them. "I once tasted for hare, fish, and pheasant, like you, but my appetites have grown. Much more meat on the bones of you foolish

Ojibwe." The other massive hand plucks the rabbit from the heap and squeezes it, crushing the meat as it funnels out between its fingers. "This... This is what *our* food eats. I have provided you the best flesh there is, but you sit there starved. What mother would let her milk spoil when she has all the ingredients to muster a new batch?" It pulls the dead animals back into the night.

Tahki crawls to the fire in defeat, reaching out to the kettle with a trembling mitten, admiring the image of the buffalo cast into the iron lid. She pulls it off, staring into the inevitable dark broth inside as her brother's bloated hand rises from the bottom in a dizzying cyclone, waving a sick hello from beyond. A whimper escapes her, and she tosses the lid back over the gruesome meal, then glares into the night.

"You may have the tongue for *Ojibwe*, foul creature, but I do not! You can hide out in the darkness between the pines, but I know what your greed and hunger have turned you into. I will not eat my own like you have." She tosses another log on the fire, compensating for the breeze.

"Mmmmmhhmmmhmm." The thing's deep laugh soaks up her voice. "I did not melt the snow in your kettle, *nuntanuhs*. I did not pluck your brother's hand from the ground and stew the broth I smell." It trails off and the branches rain down, re-patching the wigwam with their pine embrace. "Tell me, did that infant clutched to your breast make that meal?"

Tahki's stomach churns and she retches at the rising steam. "No," she admits.

"Then you. If you have no tongue for *Ojibwe*, why melt the snow? Why add the meat? Baby drinks milk, not broth. I have chewed my share of flesh and I assure you it does not soften enough for an infant's gums; no matter how long it stews. Mmhhmhmm."

The deep laugh vibrates Tahki's bones, and her nerves unravel. "W-why are you doing this to us, you twisted devil?"

"I have done nothing to you, girl!" it screams, its voice raining pine needles down from the forest canopy above. "You ungrateful vermin! I gave you heat when others would have froze!" Logs rain down, shredding the walls as they pile into the fire, letting forth an eruption of sparks that explode in all directions and fill the small structure with smoke and soot.

Tahki crawls to the flap and fingers at the knots with her awkward mittens, ignoring the thing as it takes on her brother's voice. "Your wood ran out weeks ago, Sister. You could barely strike a flint with those starved arms."

"P-please," she begs, choking on ash. She gives up on the knots, ripping the flap open to the cold bite of winter and crawls out of the flaming wigwam into the snow as the thing's frenzied screams dart past, its black mass whipping around her.

"I gave you food when others would have starved!" Another barrage of logs rain down around her and she locks eyes with one as its frosted bark transforms into torn skin, its knotted wood core curdling into splintered bone. She screams as the log reveals its true nature and turns into her brother's displaced head, rolling towards her with tortured, frozen eyes staring back from sunken sockets. One by one, the once suspected lumber forms into the arms, legs, and frozen faces of her family, long torn apart and left to freeze in the drifts of snow all around. Tahki wails, unable to look away as the thing darts from treetop to treetop, tossing the massacred body parts into the air like solstice offerings. She begs for help, knowing none will come and buries her head into her knees, waiting as the assault slows, then comes to a stop. The thing perches on the bowing branch above and its robes cascade down, encompassing her, offering brief reprieve from the cold. Tahki looks up into the dark and the thing's hood pivots down, gassing her with its foul breath as it whispers, no longer pretending to be anyone but its true, heinous self.

"I am no twisted devil to you, *nuntanuhs*. A devil would have swallowed you up months ago."

She tries to crawl away, but the heavy robes nudge her sickly body back and forth, jostling her in their grasp.

"And when it was done with its feast of your people, it would have picked its teeth clean with the ribs of your child." It whips its robes back and waves a hand through the air, commanding the snow around the wigwam to suck the ash from inside and confine the flames to the pit where they belong.

Tahki dives back into her home and stifles a scream as she kicks the pieces of frozen flesh from the flames, excavating the kettle nestled deep amongst the sizzling fat and muscle.

She collapses and breaks into sobs, pulling and twisting at her tangled braids, desperate to feel anything but hunger and terror as she writhes on the ground.

"Just one small taste," it whispers from outside.

Tahki looks upward at the set of glimmering teeth suspended in the darkness, grinning and clacking together as it speaks through the severed holes of her home's walls. "It tastes pleasant. It will fill your breasts for your daughter. For *your nuntanuhs*"

Tahki's cries fade to whimpers and she pulls the lid from the kettle, filling the wigwam with the meaty-smelling broth that to her horror, makes her mouth water. "I… I can't."

"No. Certainly not," it whispers. A sprinkle of tree nuts and dried berries trickle from above, into the liquid with a final garnish. "Not without something for texture."

Tahki reaches out but pauses. "Just once. Enough to gain me the strength to forage. Will you let us go then?" she asks.

"Oh yes, as soon as morning," it lies, its voice like grinding stones.

She reaches out, dipping her mitten into the broth and it warms her fingers within. "Do you promise?"

"I promise."

She brings her hand to her lips, wrapping them around the warm leather, and suckles like her babe on her breast. The flavor fills her mouth, and her eyes roll to the back of her head. In an instant, her cramped legs loosen and her free arm pulls herself up. "Oh," she mutters and dips it back in. The boiling liquid scalds her fingers, but she barely feels it as she lifts the steaming sponge to her mouth once more and drains the broth over her tongue. She clambers to her knees and hunches over the kettle, throwing her mittens off and plunging her hands into the boiling broth for the morsels of flesh lying on the bottom. Piece after piece she shovels into her mouth as her tongue swells and throat scalds. A shift in her chest floods her breasts and her daughter draws milk, sucking and swallowing almost as ravenously as her mother. Tears of joy fall from Tahki's eyes onto her blistering hands. Her stomach bloats, but she keeps reaching, picking apart the bones and sucking them clean, unable to feel remorse for what she does, or the searing pain brought from it.

Ravenous minutes pass and she lifts the kettle from the fire and runs her lips across the rim, her tongue smoking and sizzling against the iron until there is nothing left to drink. Then she raises her hands to her mouth and sucks at the webbing of her fingers, extruding the salty dirt from between them, desperate to get one last taste. And when the flavor of her brother's fingers is nowhere left to be enjoyed, she chews and gnaws the tips of her own, her teeth stripping the flesh with ease, her fingernails popping off and adding texture with each pump of her jaw.

The thing cheers her on and lets out one last self-indulgent laugh as Walter watches, frozen at the horror before him as the humanity in Tahki's eyes drain and she turns towards him. She flashes a crooked smile and reaches into her robes with bloody hands, pulling the piece of bannock out.

Walter gags and tries to back away, but instead finds himself grabbing hold of the bread. His fingers break through the hard surface, sinking into its warm interior as he lifts it to his trembling lips with little control and even less understanding as to why. Then he takes a bite.

A-BLOCK

Walter wakes with a violent wretch, gagging on the phantom smell of meat that lingers on his tongue. He leans over and spits, spotting Dakota rocking back and forth on his cot, kneading his flushed palms. "You been having some bad dreams, Old-timer?"

"Mind your own business, asshole."

"Attitude like that won't get you far on this side of the wall."

Walter looks out at the stretching windows across the hall and his vertigo twists his empty gut. *Top floor.*

Dakota winces and his hands twitch. "I got a pretty mean left hook, don't I?"

"That was nothing; call me when your big boy muscles come in."

"Yeah, yeah. You still able to count smokes or did I knock that part of your brain loose?"

Walter laughs. "You working the night shift, too? Charging these poor bastards to light two cigarettes a day doesn't seem very neighborly."

"Night shift?" Dakota repeats. "I really must

have scrambled that brain of yours real good. No count done yet. We haven't lit a single smoke today."

"Yes we have. Right before—" Walter pauses, taking note of the morning glow streaming into the block. "Wait… what day is it?"

"Sunday. You forget to take your pills Old-ti—"

"For fuck's sake! You're telling me I've been out cold since yesterday?"

"Told you I got a pretty mean left hook."

"Dammit, kid! I'm getting real fucking sick of being clocked out!"

Dakota points at Walter. "Hey, that's all on you. You got a knack for finding trouble."

"Is it really Sunday?"

"Yes!"

"You're telling me I've pissed away four of my five good days?"

Dakota stares. "What are you talking about, Old-ti—"

"Don't! Don't you dare! Stop calling me that! I swear to God I'll—"

A barrel-chested man fills their open doorway and cuts Walter off. "Couldn't rough it with the good boys and girls, eh, Dakota?"

Dakota stands and grabs the two cigarettes from the visitor, then pulls a lit one from his pocket. "Jesus, how the hell are you even bigger than the last time I saw ya?"

The man laughs. "How long were you gone for? A year?"

"Bit longer than that," Dakota answers. "And I was a good little Indian the whole time, thank you very much."

"Then what's your sorry ass doing back?"

"Got roped into a deal with the Shit-talker I had no skin in." Dakota flashes Walter a look and another inmate joins in, taking the next spot in line.

"What's he like? The Shit-talker?"

Dakota scratches his head. "Fuck if I know. I thought he was an Asshole, over here. Those pipes carry a voice a long way."

The inmate shrugs. "If he is, I ain't seen him." They turn, shuffling off with their smokes, and Dakota leans back, breathing a sigh of relief as his flushed brow seems to cool.

"You gonna sleep in or earn your keep, Jamestown?"

Walter rubs the crust from his swollen eyes. "I don't have time for this." He pats his pockets down but comes up empty. "Dammit. Where's my cigarettes?"

Dakota grimaces and grabs a pack of Big-Reds from a customer. "Some of the boys here took 'em off ya on the account of you being in a coma and all."

"Well, I'm not!"

"No shit."

Walter bites his cheek and considers throwing a fist into the wall, but instead takes a deep breath of the secondhand smoke and collects himself. "You got a cigarette for me, kid? Please."

Dakota shakes his head and motions for him to sit. "Nothing's free in Cold Keep. You wanna smoke, help me count."

Another breath and Walter gets himself in

check. "Fine. Let's make this quick." He grabs the bags of chips from the next man in line and gives Dakota a nod.

Another inmate flashes a genuine smile as he passes by. "Welcome back, Dakota. It'll be nice having a dart before breakfast again. Wayne is slower than cold maple syrup when it comes to getting that cherry in A-Block. Some mornings he comes strolling in on his last drag and we gotta pray the thing don't go out before lighting off of it."

Dakota nods. "Thanks. I appreciate being appreciated."

The men file by one after another as they continue to hand Walter their payments. "You didn't tell me you were an Asshole, kid."

"Seeing as we have known each other for all of three days, I figure there's a lot you don't know about me, Jamestown. You hear the mean little nickname some of the boys in here call me yet?"

"Yeah, I heard it." Walter swallows. "Kid-killer."

"You're no dummy, so why you surprised they would put someone with a nickname like mine in A-Block? What you should really be wondering is how I ended up in B-Block with you goodie goodies in the first place."

Smoke fills their cell as they count and the haze washes over Walter, making him smile. "Struck a deal with the Shit-talker I'm guessing. Same as me."

Dakota shakes his head. "Nah, Shit-talker wasn't around then, besides, you heard Uncle Bill; good boys only come here, not the other way around."

A thick hand lunges through the bars and grabs Walter by the throat. "You're the son-of-a-bitch that robbed my eye!"

Dakota acts fast and brings one of his cigarettes down on the man's forearm, burning his wrist and severing his grasp as Walter breaks free and coughs, looking at Chicago's one eye, the other hidden behind layers of gauze. "Keep your goddamn hands to yourself!" he shouts, readying his fists.

Dakota joins the men on their feet and holds out a hand. "Now Chicago, he was just playing the game, same as you."

"Then why's he still got both his eyes?"

Walter clears his airway and finds his voice. "Not my fault you couldn't hold your own in a simple game of jacks!"

Dakota throws his hands up in defeat. "Never mind, he's all yours."

Chicago takes a step for the door, then stops. "You're lucky I don't hand out beatings on the Lord's Day, Edwards. Come tomorrow, we'll see who's holding their own. You bet your ass."

Come tomorrow, I'll be long gone, Walter thinks, wishing he had a few more days to show the man a real fight.

Chicago looks at Dakota, changing the subject. "They finally kicked your sorry ass out of B-Block I see. You know," — he looks back at Walter, — "little Kota here went wee-wee-wee all the way to solitary when us Tribesmen caught wind of his rap sheet. Isn't that right, Kid-killer?"

Dakota mumbles to the floor like a scolded

child.

"What was that?"

"I said, 'Any man in my position would have done the same.'"

"Any man in your position?" Chicago presses his forehead against the bars, watching Dakota like an animal trapped in a cage. "And what position is that? The position of a man who murdered three of his own people's children in cold blood? Or was it the position of a coward running from what he did the moment it was done?"

Dakota rams his forehead against Chicago's. "You know damn well it didn't go down like that! What I did—"

"What you did is done! And until they bring the gallows back you got a nickel to pay, killer. This time there's no running off to solitary because solitary is for the best of the best now; for the boys who earn their ticket away from the Boot. Not for some reservation dog running to hide." He pulls back and smiles at Walter. "With his face in the tabloids after what he did, Dakota here was practically famous for fuck's sake. I woulda gutted him like a trout first chance I got, but Uncle Bill didn't think it would be a good look for Cold Keep having him lynched day one and all. So they put him in the Ritz, up in solitary. And when that devil came skulking in that first winter, they cleared out all the cells and Kid-killer here got grouped in with the Bastards. And there he sat in B-Block ever since, happily ever after."

Dakota grabs Chicago's jacket and pulls him against the bars, his other hand hovering a cigarette an inch from his eye. "You want me, you'll have me," he says. "I'm no fool. But when you come for your pound of flesh, you and your men better catch me by surprise because I'll take a piece of you with me. You can bet on that."

Chicago laughs and breaks away. "Oh relax, killer. Marvin bought the Tribesmen out."

"Marvin?" Walter lets the name slip.

Chicago squeezes a fist and blinks. "Does this conversation look like an ice-cream-fucking-social to you? Yes, Marvin. Marvin Wilmore. What business you got with him?"

Walter slouches, attempting to seem no longer interested. "Oh, I thought you said 'Martin.'" He waves his hands, passing the conversation back, and Chicago turns to Dakota, shaking his head.

"Well, *Marvin*, not Martin, had bought out most of the crews last year. He's running the show now. We've been told there's a cease and desist when it comes to putting the harm on you. For the time being at least."

"And why the hell would Marvin, of all people, want me in safe hands?" Dakota asks.

"Fuck if I know, but he must have wanted you bad considering what he did for the Shit-talker to get you back in A-Block. You wanna know why, go ask him yourself; he's been spending most of his time in the chapel these days, Sunday or not. Either way, killer, it would be in your best interest to stay out of the Tribesmen's sights. Orders are not to kill you, but that don't mean me and the boys won't beat your ass bloody." Chicago turns and points at Walter with a wink, then strolls down the catwalk, throwing his half-lit smoke off the platform to the block below.

"Alright, shop's closed, you fuckers!" Dakota yells to the line of waiting men. "Share your cherries; the Tribesmen will mind their own today." The inmates grumble and disperse as Dakota slaps Walter on the shoulder. "Looks like I owe you an apology." He wanders over to the toilet with a drunken stumble and pukes. "S-seems I was bound to end up in here with or without you," his voice echoes from the bowl between heaves.

Walter paces the cell. "Don't think on it, kid. You might want to consider a different line of work though, these cigarettes are gonna be the death of you."

Dakota laughs. "Only things keeping me alive, more like it."

Walter takes a smoke and turns to leave. "Just drop my cut under the mattress."

"Whoa, hold up now." Dakota stands at attention. "Why you always rushing around, Jamestown? Got some secret exit out of here I don't know about or something? You only been here a few days, and without a spoon I doubt you have been doing any tunneling. I'd suggest getting your ass in a shower, you're getting pretty beesh! And when was the last time you ate a meal? You look like a stiff breeze could knock you over."

"Ate a meal?" Walter asks. "You tell me, kid. You've been by my side since the moment I got here. You see me eat any food? I either got no fucking spoon to shovel the shit I'm served, or I'm too busy having the daisies knocked out of me to have an appetite." He strolls over and kicks the empty tray in the corner. "Looks like I would have had something if my roommate wasn't such a damn glutton!"

"How was I to know you were gonna wake up! I'm sorry. Didn't want it going to waste was all."

"Yeah, yeah."

"Well, they're serving grits now. Go get some then!"

Walter shakes his head and goes to turn.

"What about that shower?"

"Like I give a damn what a bunch of criminals think of my body odor." He puts the smoke between his lips. "Got a light?"

Dakota smiles at the hanging cigarette and shakes his head. "Fresh out."

"Oh, come on. Don't get bashful on me now. Striking these smokes is what makes you such a hot commodity in a place without warmth. How you do it, anyway?" Walter leans in and Dakota leans back.

"I wouldn't tell my own mama if she were sitting here now, so I'm sure as shit not telling you, Old-Timer." Dakota lifts his hand, covering Walter's black eyes as the cigarette takes hold of a flame somewhere beyond his calloused palm and the tobacco delivers its dizzying calm. He drops his hand and Walter crosses his eyes at the lit cigarette hanging from his lips.

"See, that's it right there, kid. You got your secrets and I got mine. Don't go concerning yourself with my escape plan, how long I got in here, or any of that nonsense. Besides, by the sounds of it, you got a hell of a lot longer to serve than me, so don't worry about my release date, worry about yours."

Dakota flicks a pack of gum at Walter's head.

"No, now *you* see. It's that smart mouth of yours right there that's gonna get you shivved. My story's not as cut and dry as murdering a few kiddies, and it certainly wasn't in no cold blood neither; not like how Chicago sold it at least." He storms out of the cell with Walter hot on his heels.

"Alright, alright, let's just relax. You're not wrong, kid. I've been told my tongue tends to wander from time to time; I didn't mean anything by it." They strut down the catwalk and Walter looks over the railing, his vision spinning as he descends the stairs, then exits the block.

"Is what it is, Jamestown. Now you and I could get along real good if you just shut up every once in a while and served your time in silence. Unlike those Bastards in B-Block, people in here actually take a liking to me, minus the Tribesmen. But they been called off so as far as I'm concerned, it's home-sweet-home. Turns out murderers don't much mind the company of other murderers. So fit in or fuck off."

Walter laughs as they pass the green French doors looking down on them from atop the staircase, and he glances up, watching the colorful beams of sunlight shine through the crooked glass dome above. "You uh… you a religious man, kid?"

Dakota spins on his heels and grabs Walter by his collar. "What did I just say?"

Walter tosses Dakota's hands and throws up his own. "Whoa, whoa, what's your problem?"

"You're lucky Chicago's got more brawn than brains, cause I sure as shit heard what you said in our cell back there. Loud and clear. You said

'Marvin' there weren't no 'Martin' coming from those lips of yours." He turns, storming through the lobby. "So, is he your man on the other side then? Your long-lost pen pal?"

Walter looks around, lowering his voice. "Keep it down, kid."

Dakota slows, letting Walter catch up. "I've known Marvin for some years, Jamestown, and let me just say this"—his voice twists into a warning— "whatever crack pot story about a long-lost war buddy you were spinning before, nobody's gonna buy if his name's attached to it. Marvin doesn't have no friends, and I know for a fact he dodged the draft like the coward he is."

Walter says nothing, and Dakota puts a hand on the back of his frostbitten neck. "You want your man, you'll find him in there." He points clean across the cafeteria to the two wooden doors set amongst the stones. "Just leave me out of it."

Walter's heart skips a nervous beat as the urge to eat abandons him entirely. *What's twenty-four more hours on an empty stomach?* He goes to leave Dakota behind but turns, feeling the need to defend himself. "I used to be able to hold my own, you know. I could scrap with the best of them, kid. At least until—"

"You got old?"

"No, dick head. Until…" He pauses and shakes his head. "Never mind. You Cold Keep boys just fight dirty is all."

He crosses the cafeteria to the chapel, his feet growing heavier with each step as the smoky haze stings his eyes. From the other side of the oak doors, the muffled melody of an organ plays out and the inmate's hymns sing along. For a moment he considers turning away, but his arm lurches, giving him no choice as the door swings open, and with it, the strangest thought crosses his mind.

I wonder if God considers smoking a sin.

HYMNS

The organ's melody washes over Walter as he leaves behind Cold Keep's stone facade and reluctantly steps into the chapel's warm oak embrace. The inmates sing as one, their voices all blurring together to create more of a gospel drone than actual words as he paces the back, surveying the silhouettes for Marvin's slicked back hair and jutting sideburns. Unable to spot his man, he turns for the door and the last notes die out, leaving a voice to call over the crowd that twists his gut.

"Thank you, please be seated." Marvin rises from the organ and Walter slides into one of the pews, avoiding his sweeping gaze as he approaches the pedestal and adjusts the oxygen tank by his side.

"Thank you, thank you all for being here to praise this damn fine Boot-less Sunday with me. Isn't it—" He pauses, adjusting the tube under his nose and clears his throat. "Isn't it wonderful knowing all of our prayers have been answered?"

Walter's tongue dries out and his jaw hangs slack.

"We deserve this, we truly do! And because it's such a glorious day filled with such a lifting of heavy burdens, I've decided to preach about something each and every one of us possess within us. Forgiveness."

Walter rubs his eyes and leans to the inmate beside him. "What's—what's this guy's story?"

"Shhh!" he hisses, unwilling to spare a moment from the man on stage.

Walter shifts, head spinning as that late autumn afternoon comes flooding back, sending images of Kevin's mangled body tearing though his mind like the bullet in his shoulder. Marvin's gin-soaked breath wafting down on him as its stench mixes with the smoking tires, solidifying into the tar and pine that has plagued him ever since. He jolts upright, bringing himself back to the chapel and the terrible man on its stage continuing to preach.

"The Good Book is filled with stories of forgiveness. Wonderful tales that serve to fill us with joy and reassurance that retribution is just a prayer away."

Walter shakes his head, watching Marvin pace back and forth across the stage and trail his oxygen tube behind him like a misunderstood jump rope. "What the fuck have you become?" he hears himself ask with a breathless whisper.

"'Father, forgive them, for they know not what they do.'" Marvin looks across his congregation. "These were the words spoken by Jesus when He was up on that cross. Or what of the prodigal Son in the book of Luke? He took his inheritance and whittled it away on whores and drink, only to come back to his daddy and beg for a place at his feet as a servant, for servants at least got bread and water each night. But his daddy instead welcomed him back with open arms, *forgiving* his son's life of sin and praised his return to the faithful."

"Amen!" someone calls out.

"And when Jesus asked a disciple how many times he was expected to forgive, he guessed seven. But Jesus just smiled and said, 'not seven, but seven times seventy.' You see, forgiveness is everywhere; not only in the Bible, but all around. And I, for one, cannot think of sinners in need of forgiveness more than us wretched men in Cold Keep, can you?" He lets out a raspy laugh, and Walter imagines snatching the book of songs from the worshiper next to him and burying the spine into Marvin's skull until it gives way and caves in. He closes his jaw on his tongue and severs the thought, hoping God wasn't watching him at that moment.

"Years of my life were wasted being someone who I was not. I gambled, drank, smoked, fucked, cheated, and stole. I did it all."

And murdered. Walter grips the arm rest and holds himself down.

"Hell, I even murdered. And after all of that, I came to my Savior's throne and I laid down at His feet. I prayed and begged His forgiveness for the things I had done, for the people I had wronged."

Walter forces his teeth deeper, but the pain does little to calm him as the tar and pine climb up his throat.

"And you know what Jesus did?" Marvin asks.

"He forgave!" the many voices call as one.

"That's right. He forgave!" Marvin slams the Bible down on the pedestal. "He forgave me for all my wrongdoings and set me free of my guilt!" He walks to the edge of the stage and awkwardly lowers himself onto the steps as his ear to ear smile fades, his face turning to one of concern. "In fact... the good Lord may have done too good of a job, boys."

The electricity in the room crackles and the inmates hang onto every one of Marvin's words.

"Seems I must have prayed a bit too hard, cause the good Lord struck me down with a fierce forgetfulness not long after arriving to Cold Keep. Little things at first, like where I misplaced my spoon, then bigger, like where my cell was or if I showered that morning. Soon enough I grew scared of the man I was becoming; I still am. But, through my fog I never forgot to thank Him for answering my prayers. For He not only forgave me but unburdened me of the memories and actions that brought me to this terrible prison in the first place. A miracle in itself. Amen."

"Amen!"

You don't get to live a guilt free life, you son-of-a-bitch. I'll remind you. Walter jostles in his seat and his nails dig into the pew's hard oak. He lets off and grabs the Bible from the bench in front of him with the urge to bring the spine down on Marvin's head again, this time not caring if God watches or not.

As if hearing his thoughts, Marvin's gaze wanders across the crowd and settles on him. "Ah, the rumors are true. We have a hero amongst our ranks, men. The man responsible for ridding A-Block of the Boot is here. Help Mr. Edwards on stage so we can show our appreciation."

Like a whirlwind, the inmates swoop in, and Walter finds himself stumbling on stage towards Marvin's open arms. The cloud of tar and pine thickens in the new altitude, and he chomps down on his tongue even harder, his teeth burying deep into the muscle, warding off the red and blue closing in on his peripherals as Marvin wraps his arms around his rigid frame.

"Quite a move you made jumping ship after losing that game of jacks the other day, Edwards." Marvin lets go and claps a hand over Walter's scar tissue beneath his jacket, then raises his arm, as if announcing a new boxing champion. "Was that your plan all along? To throw the game and join the real men in A-Block?" He steps aside and gives Walter the spotlight.

"Well, I—" Walter pauses and pictures himself on one of those game shows from the television, a contestant trying to think of an answer before the timer runs out. "Those—those pansy ass Bastards in B-Block were not to my liking, if I'm being truthful." He stands straighter, trying not to throw up. "So… I threw the game and thought I'd join you delinquents for some real fun!"

The crowd breaks into a fit of laughter as Marvin pumps Walter's arm in the air. "Did you hear that? Edwards' got chops! And look at him, still bloodied and bruised days later, still showing off his battle wounds!"

Walter clears his throat. "Laundry swap is on

Tuesdays."

"Oh, forget that!" Marvin scoffs. "I'll be damned if I let you walk around looking like anything but the hero you are! Come with me; I have an extra shirt in my cell." He snaps his fingers at Wayne in the front row and signals to the organ. "Wayne, will you send these men off with our final hymn?" He turns to the crowd. "You criminals have a blessed, forgiving Sunday. Let's hear it again for Edwards!"

They both descend the stage and head down the aisle as the churchgoers let out another cheer.

An extra shirt… in his cell. Alone? Walter's heart skips a beat as Marvin's offer pieces itself together in his mind. *This is it.* Marvin pulls at the cart carrying his oxygen tank and the organ kicks up a deep drone that fades as Walter follows him into the cafeteria. *The son-of-a-bitch really doesn't know who I am.*

"Not much for the public eye, are you, Edwards?" Marvin asks.

Walter catches Dakota's eye as he rises from one of the tables, but he waves, backing him off.

"Well?" Marvin asks impatiently.

"Uh… yeah, you could say that. Making friends has never been one of my talents." Walter thinks back to the utility garage and its many sharp screwdrivers, cursing himself for not picking one up in his mad escape back to Cold Keep.

"It's hard making friends at our age. I don't gotta tell you," Marvin says.

"Are you really losing your mind?" Walter asks, not caring how the question is perceived.

"Losing your memory, I mean."

"Yeah…" Marvin frowns. "It's withering away alright. I got my good days and my bad days now."

"How much do you remember outside of Cold Keep?"

"Some. I remember my daddy's beatings after coming home with the wrong brand of pipe tobacco. My first smooch with Sharla Monument on the Ferris wheel when I was twelve. Some days I even remember my wicked excuse for a mama, some not so much. Each morning when I wake up, I try to picture her face, and if I can't, it's one of my good days. One like today."

"You and your mama not get along, I take it?"

Marvin flashes a sad smile and says nothing while his tank skitters sideways, its wheels dragging as he gives it a kick. "I got a confession to make, Edwards…"

Walter holds his breath, readying a clenched fist by his side.

"In my sermon back there, I said it was a blessing being struck with my forgetfulness. But in truth, I don't believe it is. It's much easier being a good man when you can't remember how you fucked up your life so bad, how the people who were supposed to protect you instead hurt you time and time again. But more often now, I think it's the Devil that did this to me. Not a blessing, but a curse. Some mornings I don't even recognize my cell; I just wake up wondering where the hell I am, only to find out I threw my life away with a face that's aged considerably overnight, and I piss myself every time, hand to God. But what really scares me most is this stranger… a horrible man living in my own head. The Marvin who *does* remembers his mama. Except he was here first, and I'm just the visitor, the person who doesn't belong." He drifts off for a moment then blinks the fog from his eyes. "So yeah… I got days I remember my mama, and I got days I don't remember much of anything at all." They stop in front of a cell and Marvin raises an arm, welcoming him in.

Walter nods and swallows the stone lodged in his throat. "Thanks."

"Since we're on a line of questioning, I heard you risked your ass going out into that rec yard yesterday. What in God's name would make you do something like that?" He bends down and rummages under his cot.

"You been speaking with the Shit-talker?" Walter asks over the sound of his racing heart.

"The other guy," — Marvin taps his temple, — "the one who remembers his mama has got a close working relationship with him, so I've been told. He's got me wrapped up in some shit that I don't bother asking questions about. I just run errands for this grand plan he's been cooking up. I'm telling you, it's tiring having two of ya in the same skull."

Walter scans the cell, searching for anything heavy or sharp, but Marvin stands with a clean shirt in his hands. "See how this feels." He hands it over. "I'll grab you a new pair of socks from next door; I'm sure my neighbor won't mind."

"I'm fine, don't—"

"Hell with that. A man's only as good as his

shoes and the socks inside of 'em. I'll be back in a jiffy. You get out of those bloody rags." Marvin steps out of the cell and takes a hard right as his voice sings out. *"Black socks, they never get dirty. The longer you wear them the stronger they get."*

Walter bounces around the room, silently scavenging the small space, and swipes the Bible lying on the cot, swinging it through the air, testing its weight. *No. Fuck.* He tosses it back and a razorblade falls from between the pages with a metallic clatter. He stares, unbelieving, then mouths a 'thank you' to God and scoops it up, readying himself at the door.

The shuffling stops from the block and Marvin's song returns. *"Sometimes I think I should wash them, but something inside me says no, no, not yet."*

Walter squeezes the blade between his knuckles, preparing for Marvin's return as his family flashes through his mind. He stares at the portrait of himself, his arm draped over Angie's shoulder and Lorrie held in her arms. He smiles at the tiara tangled in her mess of hair and looks down at Kevin wrapped around his leg, but pauses, trying to make sense of the person staring back. He blinks and Marvin's crooked face materializes where his sons should be, his head hanging cockeyed by a slashed throat, torn open by the razor blade clutched in his hand.

"You decent in there, Edwards?" Marvin calls.

Walter shakes the thought, and a rush of adrenaline fills him as the moment finally closes in after so many years. "Y-yea—" his voice catches in his throat. He tries again but the cell around him closes in, and the words slathered across the walls come into focus, growing familiar.

Dear fucker,
Dear fucker,
Dear fucker,

Page after page of the plain white, letterhead wallpaper every inch of the room, all scrawled with Walter's hateful words pecked out by his typewriter over countless lonely nights in his motel room. Every wish of death, description of revenge, and horrible name spewed out and pinned to each available stone that makes up the four cobbled walls around him. Walter spins, dumbfounded at the pure seething anger on every page, and tears well up in his eyes as the blade tumbles from his motionless hand.

Marvin turns the corner and pauses with a disappointed sigh. "You like my decorating?" He looks around and frowns. "That's the thing about God, Edwards: He always forgives. It's the people down here on earth that are trickier to convince."

Walter turns on wavering knees and he reaches for the fresh socks, spotting the rows of self-inflicted scars on Marvin's arms.

Marvin pulls back, rolling down his cuffs and traces one of the hateful sentences on the wall with a finger. "I let the drink take me down a terrible road, Edwards. Months of my life went missing at a time, and soon enough I landed myself in here for some shit I'm not proud of. I was only in Cold Keep a month when I started getting these letters from a man telling me I killed his son while driving drunk." Silence hangs in the cell as Walter watches Marvin silently read one of the pages, then wince at the words.

"Did—did you reply to them?" Walter asks, already knowing the answer.

"Just the one. I denied the whole thing. Tried convincing myself the guy was full of shit. But really, I was just scared it was true, and deep down I knew it was. I knew I killed some poor father's boy."

Walter swallows, trying to stagger his shallow breaths. "Then why the one letter? Why didn't you write him back; own up to what you did?"

"There's no forgiving that, Edwards. No coming back from doing something like that to a man's family. There was… is nothing I can say. So instead, I read 'em. Every morning before I brush my teeth and every night before I lay my rotten head down to sleep. That's how I pay my dues. That father might not know it, but I don't let God forgive me for that one. I never even asked Him to, not once. When I die, that boy I killed will point his finger at me on the stands and the Devil will drag me to hell. I won't go kicking or screaming neither, I'll just follow him without a fuss, because I know it's what I deserve." A mixture of confusing emotions fill Walter's gut, and a scared whimper lets past Marvin's lips. "I won't let these stones around me become strangers. The thought of waking up every day in a prison I don't remember terrifies me too much." He looks up at the ceiling, holding back tears. "But they got a plan, the Marvin who remembers his mama and the Shit-talker."

"And what plan is that?" Walter asks, but Marvin pushes the socks into his hand and turns him towards the door.

"Never mind that. Just an old fool babbling. Did they have you scrubbing shit stains with the Sock-monkeys in B-Block?"

"Yeah," Walter answers, trying to keep the block from spinning out of control.

"Not anymore. You go get yourself ready for the shift, then I'll show you the ropes in the shop. You'll be pouring iron with the big boys today." A smile spreads across his face and he sucks back tears as they exit the cell. "Get changed and meet me there. March, Edwards!" He laughs and Walter turns, scaling the winding stairs.

A jumble of anger, pity, and sadness bombard him, and his palms open and close, grabbing at nothing as he climbs to the fourth floor, then turns into his cell. A deep breath pulls into his lungs, and he steadies himself against the sink, looking into the polished metal mirror. His frostbitten neck, bloodied body, and swollen face stare back, and he throws a clenched fist, caving his reflection in. "Fuck!" He turns, grabbing his cot with one hulking motion and flips it on its side. Dissatisfied, he drops to his knees and drives his fists into the ground over and over, smearing the cold cement with blood, the pain bringing him no relief whatsoever.

"Fuck, fuck, fuuuuuuck!"

HOT DATE

Walter storms through the lobby, tucking in his new shirt as Dakota catches up and hands him a smoke. "I take it your reunion wasn't what you thought it would be?"

Walter drops his shoulders and looks at Dakota with deadpan eyes. "The man's gone soft, kid. Kind, even. I hardly recognized the son-of-a-bitch."

Dakota perks up and a look of relief spreads across his face. "Marvin? Bullshit."

"Believe it. His memories gone to mush."

They turn down the corridor and hurry towards the workshop like school children late for class. "Maybe Chicago wasn't lying; maybe things *have* changed around here," Dakota thinks out loud.

Ahead, Marvin stands at the end of the hall and calls out, "Edwards, let's move!" He waves him over, but spots Dakota and waltzes their way. "Kota, is that you?" He hunches over, approaching him like a timid hound.

"Thought you said his memory went to shit?"

Dakota mumbles, putting on a nervous smile as he runs his fingers through his uneven hair, only to have it fall back in his face.

"Yeah, but who could forget a face like yours?" Walter mumbles back.

"I'll be damned. You look rough, boy." Marvin lets out a hearty laugh and wraps his arms around Dakota, looking him up and down. "What happened to your braids? Shit... those Tribesmen still giving you grief over those kids you fried?"

Dakota pulls away. "Mind your own, Marvin. I don't—"

"You've met my friend, Edwards, I see."

Walter pipes in. "Birds of a feather. The kid and I were rooming in B-Block long before coming to your neck of the woods."

A smile lights up Marvin's face. "No shit? Well ain't that divine intervention. I was—"

"Chicago already spilled the beans this morning. What are you doing pulling strings to get me back in A-Block?" Dakota asks, taking his turn to interrupt.

"Hey, Marvin!" Archie calls from the other end of the hall, gripping his club by his side. "How's your mama doing?"

They pace towards the head guard and Marvin calls back. "Couldn't tell ya, Boss-man."

Seemingly satisfied, Archie shifts his focus. "For fuck's sake, Edwards, I would say you should know better than to mingle with this asshole, but we both know you're dumber than a sack of snowshoes." He flashes a knowing glance and Marvin laughs, giving him a playful slap on the gut.

"Oh, relax, Boss-man. I'm a good influence today! Edwards here will be shadowing me in the shop."

"A good influence, huh?" Archie brushes his uniform off and gives Marvin a leery stare. "You sure he can handle it? Piss-ant couldn't even win a game of jacks." They laugh and Walter drops his head, smelling Archie's one sock planted lopsided on the ground.

"Judging by the looks of your tilt, you've found your latest victim," he says, holding back a glob of spit.

Both Dakota and Marvin back away and Archie's laugh dries up. "What the fuck did you just say to me, Edwards?"

Dakota raises his hands to diffuse the situation, but Archie pulls his club. "You better watch that smart mouth of yours, shit-head. Just because you're over here with the big boys doesn't mean I won't take this other boot off for a guest appearance. Now, if I hear that smart mouth of yours again, I'll feed you to that—"

An ear-piercing whistle lets out from inside the shop and Dakota pushes Walter along, hurrying him away.

"Dakota, you're with the Sock-monkeys," Archie barks. "Edwards, you're with Marvin; God help you." He points his club. "And *that's* your last warning, you hear me?"

Walter sets off for the workshop and Dakota sneers at him like a jealous sibling. "For fuck's sake, Jamestown. If you don't keep that mouth shut, I'll push you in the forge myself. I don't know how you don't—" His voice fades as he turns towards the laundry bay, and Walter moves ahead.

A dozen steps later, the hall opens to the giant workshop and its monstrous screaming machines, all of them shadowed by the hanging iron walkways branching out overhead, housing the few Boys-in-Blue strutting across, keeping their watch on the inmates below.

"Eyes in the sky, Edwards. Always watch for those eyes in the sky," Marvin says. Plumes of steam jet out in geysers across the shop floor, carrying the burnt orange glow up from the jungle of twisting metal, filling the room with a smolder that invokes images of hell.

"You wanna talk shop or stand and gawk?" Marvin asks as he pulls a smock from a locker and throws it at Walter, nearly knocking the cigarette from his lips. "Put this on and stay close." He takes off and Walter follows in hot pursuit, the heavy fumes filling his lungs and burning his throat.

A dozen zig zags around countless machines and they step up on an elevated platform, heated by the river of molten metal below.

"Come on, the gig is simple." Marvin reaches out, grabbing the chain dangling in front of them and wraps it around the slag-covered mold resting on the table. Two more loops secure it, and he pulls hand over hand, raising the large metal block up, reminding Walter of Doctor Frankenstein bringing his creation to life. It swings over the safety railing and over the pit with another heave, then sinks to the spout below.

"Step back." Marvin takes a deep breath, then

pulls the tube from under his nose and holds it high overhead as he spins one of the many wheels in front of him. The burnt orange glow seeps out from the spout as it opens its mechanical maw, and the small trickle of molten iron globs into the metal cast with an angry plume of black, tar-smelling smoke. He cuts the flow and puts his oxygen supply back on, then takes a deep breath. "Doctors tell me this bad boy will go off like a rocket if I get too close to an open flame." He taps the metal cylinder by his side and adjusts the tube over his ears. "Anyways, that's half the job. Now we wait for the dragon's piss to settle." He points Walter to the workstation across the table beside them. "I saw you in the service this morning; you didn't look too at home amongst those pews, Edwards. You a God-fearing man?"

Walter wanders over, surveying the identical setup, and takes his place. "Me and the Big Man don't have much to talk about these days." He stares into the rising smoke, much preferring the eye-watering sting over the sight of Marvin's glorified smirk.

"Whatever you got to feel guilty about, the Lord's forgiveness has no bounds. Any sin can be swept under a rug, hidden away. But to truly get those evil deeds out, you need to lift them high and beat the fibers until they're clean, clean, clean!" Marvin pulls on the chain and the mold rises.

Walter stares into the glowing runoff below, wondering how deep it goes and how long it would take to engulf a man about Marvin's size. He shakes his head, feeling a sudden pang of guilt, then a surge of anger. *Chicken-shit.*

Marvin swings the hoist, bringing the mold down between them, and picks up a pry bar from the floor. A few twists of the tool and the metal shell splits open, releasing another plume of the toxic smell. Inside, an iron kettle sits in its negative shell, its lid hosting an ornate buffalo that stares up with silent, judging eyes.

"Nice craftsmanship," Walter says.

"These?" Marvin huffs. "Used to be a lot nicer when they were made by the Hudson Bay boys in the 1800s, but the cheap bastards started outsourcing their work to the criminals and China-men. Quality's been going to shit ever since."

"Pretty color, though," Walter lies, his palms gripping the railing as the iron's burnt orange glow bathes his stoic face.

"Reminds me of a truck I used to have back in the day. Wasn't much to look at, but when I put my foot down that beauty would roar!" Marvin lifts his leg, stomping on an invisible pedal, and screams out an engine's roar with flapping lips. His pry bar pops the kettle out, then he reaches into a bucket with another grunt and sprinkles a handful of black powder across both halves of the empty mold.

Another blast of smoke rises and the powder sizzles, pushing Walter away as he clutches the railing tighter, his head spinning out of control as countless hours of marriage counselling rush through his mind. Birthdays and dance recitals all as good as missed with his mind focused on the man now standing before him. The *click-clack* of bones cuts through the shop's chaos, and in the corner of his eye the red and blue twists its way up the stairs, causing a string of bile to spew from his mouth and pour through the gaps in the walkway. He stands upright, steadying himself on shaking legs and keeps his head fixed ahead, not daring to look back.

Marvin laughs and claps him on the back. "Newbies always chuck on their first day. Don't feel bad. Give it a year or two and the morning headache won't go away until your first huff of the stuff." He leans over the mold and takes a deep breath. "Anyway, that's pretty much it. Rinse and repeat." He gives the catwalks above a quick glance. "Hey, Edwards... I'll be right back; don't burn your eyebrows off while I'm gone." He paces down the platform and disappears amongst the machines.

Walter lets off the railing and his stomach sucks in on itself with a wave of nervous, agonizing hunger. He grips the chain in front of him and it gives way, sending his face careening down, his lip smashing into the railing and releasing a stream of tears, both angry and sad. A shuddering breath sucks into his lungs, and the *click-clack* beckons him to look back as he desperately tries to ward off the stench and orange glow storming around him. He slaps himself across the face and reaches down, steadying his hand beneath the spout, his other gripping tight around the wheel. He gives it a turn and the jaws crack open, releasing a glob of molten metal that oozes out, reaching for his bloody and bruised knuckles. It lets loose as a heavy thud shakes the entire workstation and he springs upright, pulling his hand from the metal's trajectory.

"Jesus, Wayne! Could you be a little more obvious, please?" Marvin half shouts.

Walter turns, trying to reset his mind as his eyes focus on the new mold lying on the table in front of him.

"Oh, relax," Wayne says, scoping out the empty section of walkways overhead. "These guards have gotten so slack they might as well be gas station attendants." He smiles and strolls off with a wink. "Good seeing ya, Edwards."

Walter nods, unable to do much more, and Marvin turns his attention towards him.

"You doing alright, Edwards?"

Walter waves a hand. "F-fine. It's just the fumes. I never worked the mines, so I've got the lungs of a newborn."

Marvin laughs, unhooking the chains from his cooling mold and replaces it with the freshly delivered one. "Hey," he chirps. "Eyes off."

Walter turns away, collecting himself enough to lower his own mold.

"You spend any time out west?"

"No," Walter lies with another dizzy wave of hunger. "Just—just east. Too much of that hippie shit out west for me."

Marvin tugs at his chain and the new mold joins below. Together they turn their wheels and the orange glow radiates from the spouts once more as Walter takes a reluctant breath and holds in a scream, preventing it from escaping out over the *click-clack* whispering in his ear.

"Fisherman?" Marvin asks.

"Yup."

"I rode the coast for years. Hated every stinking minute of it."

"Whatever pays the bills." Walter exhales.

"What were you towing? Skiff? Pilothouse? Trawler?"

He picks one, hoping it will move the menial conversation along. "Yeah, Skiff."

"Tuna? Plenty of tuna on the outer coastline, but I don't gotta tell you."

"Tuna, yeah."

Marvin stares at Walter for a long moment and his mold overflows.

"You're full up," Walter notes, jolting him from his questionable gaze.

"Huh? Oh yeah…" He chuckles and they pull their chains, raising the molds up and letting them hang as the heat fries Walter's already cooked nerves.

Another moment of silence lingers between them, and Walter cracks his open with his own pry bar, then works the kettle out, letting it slip and fall to the floor. He reaches out with a stumble, but Marvin's hand comes down hard on his shoulder, stopping him from grabbing it with his bare hands. "Whoa, easy. That bastard will melt clean through your fingers." His thumb glides back and forth over Walter's scar tissue, each pass sending a sharp pain up his neck. "You sure you're okay, Edwards?"

"Yeah… Right as rain," he answers and turns away.

Marvin reaches into the bucket and tosses another fist of the black powder over the mold. The smoke ascends, and the *click-clack of* twisting bones raise the hairs on Walter's neck as his chest rises and falls, unable to stop itself from taking in deep lungfuls of the synthetic stench.

Marvin looks around and pulls out a small metal flask from his apron with a mischievous grin. "To new friends." He unscrews the cap and the pungent stench of pine wafts from its metallic lip. "A little nip to welcome ya to A-Block."

Walter stumbles back and another stream of bile climbs his esophagus, settling in his throat as he bumps into the railing, pinning him with nowhere to go. He shakes his head and Marvin shrugs, cracking his mold open and releasing another wave of burnt orange glow that chips away at his rapidly crumbling composure. "Suit yourself." He lifts the flask, pouring the clear liquid into his mouth and swishes it from cheek to cheek, hardening his soft demeanor into something more heinous and familiar.

Several moments pass and Walter forces the bile down. "S-strong stuff?"

Marvin's eyes shoot open with realization, and he coughs, spraying a fine mist of gin all over Walter, snapping his mind in two as the pine, tar, and burnt orange glow drag him back to that late autumn afternoon.

"Should have checked the latch, Daddy..."

Unable to stop himself, he looks down at the two mangled hands latching on to his ankles, his son's crushed skull pivoting on a bent neck, *clicking* as his cold, empty eyes come to rest on his. Kevin's lips spread, smiling with a mouth full of shattered teeth, and Walter screams as the broken image of his boy burns itself into the back of his mind forever.

He grips the railing, desperate to get away, and peers down at the molten river below. His foot plants on the bottom rung, preparing to cast him into the cleansing fires, the only reprieve from the horror wrapping itself around his leg.

"How's that dead kid of yours doing, Walt?"

Walter stops and his palms wring the railing dry as he slowly turns, his stunned gaze finally finding the Marvin who killed his boy after so many years of searching.

"There you are…" Without question, he pushes the pry bar through the air, eyes locked on Marvin's toothy grin, but another wave of fatigue betrays his malnourished muscles, sending the bar off course and only skimming Marvin's temple with a hollow thud.

Marvin winces, then flashes a proud smirk as a line of blood drips from the shallow gash.

Walter raises the bar again, this time determined to plant it deeper, but Marvin's meaty palm rises and grabs hold of his wrist.

A sharp whistle pierces the shop floor. "Everybody down!" Archie yells.

Marvin shakes the weapon loose from Walter's grip and it clatters to the floor as more Boys-in-Blue scream commands, descending the catwalks above.

"Gonna have to swing harder than that," Marvin says and hurriedly turns away, heaving at the mold between them.

"You two, don't move!" Archie screams and hurries up their platform, giving Marvin a shove with the end of his club. "Hands behind your heads."

Both throw their arms up, and Walter watches the drip of blood run down Marvin's cheek with little satisfaction.

"How's your mama, Marvin?" Archie asks.

"Mind your own business, asshole!"

"I asked how your mama is, shit-head!"

"That bitch can rot in hell for all I care!"

Archie's eyes tighten and the surrounding inmates stop and stare. "Edwards, what the hell do—" His question cuts short as his eyes lock onto the open mold and the dozen glowing cell keys inside. "What the hell is this?"

"Now, Boss-man, don't jump to any conclusions," Marvin starts.

The Boys-in-Blue approach, but Archie holds out a cautionary hand, pausing their descent as he lowers his voice. "What the fuck is all this? This isn't part of the plan."

Marvin blinks and feigns a smile. "Plans change, Boss-man."

Walter holds his breath, unsure of the situation unfolding before him, and reaches for his pry bar.

"Don't you fucking move!" Archie yells, raising his club. He looks back at Marvin with a face hot as molten iron. "Who the hell do you think you are changing my goddamn plans? The deal was three. Not one, two, six, eleven, fucking twelve!" He points to the dozen cooling keys, counting them off. "You trying to take over the show?" Archie looks around at the circle of inmates shuffling in from their workstations and he hammers the railing with his club. "Get back to work!" he yells, but the men stand their ground and the Boys-in-Blue shift uncomfortably as more of Marvin's congregation join their sides.

Marvin sucks his teeth. "Like I said, Boss-man, plans change."

"That's it, I'm calling it off, you ungrateful shit!" Archie swings his club through the air, but Marvin bats it away with his pry bar, then looks around at his followers closing in and gives Archie a smile dripping with pity.

"I'm sorry, Boss-man, but this train is rolling; the coal's already been shoveled in." He lifts his bar, smashing Archie across the skull and he crumbles with fluttering eyes, filling the shop with a moment of shocked silence.

"Jesus…," Walter whispers.

"At your service." Marvin smiles and points a finger. "I want a word with you before this is over, Walter." He turns to the vibrating inmates. "The big day's moved up, boys!"

Every man dives as one, swallowing up the Boys-in-Blue, as if rehearsed a thousand times. Walter swipes Archie's club from the ground amidst the panic of it all and swings it at Marvin, knocking his hand as he reaches for the keys between them.

"You almost had me thinking you were a changed man, Marvin, but you're still the same old piece of shit you've always been. Thank God!" Walter laughs with a relieved smile and swings again.

Marvin dodges it and jogs down the platform, snapping a finger at Chicago as he emerges from the crowd. "Take this asshole to his cell. I don't need him fucking up our plans any more than he has."

"My pleasure."

Walter waves his club, backing the man off, then turns to the side railing and throws himself over, taking off after Marvin. Screams, whoops, and hollers bellow out, mixing with the storm of fists, clubs, and pry bars. Unattended molds run over with iron and shower the air with a typhoon of unbridled fireworks. More ear-piercing whistles bleed in from the lobby as a siren starts up and Uncle Bill's voice wails out over the loudspeakers above.

"Get back in your cells, you filthy animals! This is no way for my civilized guests to behave!"

Walter pushes through the men as they separate for Marvin ahead like some kind of Messiah, and a handful of Boys-in-Blue rush in, all outfitted in black riot gear, some pointing their guns between huddled shields.

"It's twenty to one, boys!" Marvin shouts over the chaos. "Rush 'em!"

The crowd of adrenaline-frenzied criminals dash forward, sweeping Walter in their wake.

A shot goes off and a man in the front lines goes down.

Canisters of gas rain from above, trailing thick smoke that spreads across the ground with a layer of haunted fog.

Walter loses his pin on Marvin as the two armies collide and more shots ring out. A breath of the tart smoke fills his lungs and turns his view sideways as the vision of war plays out around him. He stands on his tiptoes, desperate to take a breath from higher up, but his knees buckle, plummeting him into the swath of stomping feet below. Another gulp of the poison turns his vision completely upside down and his grip on reality fades to black as the twisted mass of red and blue crawls over and wraps itself around him with its lonely, cold embrace.

THE MAN WHO
FORGIVES

Silent prayers join the tattered wigwam flapping in the wind, waking Walter from the nightmare that is Cold Keep. He sits up amongst the mountain of bones around him, watching Tahki reluctantly add another log to the fire. The snow drifts down through the holes above, piling on her patchy scalp as her gnarled fingertips rifle uselessly through the remains, searching for any morsels of flesh left to pick clean. She closes her eyes, then opens them, pretending to blink out of necessity rather than obligation, and peers out the flap to the crumbled storehouse. Its dried meats and berries lie strewn about the desecrated graves in the snow, the food half picked clean by the parliament of owls that have taken camp in the treetops above.

The new log catches fire and the flames rise, stinging Tahki's skin with its warmth. A sharp tug she doesn't truly feel jets through her chest and she opens her robes. Inside, her daughter's sticky lips suckle at what's left of her breast and draw the molasses-like substance out, swallowing with forceful gulps. Tahki leans in, drawing a breath of her baby's sweet scent and gently skims her teeth across the its soft scalp. A line of drool escapes past her gnarled lips and the faint howls on the wind snap her mouth shut as she sits up, recognizing the distant sound of sleds being dragged over the frozen lake. The chatter of the white man's language mix with the domesticated dogs growing closer, and she shuffles towards the flap, yanking it closed.

The dog's whining fills her ears, setting her on edge, and a gentle voice calls out in her own language.

"Hello? We come on behalf of the First Nations Ministry, the Church Missionary Society, and first and foremost our Savior, Jesus Christ. Please, do not—"

"It's been long abandoned, John," the other voice interrupts as the sleds come to a halt outside the wigwam.

"Then who is responsible for the smoke? Why are these people's rations spread over the ground and not taken with them?" The dogs die down, leaving room on the wind for the babe's whimpers to take their place as Tahki squeezes her child tight, trying to ignore her savory smell. "There. Do you hear that? Hello?" The crunching boots approach. "It's alright, we are here to help you."

Tahki darts back and forth, shuffling through the mountain of tumbling bones and grabs her mittens, shoving them over her dead fingers. A steady breath does nothing to calm her, and she slips out from her home, facing the approaching men.

"There." A Native man points as his other arm juts out and stops the European by his side.

The accomplice's blond hair and pale complexion makes Tahki pause for only a moment, then she remembers the new people to her land that her tribe had traded with only a few seasons before.

"Tansi," he says, taking a step forward as she looks back and adjusts the flap behind her.

"T-tansi," Tahki responds, the greeting coming out rounded and swollen over her scalded tongue. She takes a few steps, and the men look around, confused by the exhumed holes in the snow and the dried meats strewn across the forest floor.

"M-my name is John Ulrich, and my white-skinned friend is Benjamin Lewis. We have come to spread the word of something glorious." He peers towards the wigwam and Tahki side-steps into his line of sight, struggling to find her voice as the dogs fall silent, their eyes fixating on her with heads that hover close to the ground.

"W-what news?" she asks. The sight of the animals makes her stomach churn.

"Is everything alright, *iskwao?*" Benjamin asks, taking another step towards her as he surveys the desolated camp.

"Everything is as it should be," Tahki lies. "The wolves made their way through our village this morning and spread our livelihood across our grounds. Our men have set out to rid them of their pups and are set to return soon." She bites her fleshy lip, eyes watching the men's expressions as they struggle to piece together her broken sounding words. "Why do you bear the white man's name if you are Cree?" she asks John, trying to steer the conversation elsewhere.

John straightens up with a smile and hurries back to his sled, digging within its contents. He pulls out a leather book and returns to Tahki's side, his musk tickling her nose, causing her teeth to grind as she fights the urge to lean in closer.

"My name was Tackagouatim, of the Oui Cree," he says. "One day, Benjamin came to our village and offered to teach me about Jesus Christ."

"Christ?" Tahki repeats.

"Oh yes. Christ is wonderful. He saved me from my sins. He abolished evil from these lands, and by His side, we will have paradise for ever and ever in His grace, Amen. When I gave myself to Him, my sins were washed away by the waters of forgiveness, and with it, I was given a new name, that of John Ulrich. And as John Ulrich, I was born anew to start over and do right by my newfound Father. That's why Benjamin and I have come to these plains, to the edge of this very lake where the water meets the forest and your very home. We are desperate to spread Christ's beautiful words to your people, to allow them to join Him and be born again, like me."

Tahki backs away and looks to Benjamin, her lips trembling in response to John's promise. "Is that true? Could I be forgiven, too?"

Benjamin joins them and the men's pheromones collide, creating a delectable scent that soaks into the back of Tahki's throat, moistening her tongue for the first time in weeks. He grabs the book from John and opens it, showing her the words written inside. The pages swim with so many lines and symbols that she has to look away, but her eyes meet the watching dogs, and their untrusting stares make her uneasy.

"Oh yes, it's true. All of it. My Father sent His only son, Jesus, to die on the cross for our sins," Benjamin says.

"Cross?"

Benjamin holds his hands up, joining his fingers together. "A symbol of His love, for the sins He absolved. For mine, John's, and even yours. All you have to do is accept Christ into your heart and you will be forgiven."

"I-I would like that," Tahki whispers and leans in further, smelling their breath.

Benjamin claps his hands, joining them together in prayer, and John looks into her eyes for only a moment, then shifts his gaze to her black, frostbitten feet, half buried in the snow.

The babe stirs inside Tahki's robes, and John peers back at the dog's raised hackles and deep growls humming in unison, forming a choir of caution. He backs away, looking around the camp again, this time with concern rather than confusion.

The babe's cries erupt, and Benjamin's oblivious prayer is cut short with a gasp. "You have a child?" A smile spreads across his face and he reaches out. "What perfect timing for us to—"

"I think it best we move along," John interrupts, grabbing his partner's arm.

"Are you mad?" Benjamin pulls free. "This woman needs our help. She said herself that her people will be back soon. Besides, it's getting dark and their fire is already warm."

"Please," Tahki begs, blackened tears trailing down her hardened cheeks. "We will accept your Man. I need forgiveness. We need to be born again, to start over. Give us this chance."

John studies her pale skin. "Then repent," he says, his icy frown refusing to waver for even a moment.

"Repent?" Tahki asks.

Benjamin willingly flips through the pages of his book, reading aloud. "'He who conceals his transgressions will not prosper, but he who confesses and forsakes them will find compassion.'" He turns more of the paper, barely concealing his joy. "'If a wicked man turns from all his sins which he has committed, keeps all my statutes, and does what is lawful and right, he shall surely live; he shall not die. None of the transgressions which he has committed shall be remembered against him; because of the righteousness which he has done, he shall live.'"

"I am certain repentance is not the remedy for this woman," John barks, pulling with another tug.

Benjamin turns and throws him off. "What has come over you? It is our sacred duty to save these people. To have Christ work through us and rescue their souls from damnation! And you would rather take back to your sled? If not for this, what have we been doing out here in the dead of winter?"

John grabs Benjamin and turns him away as they argue with words Tahki no longer understands. Heated debate flies back and forth between them as her daughter's muffled cries mix with the dog's low growls on the wind. Benjamin looks over his shoulder at the animals, his anger fading as he peers back at Tahki's feet. His face shifts from confusion to concern then finally fear as he wipes his brow and speaks. "J-John tells me the men hunt for your band. Is this true?"

Tahki gnaws at her cheek as she fights against the smell of warm flesh. "That's right. The men do the hunting. They are tracking wolves out past—"

"What of the women?"

"I—I don't understand," Tahki tells him.

"Why is it just you here tending to the fire by yourself?"

"They are out gathering." The lies flow from her lips so easily.

"Gathering?" Benjamin asks.

"Yes."

"There is nothing to gather this late in the season, and everywhere I look there are hardly-touched reserves spread by those wolves that had not bothered to eat any. Why would your women be out gathering when you have so much left, and with the sun made to melt the snow only weeks from now?"

The growls build, turning into hushed yips. Tahki takes another step back and bumps into the wigwam, searching for another lie but comes up short. "T-tell me more about your Man. I want to know," she says.

John turns for the sleds. "Let's depart, Benjamin; our words will only fall on deaf ears here."

Benjamin follows, and Tahki drops to her knees. "No, please. Please don't leave us! Forgive me. I can't live with this—*as* this monster any longer!"

Benjamin pauses, looking back at the babe wailing almost as loud as her mother.

"Benjamin!" John calls over the cries. "We need to leave, now!" The yips build and the dogs tug at their leads, jostling the iron rings that group them together and ring out.

Tahki opens her robes and her ribs protrude, each bone visible beneath her tissue paper skin. She peels her daughter from the layer of black sticky film on her chest and holds her out. "She will not survive with me," she says. "She will soon be all that is left, and my hunger is too strong. If you will not save me, save her. Introduce her to your Man. She has done nothing wrong."

"Benjamin, leave it! We have—"

Benjamin spins to face John on the back of his sled. "What use are you if this is how you greet a gift from God? Why would Christ choose you if this is what you decide for an innocent soul? I do not care what you make of this woman, or what you claim her to be. This child is none of that, can't you understand? Are you that blinded by fear?" He strides to his sled and pulls a thick pelt from its base, then walks back to Tahki, looking down on her with compassion. "For your sake, I hope your men come back from their hunt, but the condition of your camp tells another story, girl. We cannot help you, but Christ will see to your child, I promise you that."

"Thank you, thank you!" Tahki gently lays her daughter down and she spares herself one last smell of her tender skin as Benjamin wraps the pelt around her.

"Be well and know what you have done here today was in part a miracle." He turns, gently nestling the baby into his jacket and steps on the back of his sled. Without another word the dogs take off, both sets flying in the direction they came as their howls fade into the distance, and Tahki watches the lanterns shrink across the frozen lake.

"Mhhmmmmhhhmmmhm…"

The canopy above moans and she looks up at the thing silently watching from the treetops, its robes tucked under its arms. "There were two of them, *nuntanuhs*, and two of us…," it whispers with the missionaries' stolen voices.

"Have your meal," Tahki spits. "I have spent the last of my humanity. What you have made me is nothing that will ever see an eternity of paradise, of that I'm sure. Just leave the one to deliver my daughter to the wonderful place they spoke of and save your hunger for the other."

The thing leaps from its perch without a sound as the mountain of stitched furs settle around it, then takes off, following the tracks in the snow.

Tahki crawls back into her wigwam and shuffles through the bones, taking her seat next to the dwindling fire as she stares at the kettle amidst the hot coals. Its ornate metal lid stares up at her, the metal buffalo in its center calling out, beckoning her to grab hold. Desperate for one last moment of humanity, she brings her palm down on the image, feeling nothing as her frozen flesh thaws, then sizzles against the brand, searing the animal into her skin forever. She lets go and grabs for another log, but stops, instead choosing to watch the flames die. And as the last of her babe's warmth fades from her chest, she decides that giving her daughter to the Man who forgives would be the last human thing she would ever do.

Walter sits, watching her give in to the cold with pity when the sudden presence of the warm bannock barges uninvited across his tongue once more. His teeth bare down on the bread and he chews, tasting copper as Tahki's unearthly gaze turns on him with a damning smile. The lump slides to the back of his throat and Walter grabs his neck, screaming out in desperate protest as the yeasty flavor reveals its true bloody game and goes down with a gulp.

KILLING KOOKY

A mixture of blood and mucus spill from Walter's mouth, down onto the cold cement as he coughs, gasping for air. A vile symphony of bloodshed echoes out from the block beyond their cell and the crackle of tobacco sizzles in the darkness, lighting up Dakota's bloodied brow on his cot.

"Gotta keep those nightmares in check, Jamestown."

Walter sits up and rubs his throat, still tasting the riot grenade. "If—if I get put on my ass one more time, I'm going to lose it."

"I know you said you used to be a scrapper back in the day, but seeing your shit-ass get knocked out three times in one week makes me wonder."

"You don't look like no Rocky Marciano, yourself, kid. I'd like to see you go toe to toe with one of those riot grenades."

Dakota chuckles and massages his palms as he sucks back on his cigarette.

"I thought you said you didn't smoke," Walter says.

A large cloud spills from Dakota's mouth and fills the cell. "Thought I'd start, being the end of the world and all."

"Is that busted-up mug of yours on the account of me?"

"Don't flatter yourself. Word is you tried clubbing your buddy—who, by the way, is not as soft as you led on—and that you might've finished the job, too, if you hadn't botched the swing." Hurried footsteps rattle the iron catwalks, but Dakota ignores them as he continues to mumble with daydreaming eyes. "No telling why Marvin didn't split your skull open, though."

"You didn't answer my question," Walter says. "What's my below batting average got to do with your busted-up face?"

"Marvin and his cronies came sniffing around for my secret," Dakota answers.

"Your little fire number?"

"Yup." He flicks the end of his cigarette, sending a small shower of embers through the air. "My little magic trick is the only thing keeping me alive it seems. That's why Marvin wanted me back in A-Block"

Walter pulls himself to the edge of his cot and Dakota reaches over, handing him a lit smoke. He takes it, then with three deep puffs he exhales, and Dakota drops his thoroughly tenderized palm.

"Almost had him." The feeling of failure cuts deep into Walter's gut, but is quickly carried away with the rush of forgiving tobacco.

"Knew something wasn't right the second Marvin was involved," Dakota says. "Men like him don't make friends, only enemies. I told you that, and there you went, clubbing him over the head not twenty minutes later."

"Oh, come on, now, it was thirty at least." Walter looks at his cigarette and changes the subject. "That really your first dart?"

"I said I wasn't a smoker; never said I hadn't had one before."

"Fair point." Walter blows a smoke ring and watches it waver, then turn into an oval and dissipate. "I started smoking when my grandmother got sick; so sick she couldn't even lift her arms to light her own. She would have me come into her room, sometimes in the middle of the night, and get me to spark them up for her. I'd get it lit, then would rest it between her lips. In through the mouth, out through the nose. One time I saw her finish a whole one in just two drags, I swear to God." Clouds of tobacco pour from their mouths, filling the dark cell with an even darker haze. "I remember hating the taste they would leave in my mouth. Pops refused to do it, said he resented the damn things for taking his wife from him. But she'd been smoking for sixty years and wasn't gonna stop at the bitter end; so I helped her."

"Find what you love and let it kill you," Dakota says.

Walter nods. "But, after some time my hate for the taste grew a little sweeter, and before I knew it, I found myself inhaling a little extra smoke before handing each one over. I would hold it in till she took her first puff, then let it out at the same time as hers, mixing it in so she wouldn't see. Not long after that, I was stealing entire rows, then packs. Shit, my grandmother was halfway to the moon, it's not like she noticed them missing, or maybe she just didn't care."

Dakota fingers the butt of his cigarette, ashing it onto his lap with glazed eyes. "I guess I can see the appeal."

"But that's just it, kid." Walter points his cigarette. "For thirty years I was smoking a pack a day. Over two-hundred thousand cigarettes in that time, and not one of them, not a single one made me feel like the ones they are doling out here in Cold Keep. You don't get it. Prisons don't run like this, kid, they just don't. Everyone walking around with their heads in the clouds while a fucking demon picks their bones clean. It makes no sense, none at all. You all just sit around and let it happen, day after day. Then I figured it out." He stares at his ash and smiles.

"Figured what out?"

"Every time I got to feeling angry, you would be there with one of those smokes that calmed me down real quick. Hell, even if you ain't smoking the things, the fog in the air from the ones who are is thick enough to keep anyone sedated."

"I don't understand, Jamestown."

"These aren't normal cigarettes, kid. They're putting something in them to keep us docile. To keep us from raising too many hands. Isn't it obvious?" He sucks the orange filter as it meets its end and burns, adding a tangy bitterness to the smoke. "And honestly… I kind of like it…"

"Yeah well, smoke up, because I got some

bad news for you." Dakota leans forward, looking at Walter from between strands of blood-soaked hair and reaches over, turning his head towards the catwalk.

His eyes focus, making out the worn laces that stretch over the railing and fall back down, weaving in and out of the rivets of Archie's old boot. He frowns, numb to the object as it sways back and forth just outside their cell and a small laugh builds in his throat, growing louder and fuller as Dakota joins in. The room spills with the hearty chuckles and potent smoke from both men, and as Walter takes another deep breath of the ambient haze, he lays back on his cot, no longer caring if the world were to fall out from under his feet at that very moment.

A moment passes and he sighs. "That swing I botched was my last chance at getting my life back… Ah jeez, I'm sorry, kid. I really did get you killed, didn't I?"

"Yeah…" Dakota admits. "But at least I was right."

Walter shakes his head, standing from his cot on wavering legs and un-strings his boot, tying a loop in the lace.

"Didn't take you for a cowboy," Dakota says.

Walter locks onto the iron key resting just beyond his reach and throws the lasso, ignoring him as it makes it halfway, then fall to the catwalk. He pulls the lace back in and throws it again, hearing Dakota huff behind him.

"Been watching men try that little number for a while now. It's not gonna work."

Walter turns, anger bubbling up as the haze

of tobacco clears from his mind. "So, what then? Just roll over and wait for that fucking thing to tear us apart? I don't know about you, but I have a daughter who is gonna be awfully curious as to where her daddy's gone off to. It won't come tonight, will it?" He whips the lace out again.

Dakota edges himself to the end of his cot. "I'm sorry for your daughter, truly, but I'm coming up short in the sympathy department, friend. You came in here with a vendetta that fucked us all. If my final day wasn't already long past due, I'd be fixing to kill you myself, right now. Now I'm sure whatever Marvin did, he had it coming, and I don't blame ya for it, but—"

"That son-of-a-bitch murdered my little boy!" The words send a shiver down Walter's spine as they spill from his lips. "Marvin ran him down, and when I found my son's body wedged under the bastard's pickup, he took a pistol to me like a dog in the street, trying to tie up loose ends." He pulls his jacket and shirt aside, exposing the scar on his shoulder.

Dakota's eyes soften and he throws his cigarette down. "Jesus, Jamestown... I—"

"Save your breath, kid... It's page twenty-seven news."

Dakota stands. "I have a son, too. I know how blind a man can become when there's something holding him back from his kin."

Walter pauses, clutching the laces in his palm and looks back at Dakota's tear-filled eyes as he continues to speak.

"Kid-killer... It's true. But it's not like they

make it out to sound." He shifts and looks away. "It was an accident. My son was only two, and the wife and I already feared the day big brother would sweep in and whisk him off to one of those residential schools. We heard the stories of teachers pricking needles into the tongues of children who dared speak their own language. And when word got out about how the black lung was sweeping through the classes, and how they tried to cover the whole thing up, I promised my wife I would be gunned down before I let 'em take him. But we were too busy worrying about what would happen then, when we should have been worrying about what would happen that very day. I came up from the mines on a Tuesday, and before I was even a mile from town, I could hear her howling to the moon, wailing away."

Walter stares, eyes glued to Dakota's trembling lips. "Your wife?" he asks.

"Not just her. All over the reserve. The cries of the mothers who just had their babies scooped right out from their arms by the child-welfare-something-or-other pricks. The men that took it upon themselves to relocate our sons and daughters to orphanages; to be picked out like stray cats and dogs by white families who knew nothing of our people or stories. Those snakes waited for us to be deep underground when they came with barrels pointed and trigger fingers itching. And just like that, our entire world was taken from us again. All because I wasn't there."

Dakota shakes his head, and Walter takes a steady breath, choosing his words carefully. "I know, kid… At first, I blamed that goddamn latch on the screen door. 'Should have checked the latch, should have checked the latch,' I told myself for months. It always closed, never once had it not." He fingers the loop in the lace and throws it aside with disdain. "I was snoozing away, and my boy wandered out into the front yard, onto the street." A tear lets loose from his swollen eye, and he shakes the thought.

"What are you saying?"

Walter sucks back his weakness and looks at Dakota, his sadness shifting to resentment. "What I'm saying is, it's a hell of a lot easier blaming someone else than it is blaming yourself. I struggled, nearly strung myself up one night over the guilt. But when I turned that guilt to anger and focused it on the man who deserved it, I suddenly found a purpose again, a way to get my life back."

Dakota looks around the cell and laughs. "And how is that working out for you?"

Walter sighs and manages his own laugh doused in self-pity. "Yeah… not so good, I guess."

"Blaming someone else might work for you, Jamestown, but I don't have that luxury. No one else to point a finger to because that's not where my story ends. Not by a long shot. I searched up and down for my boy after that day. I visited each and every orphanage for miles, and soon enough the missus started questioning if I would ever bring him home. She never said it, but I knew the resentment was building when her kisses grew colder each time I came home with empty arms." He picks at the corner of the cot, working a small hole in its cover. "Then one day, I opened the paper to the adverts, like I had my whole life, and there he was, standing in the third row with the other stolen boys and girls; right after an article about trout migration patterns. Fucking trout; can you believe that shit?"

Walter nods and lends a sympathetic frown. "Yeah… all too well."

"He was in some ad for an adoption program out in Saskatchewan. I ran to the bus station so fast, and within a night I was standing outside that orphanage, my naïve ass thinking it would be as easy as signing some papers. But the old bitch at the desk made it clear they weren't looking for any red-skinned fathers at that time, so I threw a fit and they tossed me out."

"Were you surprised?"

"Yeah, sorta. But you know what I did after all that searching, just to be told to walk away?" He pulls another cigarette from his pocket and puts it in his mouth, this time letting it hang unlit.

"Tell me," Walter says.

Dakota drifts off, losing himself in the story. "I wait till it's dark, and I go to the back of that home with a book of matches in one hand and a cup of gasoline in the other." His voice shakes and drifts back and forth from anger to sadness. "I go up to the shed in the garden, nowhere near the house, and I light it up. The flames take and soon enough, the staff comes running out waving blankets, throwing their buckets of water. So, I take advantage of the panic and go around front; when suddenly the screams of fire engines grow louder and I see the blaze crawl over the rooftop above, no longer on the shed, but eating up the main house somehow. So I barge in, kicking doors open, throwing kids out of their beds as I look for my boy, and with each second that passes, the smoke gets thicker and thicker until I can't even see my hand two inches from my own face."

"Mother of God," Walter says, nervously rubbing his knees as he bends over, fighting a wave of nausea.

Dakota hauls on his unlit cigarette, eyes building tears. "I'm breathing so hard that it's burning up my lungs, but I keep searching. Bed after bed empty as the children flee in terror, until eventually the smoke gets to me and I go down. And as I'm lying there, sprawled out on the ground, I see my scared little boy crumpled up under that bed I collapsed next to, clutching his legs to his chest crying, choking on the smoke." Dakota wipes another tear and drives a fist into his leg. "And the last time my boy ever looked at me, it wasn't with love or tenderness, but fear and confusion, eyes wide and wondering why his protector, his own daddy wasn't doing a thing to help him... Next thing I knew, I woke up in cuffs at the hospital and they're telling me I killed three children with that fire. One swift trial and a million pointed fingers later and I'm in Cold Keep with a band of Natives trying to cut my throat for what I did, and a belly too yellow to do it myself." He throws his cigarette aside and nods at Walter with tired eyes. "So, I guess they're right... I'm a kid killer, but I'm not the monster they paint me to be. Not a monster like that, anyway."

Walter blows a breath, and a pang of understanding untwists his gut. "I'm sorry kid, I—"

"Looks like sleeping beauty's awake!"

Marvin's sickening voice interrupts as he strides up the catwalk. Walter turns and lunges through the bars for the scarf wrapped around his neck, but comes up short as a billy club bats him away. Marvin laughs, adjusting his riot vest with a nod of thanks to Chicago and his well-timed swipe.

"Another round, boys?" Dakota raises his fists.

"We don't want any more bloodshed than need be, Dakota," Wayne says, hobbling into view in his own thrifted gear and dragging a bloodied Archie behind him.

"Jesus, Wayne, you in with these scumbags?" Dakota asks with a disappointed click of his tongue. "Archie might be a dickhead, but the man's got a family for God's sake."

Wayne looks away, his face dripping with guilt. "So do I, Dakota. That don't make a man special these days."

"Shut the fuck up, all of you!" Marvin spits. "I'll deal with you in a minute, Kid-killer." He looks at Walter and digs a photo out from his pocket, tossing it down.

Walter's heart melts at the image of him holding Angie, Lorrie, and Kevin in his arms.

"I thought you looked familiar, Walter. Hindsight's not so sharp sending me a picture with one of those mean letters of yours." He leans over the handrail, stretching his back. "You romantic schmuck! You really been thinking about me all this time? I'm flattered!" He turns to Chicago, showing off his shotgun, snowshoes, and the crooked oxygen tank slung over his back. "Look at him, Chicago.

You see the fire in those eyes?"

"By the looks of the wallpaper in your cell, you've been thinking about me too, *sweetheart*," Walter quips back.

Marvin waves a hand. "Nah, that's the other guy you're mixing me up with. The one back here." He smiles and taps the base of his skull.

"So, what?" Walter asks. "You do the dirty work and the nice version of you brainwashes all your little church mice into following your word?"

"*Obeying* my word," Marvin corrects. "I'm sorry to disappoint you, Walt, but I'm still the same old drunk that squashed your kid like the flapjack he was." He starts to laugh but Walter cuts him short with one of his own.

"Disappointed? No, no, no, Marvin. You got it all wrong. I'm not disappointed... I'm relieved!" He licks his cracked lips and smiles.

"And what do you got to be so relieved about?" Marvin looks his cell up and down.

"That you're still in there!" Walter taps his temple with a rigid finger. "I'll admit, I was disappointed—no, devastated, when I saw you went soft. But it turns out you just went kooky."

"No difference in my eyes," Marvin says.

"But there is, Marvin." Walter paces the cell. "Ya see, soft was an issue for me. But I got no problem killing kooky."

Marvin chuckles. "Look around. The game's over; you lost. You're trapped, and there's not a single Boy-in-Blue left breathing to let you out. Not to mention that I got the keys to the kingdom." He points at Archie, then punches him in the gut as he slumps from Wayne's grasp onto the catwalk. "We weren't planning on making a break for it for at least a few more weeks, but you just had to go and set the whole thing off, didn't you? Got me caught in the middle of making a batch of—"

"Keys," Walter says and reaches out again, this time catching Marvin's scarf and yanking so hard his face smashes into the bars.

Chicago's club comes down, severing his grasp, but Walter barely feels it as Marvin pulls away and grabs at his face.

"Dammit!" Blood drains from his nose, and he pinches its brim, steadying the flow. "You see, Walter? That's why nobody wants to play with you! Twice in one fucking day you bust up my head!" He stands straight and composes himself. "Now, I'm gonna let that slide, cause of murdering your boy and all, but as far as I'm concerned, we're square."

"Square?" Walter scoffs. "We are so far from square that you look like a goddamn circle from where I'm standing, you piece of shit!" He lunges again but Dakota pulls him back and Chicago's club swings, missing its target.

Walter points at Archie. "So what good is he to you, then?"

Marvin looks at the incapacitated guard. "Who? The old Shit-talker?"

"No, Archie," Walter says, enjoying the sight of blood dripping down Marvin's chin.

"One and the very same. Old Boss-man here set this whole thing up. Well…" Marvin pauses and looks around. "Not quite this exactly. I tweaked his plans a bit to better our odds."

"Why the hell would Archie help someone like you get out of Cold Keep?" Dakota asks.

Marvin reaches, twisting the knob on the cylinder strapped to his back and the tube under his nose hisses louder. "I wasn't the bastard's first choice, that's for sure, but once word got out that a guard was looking to clear his conscience, it was smooth sailing for a pastor with a failing memory. Ya see, Walt, I'm the only one thinking clearly around here!" He tugs on his oxygen supply and pinches it off briefly, then takes a deep breath. "I'm the only one breathing clean air, air free from those silly sticks you idiots have been smoking! So I was the only one with the brain cells left to take Boss-man up on his offer."

"Well, you got the keys, now leave the poor bastard alone," Walter argues.

"Yeah, but too many to count." Marvin holds up the cluster of keys, all clattering together like an unruly wind chime. "We don't have much time for trial and error, I'm afraid." He snickers and looks at the picture on the ground. "I gotta know, Walt, was it a coincidence or divine intervention that brought us together?" He taps at the bars, watching him like a fish in a tank. "Ah… Neither… It was good old-fashioned revenge, wasn't it?" He dabs his leaking nose with a finger and waves his question away. "Forget it. It's too late to wash away those sins now." He reaches his bloody finger out, as if to anoint Walter with oil.

"Rot in hell." Walter spits, and the glob tangles in one of Marvin's sideburns. Marvin brushes it away with another snide laugh.

"Ya know?" Dakota cuts in. "For such an

ugly prick, you sure laugh a lot. You would think having the face of a dog would bring you down, but not you, Marvin. Good for you." He lets out a laugh of his own.

"Shut the hell up, Kid-killer!" Marvin turns and pulls the key out from the swinging Boot. "Now, I said leaving you two to rot in this cell was the way to go, but Chicago here has really been missing that eye of his. And because of that, he insisted on hanging the Boot for you boys to ensure that demon finds its way to you personally. Didn't you, Chicago?"

Chicago nods. "Like I said, you're lucky it's the Lord's Day, or else I would have dealt with you myself." He pulls a shotgun from his back and wails on the bars with its muzzle, the men inside ducking from its path.

"Alright, Chicago, calm now," Marvin says and unlocks the cell door. "See, us boys here got everything we need for our hike out. Don't we boys? Snacks for the road provided by Georgina, may she rest in peace." He points to a sack slung over Chicago's back. "Nice, warm gear donated by the Boys-in-Blue, may they rest in hell. Jeez, we even got matching snowshoes courtesy of Walter himself. Only thing missing is a box of matches to keep us warm out there on our long trek back to civilization." Marvin looks at Dakota with undressing eyes. "Can you believe there wasn't a single match amongst all these guards in here?"

Walter and Dakota take a step back as the men flow into the cell.

"You got the last thing we need, Kid-killer,

so why don't you make this easy and just hand over the matches?"

Dakota's humored wheeze fills the room, and everyone pauses. "You think I have been hiding a box of matches up my ass all this time? A single jumping jack over the last four years, and I would have burst into flames!"

Walter breaks into a fit of laughter, and Dakota's wheeze transforms into breathless gasps for air.

Marvin lunges, grabbing Dakota as Chicago and Wayne throw Walter down, pinning him to his cot. "Let go of me, you—" A stray fist punches him in the jaw.

"Tell me how you do it!" Marvin screams. He draws his shotgun and points it at Dakota. "Tell me now, or I swear to God I'll empty your skull!"

Dakota stifles his laughter and stares at Marvin's twitching eye, then composes himself enough to speak. "Go on then, do it." He takes his turn to spit, this time directly in Marvin's face.

"Bullseye!" Walter yells as the pair begin their cycle of laughter over, and Marvin screams, gripping his gun tight.

"That's all folks!" Dakota screams and tips an invisible hat.

Marvin steadies the weapon and squeezes the trigger, stopping as a distant, horrible scream permeates the prison and churns every stomach in the cell, causing them all to grip at their bellies at once. "Fuck, it's here!" Marvin grabs Dakota and jostles him. "Bring him with us. We gotta move!"

Chicago and Wayne grab Dakota and pile out

of the cell behind Marvin, leaving Walter to breathlessly crawl to his feet and throw his beaten body against the door as it slams in his face.

Marvin turns and drops the key back into the Boot with a self-satisfied grin, then he and his accomplices break into a heated argument over who's to carry what.

Dakota takes advantage of the panic and pushes his face against the bars. "Jamestown, listen," he whispers. "If you get out, promise me you will help Eddie."

"Eddie, I mean—"

"Help Eddie and he will lead you to me."

"No offense, kid. But I think this might be where we part ways."

"No! You get him out of here, away from that thing, and I promise I'll help you bury this creep for good."

"Shut up!" Marvin barks and shoves him forward.

Walter looks at the snowshoes slung over the men's shoulders and scoffs. "I've seen how fast that thing moves, you idiots. It will pick you clean before you can make it into the woods!"

Marvin looks back at Walter. "Don't you worry about us, Walt. We've bought ourselves some time." He goes to turn, but freezes in place as a softened look washes over his face and his eye begins to twitch. A moment of silence passes and finally he blinks, looking around with concern. "Edwards? What—what the hell is going on?"

"Oh, for fuck's sake!" Chicago curses and shuffles over. "Where is it?"

"Where is what? What happened down there?" Marvin asks, looking over the railing with tearful eyes.

Chicago pats him down and pulls his metal flask out from one of his pockets. "Here, have a drink." He opens the flask and raises it, but Marvin pushes it away.

"Get the hell away from me, what are—"

Another scream shakes the entire complex.

"We don't have time for this shit!" Wayne yells.

Chicago jabs Marvin in the throat and yanks his head back by the greasy hair. With one swift pour, he empties some of the gin into his gullet and lets off, working the liquid down his throat with his free hand.

Marvin shakes his head, choking on the liquor, the muscles in his neck spasming as hardness reclaims his face and his eyes sharpen once more. He pushes Chicago back and straightens himself up with a shake, then nods to his goons. Without missing a beat, he draws Archie's stolen club from his hip and tosses it into Walter's cell.

"It's only fair you have a fighting chance when that thing comes sniffing. Bygones be bygones and all that. You just tell that dead kid of yours I say hello when you see him, Walt."

Walter fumbles with the stick, then lunges for Marvin, screaming and cursing his name as the men descend the stairs and exit the block, leaving him to die alone.

"Come back here, Marvin! Come back!"

REACH

"Come on, come on!" The lace grazes the key and falls. "Fuck!" Walter tosses it aside and hammers on the bars with Archie's club, his breath forming crystals on the rapidly cooling air.

"It's here," someone whispers.

"Shhhh!" a dozen others call back.

The bones *click* against the cement, each step ushering more of the frigid cold into the block, accompanied by a rotted stench that silences every inmate with a gag.

"Cages closed, sealed, locked. Treats inside so many, many, many," the crooked voice whispers with its spoiled tongue.

Walter picks the lace back up, his eyes fixating on the Boot dangling only feet away. "Please, *please*." He squints through the darkness, and the block trickles with cascading screams, each working their way down the hall as the sound of rushing air flows through the thing's festered nostrils.

"Where, where, where?" it asks, tearing a

hole through Walter's nerves as the loop lets off his fingers and wraps itself around the key.

"Oh thank you, Jesus!" He flexes every muscle at once, stopping himself from jerking on the string, and instead pulls gently, narrowing the loop with stifled panic.

The thing's Siberian stump feet *clack*, its frozen flesh dragging up the aisle as another draw of breath searches for the Boot and its musky stink. "There you are… Up, up, up."

Walter heaves, his stomach offering nothing as the smell putrefies and the catwalk rattles, shaking like a tin house with a copper roof. He steadies his hand and the loop closes, nearly hugging the key as the inmates' scream from levels one, two, and three ascend. The lace cinches tight as the gnarled fingers reach out from the inky swell below, wrapping themselves around the railing next to the swaying Boot, and a familiar boyish voice greets him with a "Hello."

Walter throws himself back and yanks the lace, launching the key. He reaches for it as it hurdles through the air, but the impossibly long arm extrudes upwards, twisting its ungodly appendage and snatches it inches from his grasp.

"Almost…" It rips the line from his grasp and Walter shuffles back, his frostbitten neck coming up hard against the stones as his hip careens off the sink, bringing him to his knees. Outside, the key rolls between its knuckles like a coin about to disappear, then glides into the keyhole with remarkable precision, snapping the lock open with a turn of its crooked wrist.

"Get back!" Walter swings Archie's club and the bone-tipped fingers flick it away, sending it clattering to the floor. "Go! I said get back!" A cold sweat washes over his entire body as he fumbles for the photo and buries his face deep into his knees, happy to die staring at the people he loves most.

The thing pulls itself over the railing and opens the door with a tortured squeal, sucking the last flicker of hope from Walter's rapidly beating heart. He gags, his stomach offering nothing as his chest heaves, readying itself to be torn apart, but still, he stares at his wife and kids, remembering the birthdays, dance recitals, and school meetings with a sad fondness.

It leans into the cell and its breath tugs at his hair, lifting the strands with each pull. "You smell… freshhh."

Walter holds his breath, ready for the thing's jaws to close around him as the words ring true, and the smell of laundry fills his lungs.

"Fresh…. *Fresh!*"

He reaches into his pocket, feeling his fingers rake through the forgotten grains of detergent. He hurls them through the air and a cacophonous wail ripples out across the penitentiary as the thing throws itself back, plummeting over the railing, into the aphotic block beyond. The prison trembles as the thing comes to a dead stop four floors below, and Walter gets to his feet like a deer on ice. He snatches Archie's club and leaps from his confines, peering over the ledge at the wicked, faint outline below twisting and clawing at its eyes. Its half-formed words scream out, mixing with animalistic howls as it writhes, its ribboned scalp flopping over its face like a tattered shawl left outside to rot.

Walter breaks away from the terrible sight and launches himself down the stairs two at a time, circling around and around as the remaining, non-church-attending inmates call to him, hands reaching from their cells, trying to stop his mad dash to the only exit. The stairs end and he tenderly meets the ground floor where the thing continues to thrash back and forth, black tar-like syrup extruding from its face and covering everything with a slick sheen. Walter stares at it for only a moment before the pure horror forces him to turn and hug the wall. He gently steps one foot over another, avoiding eye contact with the terrified men huddled against the backs of their cells, and works his way towards the lobby.

The thing stops and snaps its one scattered, gouged retina in Walter's direction, the other nowhere to be seen. "Fresh... so fresh..." It lets out a tortured howl and Walter propels himself onward, struggling to gain traction on the greasy floor as the frantic jostle of bones find their footing behind. He slides past the remaining cells, not daring to look inside as the red and blue hammers at the bars in each one, their *click-clack* joining in on the cold pursuit.

The egress spits him out into the lobby and he heaves against it, sliding the door on its rails as the thing's raw cruelty cuts through the darkness one last time and disappears with a heavy thud on the other side. A plume of mortar lets loose from the supporting wall and peppers Walter as he holds steadfast against the blockade, knowing his body would do little to stop it if the thing knew how to slide the door instead of pushing through.

The screaming and pounding continues, but it fades in Walter's mind as he stands frozen, staring out at the lobby he no longer recognizes. Inmates and Boys-in-Blue alike lay in heaps, bloodied and torn, beaten to death by each other's hands as the snow floats down from the open dome and swallows the violence with its forgiving, white duvet.

The pounding stops, and Walter collapses, fighting to find his breath as the thing whispers to itself from the other side. "I wonder, wonder, wonder..."

A shudder lifts him back to his feet and his eyes fixate on B-Block. Inside, the desperate, pleading inmates call out, hundreds of voices building into a hopeless ensemble. He shuffles over the bloody wreckage and his eyes follow the trail of claw marks in the wall to the open dome overhead, picturing the thing's fleshless fingers gripping at the stones, pulling itself in and out of Cold Keep.

Should have checked the latch.

He steps into B-Block and pauses, almost swallowing his tongue as the moonlight reflects the hundreds of dead eyes staring back from down the long hall. He winces, afraid to look, but they come into focus and turn into keys, hundreds of them swaying by their laces from the catwalks just outside every inmate's cell. *Don't you worry about us, Walt. We've bought ourselves some time.* Walter repeats the words in his mind as Marvin's sickening escape plan pieces itself together.

Before him, a sea of whipping laces and reaching arms span out in countless pairs, all fading into the long darkness and lending an overwhelming sense of false hope that further thickens the air.

"Hey," an inmate whispers. "Mister, let me out of here, please."

Walter spots the terrified man standing on his tiptoes, arms stretching through the bars for the key hanging just out of reach. He goes for it, but years of locking criminals up rather than setting them free makes him pause and reconsider. "I-I'm afraid I can't do that," he stutters.

"What do you mean you can't? Just pass it over, dammit!"

Walter shakes his head and turns. "It's not getting in here, I promise." The man bargains some more, but Walter ignores him and continues on.

One by one the inmates call out, begging for release as he hurries by, scanning each small room for the person he came to see. Giggles fill the gaps of silence, and two hands reach out from their cell, ahead, not for the key, but to play a game of patty cake with seemingly nobody.

"Eddie, is that you?" Walter calls and a half a dozen voices shush him. He treads forward, rounding the cell to Eddie's contorted smile shining out as he tries to push himself through the bars like a dog trapped in a crate.

"Good morning, New-boy."

"It's night-time, Eddie."

Eddie pulls back and tips his invisible hat. "Good night, New-boy. I thought you moved. I thought it for sure." He reaches out and pulls Walter in for a hug.

"I did move, Eddie, but I came back for ya."

Walter pats him on the back and gives him an awkward sway.

"Really? I must be something special if you came to see me, New-boy!" He lets off, clapping his hands, but Walter catches them between his own.

"You are, Eddie, you are. Now, listen. I need help finding the kid. We got split up and he said you could help me."

Eddie's eyes narrow, then widen. "You mean Kota, New-boy?" His face lights up and he bounces up and down.

"Yeah, that's right."

"Oh, I've missed Kota. I've missed him so much. Let's go find him!"

"Attaboy; let's move!" Walter plucks the nearby key from its lace and opens the cell to a flood of angry objection from the inmates all around.

Eddie bursts free and grabs him with another hug. "Freedom! Oh, thank you, New-boy! Thank you!"

"Alright, alright." Walter straightens him out and pushes him back. "You know a way out of here, Eddie?"

Eddie laughs and points towards the lobby. "Through there. You know that!"

Walter grinds his teeth and takes a breath, suddenly craving a smoke. "I do, but I'm talking about Cold Keep, not B-Block."

Eddie's smile disappears and he looks at Walter with a baffled frown. "You know this is a jail house, right, New-boy? You need better keys than that one if you're gonna walk out of here in a hurry." His smile returns, and he knocks Walter's skull with a playful rap.

Walter slaps it away with Archie's club and grabs him by the shoulders. "Think, dammit. Marvin and his church goers must have left a door open somewhere. Let's move." They hurry back down the block as Walter drags Eddie by the hand, stopping him from starting a conversation with every angry inmate they pass, then pause at the exit.

"We gotta be real quiet when we go out there, Eddie. You know what's out there, don't you?"

Eddie's palms shoot up, closing together like a set of massive jaws in front of his face.

"That's right. So no more clapping, hugging, or giggling, okay? Just follow me, quiet as a church mouse."

Eddie bobbles his head and slaps a hand over his mouth.

"Good, let's go."

The lobby lays silent, and Walter pokes his head out, scanning every inch, then steps into the eight-sided chasm on careful feet.

"Oh, no." Eddie whimpers under his breath, seeing the arms, legs, and frozen faces of Cold Keep's men jut out from the drifts of snow at twisted and broken angles. An agonizing scream rings out from across the lobby and their attention snaps to the tomb that was once A-Block. Eddie jumps back, huddling behind Walter's unsure stance. "Is—is it in there, New-boy?"

"It's in there, alright," Walter admits. "We better get moving before—" The cold metallic clink of a key popping open its lock echoes out from behind the door and another terrified inmate lets loose his final, agonizing scream.

"Jesus," Walter gasps, fighting off a wave of nausea. "It's figured it out."

"Figured what out, New-boy?"

"You remember when Dakota said it was only a matter of time before that thing figured out Archie's key opens every cell in this place?"

"Yeah. I remember."

"Well…I think the powder keg's gone off."

"Oh…" Eddie starts across the lobby on exaggerated tiptoes. "That's easy." He bends down and pulls a set of handcuffs loose from a guard's belt, then reaches for the door.

Walter pulls him back. "Whoa, what are you doing? Those are innocent men in there, Eddie. You can't just—"

Eddie turns on Walter. "No, they're not. Those are the bad boys. The killers, rapists, and the worst of the worst, don't you know that, dumdum?"

Walter bites down and splits his lip. "That doesn't mean they deserve to be torn apart."

Eddie raises a cupped palm to his ear and another scream lets out from inside. "It's gonna get out of there, New-boy, look." He grabs the handle and slides the door open and closed on its tracks.

Walter raises his hands, begging him to stop. "Okay, Eddie, please!"

"And when it does, New-boy, it's gonna go through the good boys in B-Block next. Boys who deserve it a lot less than the Assholes. They gonna get eaten up in there if we like it or not."

Another shudder cuts through Walter as a guilty tear runs down his cheek, burning the many cuts and bruises on its way. "You're right, I know…" He steps to the door with an unsure wobble and grabs the cuffs from Eddie. "Just… let me." His teeth saw through another layer of flesh as he gently clicks the bracelets around the handle, sealing the fate of the remaining Assholes inside.

C'EST LA VIE

The pry bar slips from between the steel plates and stops hard against Walter's shin. "Motherfucker!" He throws a fist into the doors marked *Processing*, holding in a muffled scream. "Come on, Eddie, think hard. There's gotta be another way." He pulls out the key, trying it again.

"You did that already, New-boy. That thing only works on the cells!"

Walter turns. "I'm wide open to any other ideas here!"

"Get a better key!"

Walter hurls the bar across the lobby and shatters one of the windows atop the staircase, leaving only metal safety mesh in its frame.

"Be gone, you mongrels!" a voice shouts from inside.

"Who's that, New-boy?"

"How should I know?" Walter turns his ear, and they step over a bludgeoned guard.

"Hello up there?" Eddie calls out, earning himself a nudge.

"I have no quarrel with you, heathens. Leave me to my own curiosities!"

"I think that's Uncle Bill, New-boy! Nobody else in here talks like Uncle Bill talks." Walter nods and they summit the stairs, closing in on the crooked doors that hang from their frame. With a gentle nudge they open, revealing papers, bedpans, and beds strewn across every inch of the once organized room, now a broken overturned mess. They push forward, stopping at the guard slumped over in a wheelchair, a line of congealed blood trailing the hole in his skull and pooling in his lap.

"You think he done that to himself, New-boy?"

Walter grimaces and nods at the man's hand gripped around a gun that's no longer there, reminding him of the phantom trigger he pulled on the Laidlow kid only days before.

"They must keep that Boogeyman in that cage, there." Eddie points across the wreckage to the empty lockup, its shelves picked clean of its riot gear and guns.

"That's not a cage Eddie." Walter waltzes over and leans through the doorway, kicking an empty box of ammunition. "Not a crumb, not even—" He pauses at the small cylinder lodged beneath the bench and digs it out. "Riot CS Smoke," he reads, the words bittering his tongue. "Would have preferred a grenade."

"Let's go back," Eddie whispers, tugging at Walter's free hand.

Walter tucks the canister into his pocket and pulls free. "If anyone's got spare keys, it's Uncle

Bill. If you're too chicken-shit to follow, just stay here and be quiet." Walter holds his club high and proceeds, Eddie hot on his heels.

"Who's there?" Uncle Bill's southern drawl carries out from the back doors.

Eddie reciprocates with cupped hands. "It's me, Uncle Bill!"

"For fuck's sake!" Walter stands upright, abandoning his readied stance. "What did I *just* tell you?"

"Who's there? Go back to your confines, and I'll be sure you get double pudding for dinner tonight!"

Eddie turns on his heels and makes for the exit, but Walter grabs his collar and drags him back.

"We don't want any trouble, Uncle Bill." He barges inside with the club ready to swing, but the short hallway and its rows of reinforced doors stand at attention, silently staring at each other with years of rusted solitude.

"I've been here before, New-boy. This is where they send the Best-boys."

"It's solitary confinement, Eddie. It's not for good boys, it's for—"

"Best-boys," Eddie corrects him.

"No, Jesus. They got this place running so backwards it's enough to drive anyone batty."

"I said state your name!" Uncle Bill demands once more, his voice echoing from the last door on the left. They proceed down the abandoned hall, coming up on the small hatch framing Uncle Bill's cracked glasses and matted hair hanging in his prideful face.

"Well, I'll be damned. If it isn't the big cheese himself," Walter chuckles.

Uncle Bill runs a hand over his head and adjusts his crooked tie. "Edward and Edwards, what an odd coupling, indeed. How are we this evening, gentlemen?"

"A lot better than you!" Eddie spouts over Walter's shoulder with a satisfied giggle.

"Mind your manners, you witless maroon! I should have—"

Walter's fist threads through the hatch and socks Uncle Bill in the mouth, sending him stumbling back. "Oh, dear God!" he gasps. "I'll… I'll have your ass, Edwards. Don't you—"

"The man's name is Eddie. You got that? Now, I've had a long few days, so if you would kindly shut your mouth, we can work on getting you out of there." He pulls his key out and Uncle Bill wipes his fat lip, turning his bloodied nose up.

"You think I want to be out there with you savages and that devil running loose?"

"You mean the one you've been letting in through that skylight each night? The one that feeds on the inmates who make the least goddamn kettles, license plates, or candlesticks in that shop of yours, Willy?" Walter winds his fist up again, but Eddie holds him back. "Well, look what it's got ya, you greedy prick! You've been scaring these men straight for so long that none of you idiots in charge could have fathomed them acting out, let alone killing the lot of you in one fucking afternoon! How many guards are you supposed to have in a facility this big, Willy?"

Uncle Bill straightens his suit and adjusts his glasses. "That's Uncle Bill to you, inmate."

Walter grabs the riot canister from his pocket, and with one sharp tug he pulls the pin and drops it through the hatch.

"What—what the hell is this?" Uncle Bill asks, kicking at the vibrating cylinder.

"I asked you a question," Walter says. "How many guards does it take to run a joint this big, Willy?"

The warden's prideful demeanor sours as the canister pops and begins to spew its thick smoke around his polished shoes. "I knew you were like the rest of them, Edwards. Three to five years for tax evasion, my ass! I'll have you in here for decades if you don't—"

"You got a listening problem, Willy?" Walter slides the hatch closed and a barrage of muffled threats ring out from the other side, shifting to violent fits of hoarse hacking. "*How many*?"

Another satisfying moment passes before Walter finally opens the hatch, spilling Uncle Bill's face as he gulps the fresh air. "A hundred! A hundred guards per shift!" he shouts.

"And how many you got?"

"I—I don't know!"

Walter slams the hatch again, the metal plate catching Uncle Bill's nose as it seals shut. The desperate protesting starts over and the smoke seeps out through the crack below as Eddie watches, fingers hanging from his nervous jaw. "Twenty-two, twenty-two!" Uncle Bill cries, his voice catching on a throat full of poison.

"That's enough, New-boy. He's had enough!"

Walter opens the hatch, resisting the urge to punch Uncle Bill in the face for a second time as he comes up for air.

"Twenty-two? Twenty-fucking-two! The auditors said you have a full staff, Willie! Where are all your guards?"

"How—how do you know that?"

"Did they quit, or did you feed them to that creature, too?"

Uncle Bill clears his lungs and squints. "Please, just leave me be!"

"It's no wonder Marvin's cultists took you down so quick. If it weren't for those doped up cigarettes you've been feeding them, these boys would have turned on you ages ago."

"The smokes were Archie's idea. It wasn't me!"

"He said, she said. You both deserve to be prisoners, not employees! You wanna talk criminal? Shit, you're worse than that man-eater out there. The inmates are just a meal to that thing, but you... you're feeding off them."

Uncle Bill breaks into tearless sobs and he reaches through the hole, clasping his hands in prayer. "I had no choice! It was picking the staff off long before it got to the men inside!"

"How long? How long until you opened that dome for the first time and let it crawl in to feast, Willy?"

"I had them shoot at it, I swear. Please believe me! The boys said they could see it in the tree line, pacing out there that first winter. We tried to run it off, but it kept coming back, closer each night. Then the guards in their watchtowers started getting snatched from their posts, others on their way to their cars in the middle of the day, for God's sake. I wanted to call in the cavalry, but what would I say?" His knees buckle and he pulls himself back up, choking on the rising smoke. "S-so I did what I had to do." He pulls the handkerchief from his pocket and waves it, his eyes red and swelling from the fumes. "My guards had families, children."

"So did they! So did the inmates you sentenced to death by mauling!"

"What do you want me to say, Edwards?" A trickle of blood drips from Uncle Bill's nose and he dabs it with the cloth. "Someone was going to die, and it might as well have been the leeches on society's underbelly! The ones who already tossed away their lives!"

"Sure, the rapists, murderers, and wife beaters I could understand," Walter says, "but you had it going after the tax evaders, shoplifters, and petty criminals! No, they weren't innocent completely, but far from deserving of this! So don't you stand there and shovel that bullshit my way. You pitted these men against each other so you could profit off their blood sport, their will to live! You didn't care who got torn apart, you just cared about what they would do to survive."

"I started with the Crazies! Ask Eddie, it didn't have a taste for them!"

"And how is that any better? Feeding innocent men like Eddie to that thing?"

"Him?" Uncle Bill scoffs. "You think that man there is innocent?" He points and Eddie ducks out of the way. "Tell him, Eddie; tell Edwards why you're here. Tell him what atrocity you committed to get locked up with the rest of the certifiably insane!"

Eddie throws his hands over his ears. "I don't know what you're talking about, bad man!"

"Of course you don't! You wouldn't even remember how to wipe your own ass if it weren't for that kid-killing boyfriend of yours!"

"No, no, no. You're a mean boy, Uncle Bill! A mean, mean boy!" Eddie twists and mashes his ears, stomping around in troubled circles.

The warden stands up straight and his face hardens on Walter with prideful defiance. "It's been three years, Edwards. Three God-forsaken years of it, and you couldn't even handle three measly days! So don't *you* stand there judging *me*, you pathetic suck! I've let that thing drag over a hundred lowlifes to their graves since it first came sniffing about, and in all that time, I've only accumulated one single regret."

"Yeah? And what's that?" Walter asks.

Uncle Bill drops his handkerchief and smiles. "That I hadn't changed that devil's diet from blue to black and white sooner."

Walter hammers the club against the door, his pink face flushing purple. "You'll get yours, Willy. I promise you that!"

"I'll pay my nickel eventually, Mr. Edwards. A hundred souls don't just up and vanish without inquiries being brought forth, and believe me, they're trickling in. There are only so many burnt trees one can pass off as cremated remains, only so many empty pine boxes one can bury amongst our forest's trees before Big Brother sends someone looking for them. That accusatory finger of yours won't be the only one pointing when I'm on the stands. But I chose the lesser of two evils. I burned, murdered, and condemned the lowlifes of this world when nobody else had the balls! And I would do it again. What's done is done, Edwards. *C'est la vie!*"

"That's enough!" Walter screams. "Just hand over the keys out of here or I swear to God I'll fill that cell with gasoline and turn it into a fucking oven!"

Uncle Bill jumps back, choosing the noxious fumes over Walter's wrath, and cowers, his brittle arrogance stripping away immediately. "I would, but those crooks dragged Archie out of here with the only set! If they sealed up whatever door they left through, then there's nothing I can do."

"Bullshit!"

Walter slides the hatch, but Uncle Bill wedges his fingers in the slot, snapping one of his digits with a painful yelp. "Oh, Jesus! Please, please believe me!" He forces the metal plate open and flashes a look of agony. "Here, make—make cozy in one of these cells; it's our only chance of surviving with that thing running loose."

Walter considers the offer, but shakes his head. "Ya know, Willy, you're a lot better spoken when you're running the show. Where's that showmanship of yours now that you've got shit running down your legs?"

"New-boy…"

"We don't have time to pussyfoot around, so you better pull an exit plan out your ass right now or this cell is going to become a tomb." Walter puts his hand on Uncle Bill's sweaty brow and shoves his face back into the cell.

"No, wait, wait. I don't know, I don't know!"

"New-boy…"

Walter waves a dismissive hand. "Just a minute, Eddie."

"New-boy… I think I know a way out."

Walter turns, and Eddie looks at Uncle Bill.

"Boss-boy Archie might have the keys to the front door, but Uncle Bill's still got the keys to the back."

"That's—that's right!" Uncle Bill shouts, grabbing at the lifeline. "Bottom drawer of my desk!"

Walter pivots back and smiles at the warden. "Looks like we will no longer be requiring your services, Willy. Enjoy your cell for one."

"No, no, please!"

Walter forces the hatch closed and walks away without a second thought. "Now… where's that back door?"

Eddie straightens his invisible hat and puts on a brave face. "It's… it's in one of the cell blocks, New-boy."

Walter sighs, "Let me guess, the one with that thing locked inside?"

"Worse… It's through C-Block."

C-BLOCK

Walter fumbles with the stack of cafeteria trays and pulls his earmuffs back. "What did you say?"

Eddie spits the scarf from his mouth and yanks the guard's belt from his blood-soaked khaki's, grouping it with the other's. "I said this don't feel right, New-boy."

"We don't have time for feelings right now. Just focus on getting us to C-Block."

"What are you talking about? This is it, dumdum. We're here." Eddie points at the door, sealed behind a thick layer of sickly gray paint in the lobby's eighth forgotten wall.

Walter traces a finger over the raised outline, looking up at the faded stenciled letters above. "C-Block... Huh... It blends right in."

"I—I don't like it in there."

Walter bites his lip and fights off another craving for a cigarette. "You think it's better out here? Closer to that thing?" He points next door to A-Block. "You said it yourself, C-Block is the only way out of here. Besides, I'm not sure that door is gonna hold once that demon runs out of rotten apples to eat."

Eddie looks at the handcuffs latched around A-Block's handle, then back at Walter. "We gotta be quick then, okay? Back and in—in and back, I mean."

Walter claps him on the back. "Alright! You still got Uncle Bill's gifts?"

Eddie pulls the keys from his pocket, singling out the one engraved with a 'C' and unsheathes his flashlight. "In and back, promise?"

"In and out. No coming back," Walter says with a half assuring nod. The key turns and cracks the seal of paint as the doorway lets out a bitter belch that numbs the tip of his nose. "Jesus, it's even colder in there!"

They slip inside and Eddie clicks the flashlight on, sweeping the beam across the single level block devoid of tall windows, iron catwalks, and winding staircases. Glimmering frost clings to every surface, forming icicles that stretch down from the maze of burst pipes above, spreading their translucent sheen across the floor and into the cells lined with soft padding in place of hard stones.

"The exit's way down there, New-boy."

Walter squints, expecting the light to reveal something terrible but sees nothing other than the desolate block. "How do you know all this?"

"Us good boys in B-Block are called Bastards. B is for Bastards. They call the bad boys in A-Block Assholes. A is for Assholes."

"Yeah, I know that. What's your point?"

"Papa wasn't always nice to me, but he was

okay as long as he didn't lose at the horse track."

Walter rolls his eyes, losing patience.

"But my mama, she was always kind no matter what. She was always calling me Cute-boy, and Kind-boy, but I liked it when she called me Sweet-boy most. It was like that for a long time with Mama and me. She was real young when I was growing in her tummy; Papa, too. But later, when they weren't so young no more and I was all grown up, they made another baby. They said she was a surprise, but that didn't make no sense cause Mama's tummy took a long time to grow. You couldn't miss it if you tried. Anyway, when baby was finally born, she came out crying something awful. Always with the 'boo-hoo' all day and night, she was. And no matter how much noise she made, Papa was always nice to her, even though she made Mama sad all the time. Baby had all of Papa's love and still nothing was ever good enough for her!"

"What's this got to do with the way out of here?" Walter asks, feeling his anxiety bubble in the darkness.

"Don't be interrupting me, New-boy, I'm gettin' to it." Eddie begins his careful hike down the corridor, and Walter follows behind. "I saw how upset baby made Mama, so I helped. I went into baby's room one night and told her to 'stop stealing all the attention', to 'stop crying all the time, baby-girl.' I even told her Mama would like her better if she didn't make so much fuss, and if she was good and quiet like me, things would be okay. But she just kept on crying and crying, so I pinched her, and she stopped."

"I find that hard to believe."

"Oh yeah. For a few seconds, anyways. Then she started again, only louder. So I pinched her even harder."

Walter tries to focus on the strobing block as Eddie jostles the flashlight, telling his story with his expressive hands. "And let me guess, she started crying even louder?"

"How did you know that?"

"Lucky guess."

"I was only trying to help. Then I figured out if I pinched longer, baby wouldn't make noise as long as I held it. She would only start up again once I let go. So I just kept holding and holding."

Walter eyes his ally and his curiosity gets the better of him. "Where uh…where did you pinch her exactly?"

Eddie smiles, then frowns as he shines the light on his throat and squeezes. "On the neck. It only worked on the neck, New-boy."

Walter drops his head and sucks his teeth. "Yeah… that's what I thought you were gonna say." He steps over an abandoned wheelchair and his boot slides on a patch of ice. He waves his arms, catching his footing and an ache runs through his bruised and battered back as Eddie lets out an amused giggle.

"Anyway, then baby didn't cry no more. Didn't make any noise at all, really. I was so proud that I scooped her up and brought her to Mama's room to show her, but she got really sad again. The most sad I ever saw her. And Papa yelled like he lost a whole lot of money at the track, but I know he didn't cause it was Sunday, and there ain't no ponies on Sundays. After that, everything changed. Mama stopped calling me 'sweet' and 'cute' and instead started calling me names. Mean names... names like—"

"Crazy," Walter whispers. "A is for Assholes. B is for Bastards. And C is for Crazies."

Eddie nods. "Now you're getting it. But C don't stand for 'Crazies' no more. After Mama stopped her crying, she said I was gonna go to summer camp with other bad boys just like me, and the next day the coppers scooped me up and brought me to that room with the benches and the man with the funny hair."

"That was a judge, Eddie. You were in a courtroom."

"Yeah, that's right! And he told me about the bad thing I done, even though I explained to him a hundred times it was a good thing and that I was just helping mama be happy again. But he wouldn't listen, so they brought me all the way out to Cold Keep and put me in there." He shines the light into the cell beside them and throws his nose up.

"So you were a Crazy before a Bastard?"

"Sure was. I would—" Eddie pauses, locking eyes with the kettle inside his cell and treads over, cautiously retrieving it through the bars. "There you are!" He leans in and kisses it, his lips sticking to the frozen iron for only a moment before he rips them off. "Ouch!" He wipes a spot of blood from his lip and laughs. "I would sit in there all day long drinking my tea, and sometimes—mostly Tuesdays—I would see the Blue-boys bringing big boxes in from down there." He swings the flashlight towards the end of the hall, its glow sputtering out before reaching the end. "That's how I know where the exit is, cause I seen it a bunch." He tucks the kettle under his arm and spits at his old confines. "Maybe we will get lucky and find some hot water outside, New-boy. Kota says you can make tea out of pine needles."

Walter shudders at the thought and a sharp groan spills out overhead, sending Eddie into a panic as he whips the flashlight around, strobing the frosty block like a drug bust gone wrong.

"Relax! Relax! It's just the pipes." Walter grabs him by the shoulder and calms him with a reluctant hug.

"Huh?" Eddie looks to the shifting plumbing and lets off. "Oh… yeah, I knew that."

"Sure you did. So, if you were in here before, how did you end up with the Bastards?"

"Oh, not just me, New-boy. All of us Crazies got moved out of here. Some into A, others into B. They needed the cells."

"For what?" Walter grabs for the flashlight, but Eddie yanks it away, gripping it hard as his childish demeanor dries up and he presses forward.

"You know any other words that start with C, New-boy?"

"Carrots, cardinals, cookies. The list goes on."

Eddie's voice shifts to a nervous tremble. "At first, that Boogeyman was always tapping on the windows and scratching at the walls from outside, sometimes all night long. Then, just before they moved me to B-Block, Uncle Bill told Boss-boy to open up the skylight and let it inside. Didn't eat nobody that night, though. Just did a few laps and left. It scared me so bad I pooped my britches twice. Count 'em: one, two."

"So it's true what Uncle Bill said? That thing doesn't have a taste for the Crazies?"

"I guess not. Boss-boy tied his Boot outside my cell more than once, but it didn't like the smell of me, I guess. I offered it some tea one time, but it didn't want no part of it."

"Cold!" Walter blurts out.

"Huh?"

"You said another word that starts with C. It's fucking freezing in here."

Eddie shakes his head. "Nope, that's not it."

Walter bites his lip and tries to hurry along, eyes darting from the dark cells to the even darker corridor ahead as the metal cafeteria trays numb his fingertips. "Then why is it even colder in here than the lobby with that dog door in the ceiling?"

Eddie shakes a fist and stomps his feet. "I'm trying to tell you! After those first nights, they started moving some smart boys in from the other blocks. Ones that were normal before, but now off their rockers and howling to the moon. Oooww ow wooooo!" Something shuffles in one of the cells ahead and he stops Walter with a finger to his lips. "Shush!"

Walter knocks his hand away. "Me shush? You're the one making all the damn noise! You shush!"

They push on and Eddie grips the tangle of leather belts in his free hand, readying to strike. "Those smart boys they brought into C-Block, the ones that started acting like Crazies were saying that the Boogeyman drove 'em insane. Telling everyone who would listen how it had been coming to 'em in their sleep, bringing 'em food in their dreams. Real good food like cinnamon buns and pies; you ever had pecan pie, New-boy? It's real buttery like—"

"I prefer a plain pumpernickel. Stay focused."

"Right. Well, before long, they started nipping at each other any chance they got. More and more each day until there were hundreds, maybe thousands of boys all crammed in here."

"A thousand? Really?"

"Oh sure, maybe even more. Too many boys to count, all of 'em pretending to be crazy like me, but not like me cause I ain't crazy like them. Ain't crazy at all, just stupid."

"You're not stupid Eddie, you—"

"I said stop interrupting me! Are you stupid, too?"

Walter holds up his hands and Eddie turns with a satisfied nod. "Then Uncle Bill gets wise and says they are just putting on an act to get away from that Boot out there, because Boss-boy's boot don't come into C-Block with the Crazies. So that's when he did it. He closed the furnace vents and opened the back door."

"To cook them out."

"To freeze 'em out, more like. Boogeyman likes it cold. Kota told me it's got a heart made of ice. You think that's true?"

"Normally I would say that's impossible, but after these last few days, I don't know what impossible is anymore. What happened after they cut the heat?"

"The liars froze right up! At least the ones who didn't admit to faking their sickness. Look." Eddie shines the light into the adjacent cell and a frozen inmate stares back from his cot, his mattress wrapped around him with blackened fingers gripping at its edges, frost gleaming off his fractured face.

"Jesus!" Walter stumbles back and trips over a stray bedpan. "Those sick bastards just let them all freeze in here?"

"Just the ones who wouldn't tell Uncle Bill the truth." Eddie points the flashlight ahead, and Walter swallows the lump in his throat, continuing on with the metal trays clutched to his chest.

"What did Kota call it? Friendly glow syndrome? No... It was a funny name that made me giggle. Kota said someone like him, but not like him, once killed his whole family and gobbled 'em up, someone real bad with the friendly glow syndrome. But not all the jail birds in here were lying, New-boy. Some really would bite you real hard if you got too close. And the ones that did would just keep on chomping no matter how cold it got in here. No matter how frozen and stiff they became."

The flashlight floods the next cell, and Eddie grabs Walter's arm, gently pulling him away from the moving corpse melded to the frozen cement inside. It looks up at Walter and beats its skull against the bars, legs nothing more than knees pedaling through banks of eroded flesh with thoughtless, perpetual motion.

"Some were telling the truth, New-boy.

Frozen, but still biting, clicking their teeth all night long."

It reaches out with nothing but gored wrists, scraping uselessly at the floor, the bars sinking into a face whose cheeks had long given way.

"Can you think of any other words that start with C, New-boy?"

Walter stares at the madness for what feels like minutes, barely comprehending the scene before him. "Cannibals," he whispers.

"A is for Assholes. B is for Bastards. And C is for Cannibals." Eddie pulls him away from the nightmare. "Let's go."

"Yeah..." They pick up their pace and Walter avoids looking into any more of the cells as the wind whips around harder with each step and the icy floor turns to snow, building into a dune that climbs to the end of the block.

"There." Eddie steadies the beam on the corner of the overhead door poking out from behind the pile. He pulls two trays from Walter's hand and sits, stringing his belts over and around his boots, fashioning a set of makeshift snowshoes. He stands with a smile and climbs the small mountain on all fours, looking down on Walter as he struggles to strap the trays to his feet, fighting his bruised ribs in the process.

"You ready, New-boy?"

Walter gets to his feet and tests the shoes out, impressed with their functionality. "Yeah... let's go." He climbs and joins Eddie where the cruel breeze floods in from outside. Eddie drops and shuffles through the hole, disappearing like a fearless spelunker as Walter looks over the block, hearing one final distant scream emanate from the lobby. He collects himself and takes a parting breath of the sweet, tobacco-tainted air and shuffles out into the stench of the forest's pine.

The wind blows hard, and Eddie laughs as he slides down the mound into the white ocean below. Walter tumbles close behind, the cold biting his frostbitten neck. He brushes the snow from his face and stands, looking back at Cold Keep, the feeling of freedom overwhelming him as a cautious smile tugs at his cheeks.

Eddie bursts from the powder, out into the field with a fit of laughter as the storm swallows him whole, and Walter listens to him play, envying his innocent ignorance.

"Come on, New-boy!"

He catches up and holds Eddie in one place. "Not now, let's focus up. Which way are we going?"

Eddie stops and stares, cocking his head to the side. "What do you mean?"

"I mean, where's the kid? You're leading the way, remember?"

"I—I don't know where Kota is, New-boy. You know where Kota is. Stop joking around!"

Walter's heart sinks and his face flushes red despite the cold. "I sure as fuck do not! Why the hell do you think I brought you out here with me? You're telling me you have no idea where he is or how to find him?"

"No idea, New-boy. None."

NOT AS BAD AS HE SEEMED

"Think hard, Eddie. Why'd the kid tell me you would know how to find him? Did you two have a rendezvous picked out?"

Eddie stares at Walter through the flurry of snow with blank eyes. "A what?"

"A meeting place in case you ever got out."

"We never talked about getting out, New-boy. Kota didn't wanna leave. He's always saying how Cold Keep is where he belongs, and I belong with Kota, so why would we leave?"

"Goddamn it. That fucking kid never intended on being found, he just wanted you off that devil's menu. Why's he got such a hard-on for you anyway, huh?"

Eddie tucks his hands in his pockets and his nose fades to blue against the wind. "Kota's always been nice to me, New-boy. And I've always been nice to him. You don't—" He stops short and wanders off, his snowshoes treading over the snow as he glides his way into the clearing before them.

"Where the hell are you going now?" Walter calls after him, suddenly feeling more like a babysitter than an escaped convict. Giggles cuts through the wind and he begrudgingly follows, holding back a scream as Eddie plucks a purple Chicklet from a mound of snow and pops it in his mouth with an audible crunch.

"Found some gum, New-boy!"

"That's great. Now let's go back."

"Wait! There's another one there, see? Just one more piece, please, oh please!"

Walter bites his lip, soothing his frustration and nods, following further into the clearing where Eddie plucks the Juicy Fruit probing from the snow.

"How the hell did you see that from way over there?"

"It's easy when they're all over, New-boy. Just look around." He points into the darkness. "One there, and there, and there."

Walter squints. "Wait a minute… I think he left us breadcrumbs."

"No, dumdum. It's gum, not bread. I said over and over." Eddie stomps his foot and his leg sinks to the knee.

As if pulling a plug, the wind succumbs to the inhuman scream that blares out from Cold Keep and the snow abandons the air, falling like a million dead moths.

Walter looks to the prison revealing itself through the vanquished storm, then back at Eddie. "You want more of that gum? Lead the way."

Eddie nervously nods and shuffles towards

his next piece. "Do you think it's angry we locked it in there?"

"Were you angry when you got locked in there?"

Eddie nods and picks up another Chicklet.

"There's your answer."

The last of the snow gives way and the wall of chain-link and barbwire bleed through the night, stopping both men in their tracks.

"Dead end, New-boy."

"Not quite…" Walter points at the large hole cut out in the fence and the solidified globs of steel puddled beneath it on the ground, snow melted and exposing burnt grass.

"Where they get a blow torch, you think?"

"I'm watching the same movie you are, Eddie, I got no idea. But I'll tell you this much, if they had an acetylene torch this whole time, they wouldn't have taken our fire-starting friend with 'em, that's for sure." They step through the jagged hole and Walter turns back to Cold Keep's long-abandoned watchtowers, brilliant glass dome, and giant open gates bidding them adieu.

"Boss-boy!"

"Huh?"

"Over there. It's Boss-boy!"

Walter follows Eddie's finger to the edge of the forest where Archie sits slumped against a trunk, half buried in snow with a cigarette hanging from his lips. The pair carve their way through the field and come to a stop at the bloodied ex-guard, his hand clutched over his throat and stifling the flow of crimson blood with his palm.

"Oh no…you think Boss-boy is done for?"

"He isn't anybody's boss out here, Eddie."

Archie opens his eyes and swipes his free hand through the air. "Get back! Get the fuck away from me! You damn bastards got—" A gargled cough interrupts his barrage of insults and the nearly spent cigarette falls from his lips onto his chest.

"Boss-boy, you're still alive!" Eddie drops next to him, and Archie rolls his eyes.

"Oh, for shit's sake. It's bad enough I'm gonna die out here, but now I gotta go out staring at George and Lennie?"

Walter laughs and kneels by his side. "Let's get you back, Archie. Get up."

"You know any living surgeons around here, Edwards?"

Walter tongues his cheek and says nothing.

"I didn't think so. Unless you got a couple dozen yards of bandage and enough blood to fill me back up, there ain't shit-all you can do for me now." A gush of blood slips through his fingers and he dreamily stares up at the night sky with a frown filled with remorse. "I—I got what was coming. Maybe even got off lucky, all things considered."

Eddie picks the cigarette from his chest and places it back between Archie's lips. "You don't deserve to die, Boss-boy. Sure, you don't much like bubbles, but that's no reason to have it coming."

Archie scoffs. "Of all the fucking people, Eddie. Of all the shitty things I did, how could you possibly think I don't deserve the bullet I'm about to eat? Did you forget how many times I tried to feed your ass to that thing over the last three years? Or how many cells I strung that Boot outside of since Uncle Bill made me open up that skylight for the first time?" A string of spit spills down his chin as he breaks into a sob and the cigarette falls to his chest once more. "I—I don't deserve a peaceful death out here, not one like this."

"Why did you do it all, Archie? Why not just leave? Refuse?" Walter leans in, feeling the man's sorrow radiate off him as he struggles for breath between drowning cries.

"It wouldn't do any good, don't you understand? Warden Willy woulda just stripped those boots off my feet and promoted the next poor bastard in line. Guarding is all I've ever known. You think you're the only one with a life outside of Cold Keep? I got a dog I love, a cat I hate, a mortgage almost paid off, and a bitch ex-wife who only lets me see my daughter when I show up with a cheque. We all got responsibilities we can't just shed, so I did what I had to do. I took that Boot, and I chose the child molesters first, after that the rapists and the baby killers! Save for a few." He gives Eddie a point. "I started from the top down, dammit!"

Walter picks the cigarette back up, but he swats it away.

"Even those fucking cigarettes were my idea. I filled 'em up with enough opioids to stave off the fear I was causing you poor bastards, enough to keep you from losing your fucking minds." Tears stream down his face, freezing to his chattering jaw. "T-then Warden Willy got greedy and pitted you all against each other, and before I knew it, I had to choose the worst of the damn tax evaders and petty shoplifters.

That fucker forced me to tear my soul out one piece at a time and hang it in that Boot over and over again until there was nothing left of me to give! I was dead inside before that first winter was even over. It wasn't until I ran out of the criminals who should have gotten the chair, that I decided enough was enough. So, I helped a few boys escape the madness."

"A few more than a few got loose, I'm afraid," Walter says.

Archie shakes his head, sucking back a runny nose. "It wasn't supposed to be like this; nobody was supposed to get hurt. I was just trying to do one last good deed before I tied my Boot around my neck and wandered into the woods. That bastard Marvin knew it would be dangerous, but he agreed to the plan. But just like the warden, just like all men, he got greedy and wanted more. And how did he thank me for it all? By cutting my fucking throat and leaving me to bleed out. Assholes didn't even slice deep enough to end it quickly."

The blood soaks through his uniform into the snow as another set of tears run down his cheeks, and he looks to them, searching for forgiveness. "I didn't do any of it to be cruel, Edwards. I didn't do it because I liked it… I did it because that thing's hunger was—is never ending. It was just gonna keep devouring and devouring, and it might as well have eaten the men that deserved it, the ones who were gonna die in here from old age before the ones who had a chance of getting out and seeing their families again. I— I didn't want any of it… I'm sorry."

Eddie leans in and wraps his arms around

Archie as he collapses, weeping into his shoulder. "It's okay, Boss-boy, it's okay."

Archie lets go and looks up with glassy eyes. "Did—did Warden Willy get his in the end?"

"Yeah," Walter lies. "The thing tore him to shreds. Pecker first and everything. He even started crying for his mama right at the end." Archie smiles, and in that moment, Walter's disdain towards him lifts, leaving only pity for the man dying in the snow. "Are you sure we can't help you back inside?"

"No… I don't wanna die in there. Both of you jerkoffs just bugger off and let me go in peace."

"Okay, Boss-boy. We'll be seeing you around!" Eddie stands and turns, his face lighting up as he steps into the forest, chasing after his next piece of gum.

Archie chuckles and shakes his head. "Tell me, Edwards, you ever figure out how Dakota gets those cigarettes lit?"

"Yeah," Walter lies again. "The tricky bastard was hiding a box of matches in his prison suitcase all along. Saw him dig them out of his ass one morning." Another chuckle builds in Archie's throat as he picks the still burning cigarette off his chest and pulls out a crumpled pack of cigarettes from his pocket.

"Take these fucking things away from me. I wanna die clear headed."

Walter takes the cigarette and gives it a welcoming puff. "Mmm. Tastes like ass." An explosion of laughter erupts between the two and Archie waves Walter away.

"Oh, do me one last favor, Edwards."

"What's that?"

"Don't let them engrave 'The Shit-talker' on my headstone. Now really, get out of here so I can beg my way into heaven."

"Sure thing. Oh! I got something of yours." Walter draws the borrowed billy club and lays it on Archie's lap.

"Hello beautiful." He takes it and lovingly brushes his thumb across its scuffed surface. "Thank you, Edwards."

"You're welcome, Boss-man." Walter turns and walks off after Eddie without looking back, feeling a profound sadness for the man who wasn't as bad as he seemed.

"Eddie? Where you at?" The wind blows through the trees, filling Walter's ears with nothing but whistling branches. "Eddie?" He crosses his eyes, seeing the glowing tip of his cigarette begin to fade and he heaves on the filter, re-invigorating the ember as it fills his head with the disorienting smoke. He reaches up and squeezes the tube, feeling the moist paper between his fingers, its damp shell threatening to drown his only source of heat. Another puff, and his head swirls out of control. "Damn it, Eddie, where are you?"

SUCH DIRTY FOWL

"Come on, please!" Walter begs the dying cigarette, its smoke drawing into his lungs and melting his anxiety away. "Eddie, where are you?"

The forest's canopy moans its relentless drawl, catching the wind and whistling as he scans the moonlit thicket filled with nothing but shrouded bark and withered deadfall. The thought of leaving Eddie behind crosses his mind, but another long haul on the cigarette sends the idea away, along with his sense of direction.

The filter grows warm as the cherry works its way to his fingers and he plucks another smoke from the damp pack, carefully lighting it off the other while he dreamily sings, *"In the big rock candy mountains, all the cops have wooden legs. The bulldogs all have rubber teeth, and the hens lay soft boiled eggs."*

The cafeteria trays cut through the snow, his knees no longer bothering to lift as they launch the powder in all directions.

"The farmers' trees are full of fruit, and the

barns are full of hay."

A small, playful spin twists his vision and a warmness works its way up his back, covering his flesh with a thin film of sweat.

"Oh, I'm bound to go where there ain't no snow, where the rain don't fall, and the wind don't blow. In the big rock candy mountains!" He laughs and flashes a salute to a passing bush. "Hang in there, corporal, we can't have you going out in this cold by yourself. We still need you if we're going to head up the rations to camp five!"

A cloud spills from his broken nose and another wave of opiate-induced heat washes over him as he abandons his earmuffs, stumbling deeper into the snow with little care. *"In the big rock candy mountains, you never change your socks. And the little streams of alcohol come a-trickling down the rocks."*

The snow crunches and echoes all around, falsifying the sound of someone following close behind. "Hello?" Walter spins towards his own empty tracks and fiddles with the buttons on his outermost layer, doubling back through his carved-out path. "That's more like it! Always take the path of least resistance, soldiers!"

Another deep draw of the cigarette knocks its long ash loose, and he unwraps his scarf, dropping it next to the earmuffs. *"In the big rock candy mountain, all the jails are made of tin. And you can walk right out again as soon as you are in."*

"Mmmmmhhhmhmmhm." The ancient laugh hums from the treetops, and Walter rounds on himself again, nearly falling over.

"Who's there?"

…Who's there? his own voice echoes back, distorted and cold.

"Candy mountains!"

…Candy mountains!

He chuckles and resumes his stoned wobble, meeting even less resistance the third time through the same cut-out path. "This is more like it!"

A meek greeting calls out from a lone owl watching on with curious scrutiny, and Walter spots it in the treetops above. "Oh, hello!"

…Oh, hello!

He pauses and his brow flushes at the bird's response. "Jesus… it can talk… Calm down, Walt, you only got one shot at this. Don't blow it." He stands upright and bows. "Oh, my majestic, magical friend, I am Mr. Snickelfritz, and I come to your beautiful woods in search of Marvin; have you seen him around? Will you point your beak in his general direction?"

The owl calculates with yellow eyes and swivels its neck, getting a better look at the half naked man wandering around in the dark, then calls out, "Hoo."

"Who?" Walter asks. "The bastard I'm fixing to kill is who!"

"Hoo."

"I just told you! Oh, for fuck's sake, what are you playing at?" He unbuttons the rest of his jacket and throws it down, storming away as the freezing breeze cuts across his moist skin and eats away at his body heat. "Wait, no! It's Eddie. I'm looking for Eddie!" He turns back, slapping his forehead, but the owl hops from its branch and takes to the sky. "Dammit, I meant Eddie! Come back!" He punches the air and stomps on his jacket, taking notice of its warm inner lining. "Eddie, you're gonna freeze to death without your coat, boy!" He reaches for it too fast, flooding his head with blood and collapses into the snow with a soft thud and content exhale of smoke. "Eddie, where are you? I found your jacket…"

The forest calms, and its canopy settles.

"Are you lost?"

Walter looks up, scanning the world above, and huffs. "It's Eddie who's lost, not me."

A bulk of stitched furs spill out from between the trees, and the hood filled with shadows looms high, leaning in for a deep breath that almost lifts Walter from the ground.

"Not many of us left in these ravaged lands. You are young. Was it *nuntanuhs* who mothered you?"

"Mothered?" Walter asks, looking into the dark, liminal spaces between its shifting robes. "What the hell are you going on about?"

"Oh yes, a pup, for certain. With three maws to nourish, our river will dry up quickly." Its burdensome sleeve extrudes from the pillars of wood and points towards Cold Keep. "Or maybe *nuntanuhs* plans on sending you in her place. A smaller mouse may be exactly what we need."

Walter blows a cloud and looks around. "Have you seen that owl somewhere around here? It owes me my wish."

"I don't speak with such dirty fowl. They

have nothing nice to say. Mmmmmhhhmhmmhm."

The horrible laugh raises the hairs on Walter's arms, and he waves its breath away. "Pee-yew! What is that? Is that you?"

"No...," it answers. "It's that one... over there." The thing reaches out, pointing a stolen arm by its severed elbow, its remaining fingers signaling to Eddie fumbling with his kettle through the brush. It dismisses him and leans over, analyzing Walter once more. "Have you seen *nuntanuhs*, young one? She should be back by now." It tilts its head, and Walter waves it away.

"Bugger off already! Can't you see I'm trying to enjoy my cigarette?"

"Mmmmmhmmmm...Very young indeed." It sinks back between the trees and its voice trails off, leaving Walter to stumble to his feet and call out.

"Eddie! Over here!"

Eddie turns, his face covered in tears. "New-boy!" He dives through the snow, tripping twice as he runs over and throws himself into Walter's arms, nearly knocking the cigarette from his lips.

"Where the hell did you go?" Walter asks.

"Where did *I* go? Where did *you* go, New-boy? I was just over—" Eddie gasps. "What are you doing? It's freezing!" He scoops Walter's jacket from the ground and begins to dress him.

"It's too warm, Eddie, stop." Walter pushes him back and sucks on his cigarette.

"How many of those you smoke?" Eddie plucks the cigarette from his lips and throws it down.

"No!" Walter dives after it and the cherry hisses in the snow. "You idiot!"

"Me? You're the one in the snow without a jacket, stupid! Look at you. That smoke is making you all backwards!"

Walter picks up the butt and sucks on it, his mouth pulling the melted ice through the filter as the cold stings his lips. "Shit!" He throws it down and gets to his feet, grabbing Eddie by the collar. "That was our only way of starting a fire!"

Eddie's eyes flash panic and he scoops it from the ground, shoving it back in Walter's palm. "Quick, start another one!"

"We can't!" Walter pushes him down and the cool air rushes into his lungs, clearing his mind as he breathlessly pants. "We—we only had the one…"

"I'm sorry, New-boy." Eddie smacks his forehead, wincing with each blow, and Walter steps to his side, breathing in more of the putrid pine air.

"It doesn't matter now. Stop hitting yourself." His body shakes and he looks down. "Jesus, where are my clothes?"

"That's what I was saying!"

The last of the opiates dissipate, and Walter plucks his earmuffs from the ground, then pulls Eddie to his feet.

"I'm sorry about the smoke, New-boy, I am."

"Just forget it, it's okay."

"We can always ask Kota to light us a new one."

Walter rubs his hands, getting the blood moving in his fingers. "Yeah, if we don't freeze to death first."

"We shouldn't. It's not a long walk."

Walter pauses. "What do you mean 'not

long'?"

"I mean they're just up and over there, see?" Eddie points at the faint panes of glass to the east, shining out from the wooden structure tucked amongst the trees. "I found 'em just over there, New-boy."

Walter hollers and shakes Eddie back and forth. "Good job, boy! Good job!" They take off, and Eddie claps his hands, setting course as Walter sings a tune. *"I'll see you all, this coming fall, in the big rock candy—"* He stops, heart skipping a beat as the distant recollection of a dark hood and fur robes creep into his mind, lending an overwhelming suspicion that he can't keep to himself. "Eddie…"

"Yeah, New-boy?"

"Have you seen anyone else out here?"

"A couple trees," Eddie answers, "and one or two other escaped jailbirds."

Walter breathes a sigh of relief. "Okay, that's—"

"Oh, and a great big bear! But he was just climbing around in the trees, searching for honey or something. I asked what he was doing, but he didn't have a whole lot to say, pretty much kept his distance."

Walter shudders and coughs on a dry swallow. "Eddie… I don't think that devil we locked in A-Block was the only one in this valley…."

SMOKED OUT

"They're not gonna be too happy to see us," Walter whispers and strips off his snowshoes.

"We gotta be quiet as church mouses, New-boy. They won't hear me none in that cabin, just listen." Eddie takes a gulp of air and holds it as Walter scans the log structure. Shovels, pickaxes, and dilapidated lockers litter its walls, all covered in a fine layer of black soot.

"That's no cabin, Eddie." He kicks at the snow, uncovering a set of metal tracks running between them to the door. "That's an entrance to a mine."

"Oh... Well, whatever it is, it looks warm."

Walter nods, desperate for the balmy glow inside as his body vibrates, still recovering from the nearly naked stroll through the woods. "You wait here, I'm gonna go take a look." He takes off, pausing between strides as his boots crunch in the snow.

A nauseating mix of laughter spills out from inside, and Walter picks up his pace, peering at the chimney billowing its warm smoke above. He creeps onto the porch and peeks through the window's warped glass at Marvin, Chicago, and Wayne, all huddled around a small table dealing cards and picking at a can of peaches. The sight of the men enjoying themselves burns Walter's gut, forcing his eyes to pull away and lock onto Dakota lying unconscious in front of the gaping hole sloping into the earth in the back.

Walter ducks beneath the window and rounds the side of the building, coming up on a stack of split logs piled to the roof. A long-abandoned pickaxe catches his eye, and it breaks free from the ice with a sharp tug. He swings it through the air, getting a feel for its weight, and closes his eyes, picturing the thing sinking into Marvin's skull as the tar and pine creeps across his tongue. He rounds the corner, making for the door with his weapon, but stops, spotting the riot shotguns and their boxes of ammunition on the table inside.

"Gotta flush 'em out, New-boy."

Walter jumps and swings the pickaxe, hitting nothing as Eddie ducks from its path. "Jesus! I told you to stay put. Why don't you ever listen to me, huh?"

"It's cold over there, New-boy!"

"It's cold over here, too!"

"Not up there." Eddie points towards the chimney and turns the corner before Walter can get his footing and follow.

"Get back here!" Walter rounds the corner after him and pauses, impressed by how fast Eddie managed to climb the stack of split logs and situate himself on the roof.

"Eddie, *please* get down!" he begs, trying to stop his voice from escalating into a shout. He climbs after him, thankful the ice had solidified the mountain of logs together as he lifts himself next to Eddie, mittens already off and fingers warming over the chimney. "I'm fixing to slug you; why won't you just—" Walter stops, feeling the heat radiate off the stone pillar, then hangs his hands next to Eddie's, feeling the blood return to his fingers.

"We gotta get Kota out of there, New-boy."

"They got enough bullets to fight off a cavalry in there. What do you suggest we do?"

A smile spreads across Eddie's face and he taps his temple. "When Papa used to get rid of the bees each summer, he would use smoke to flush 'em out of their nest. He would just light up last week's newspaper and out they came running."

Walter rubs his hands and sighs. "Those bees your daddy used to flush out didn't have guns, though, did they? Smoke only makes them angry, we—"

"Yeah, but we got the special smoke." Eddie nabs the pack of cigarettes from Walter's pocket and shakes them like a broken maraca. "Smoke 'em out, New-boy. These won't make 'em angry, they'll make 'em loopy."

"Shit...that could work." Walter wraps an arm around Eddie and pats him on the back. "I'm gonna go down there and seal that door up, lock the bastards in." He fiddles with his buttons and reluctantly strips his jacket off once more, handing it over. "When I give you the signal, you drop that pack in and block up the hole with this, okay? Once those cigarettes start burning, there should be enough smoke to get their heads spinning twice over. I'll wait for those schmucks to be good and dazed before I open that door, and if we're lucky, I'll be able to get the drop on them before they come to."

"What about Kota?"

"He'll be fine. He's on the floor; the smoke will get to him last. Won't notice a thing."

Walter climbs down and passes under the window, stopping outside the door as the cold air cuts across his body. The laughter inside becomes muffled behind his pumping heart and he closes his eyes, visualizing Marvin barreling through the door, falling, coughing, clutching at his throat as the pickaxe sinks deep into his skull and drains the life from his eyes. A shudder runs up Walter's spine as he wedges the tool under the handle, then gives Eddie the nod and backs away to the window, watching the pack of cigarettes drop into the fireplace inside.

"I did it! I did it!" Eddie yells, tumbling down the pile of logs to Walter's side.

"Shhh! You hear that?" Marvin asks. "Who's out there?"

"Damn it! What happened to quiet as a church mouse, Eddie?"

"The smoke's backing up. Something's got the flue all clogged," Chicago says, his voice growing nervous.

The shotgun clicks, raising the hairs on Walter's neck, and he throws himself to the ground, dragging Eddie with him as a blast of lead eviscerates one of the glass panes, shattering it into a thousand pieces.

The barricaded door chatters and jolts against the abiding pickaxe. "It won't budge!"

"The windows then!" Wayne suggests, trying to push himself through the narrow frame where he spots the pair lying on the porch. "Edwards? Eddie? What—what are you doing?"

Eddie waves, flashing the custodian a guilty smile. "Hi, friend…"

"Move!" Marvin pushes Wayne aside as his shotgun lets loose a flurry of lead, and Walter throws his arm around Eddie, rolling them both out of the way. They scuttle to the side, taking cover next to the stacked logs, and another blast kicks the wall from inside, vibrating through them with a dull thud.

"Listen, New-boy!" They hold their breath and the men inside cough, choke, and grapple for air.

"Face me… Face me like a man, Walter!" Marvin calls out.

"Like how you faced what you did to my boy?" Walter screams back. The black smoke seeps from the cracks in the mortar between the logs, and the coughing shifts, turning into giggles as the hammering on the door comes to a stop.

"That's enough, New-boy. I think they had enough."

Walter shifts back around to the door and grabs the pickaxe, then stops, listening to Marvin giggle then hack some more.

"What are you waiting for? Kota's still in there!"

Walter holds fast on the handle, unable to hide a smile as the sound of the suffering men sputter out and fade inside. The *click-clack* creeps in from the woods, and he closes his eyes, picturing Angie's arms draped around his neck, her lips pressed against his cheek; his hands running through Lorrie's curly hair by his side, straightening the aluminum tiara on her head; and Kevin, fingers gripped around his leg, but the burnt face of Marvin staring up with peeled-back eyelids and a horrible grin flashing from between his two rows of charred sideburns.

An uncertain breath floods Walter's lungs, clearing his mind as he yanks on the pickaxe and releases the spew of black smoke that carries Marvin and deposits him into the snow. Eddie shoves Walter aside, leaping into the structure and bumping into Wayne as he tosses himself next to Marvin.

Walter scans the men, searching for any weapons, but their hands lay empty and twitch as they stare up at the stars, choking on their ash-covered tongues.

"I got them!" Eddie yells, dragging both Dakota and Chicago's limp bodies behind him, the shotgun hanging under his chin like a boy carrying too many groceries at once. He drops Chicago next to the others, tossing Walter the gun as he continues past and leans Dakota against a nearby tree.

"Don't fucking move!" Walter checks the chamber and cocks the weapon.

Marvin blinks, his dreamy expression fading and turning into an amused gawk. "Look, Chicago, it's Walt, hell-bent on getting his revenge." He sits up and shakes his head. "God, it was just a kid, Walter! Make a new one and move on already." He laughs and nudges the motionless man next to him in the snow. "Chicago?" He leans in, listening to Chicago's chest, then slaps him across the face. "Dammit, Walt! I just won fifty bucks off this loser with a pair of fours!" His fist comes down hard on Chicago's bandaged eye and he laughs. "Oh well… Yellow-bellied prick probably wasn't good for it, anyway."

Walter raises the shotgun into the air, letting off a blast that ripples across the valley and wipes the smirk from Marvin's face. He shuffles back, but Walter brings his boot down on his heel, pinning it in place. "N-now, Walter. I—I know we've had our differences, but—"

"Differences?" Walter cocks the shotgun and readies the next shell. "What you and I got goes far beyond differences, you piece of shit!" He pushes the muzzle against Marvin's cheek, nudging the oxygen tube out from under his nose. "You think you get to murder my boy in cold blood and just go on living like it never happened? You're such a fucking hypocrite; you stand up on that chapel's stage and preach forgiveness when you have never once asked for mine!" The red and blue creeps into his peripherals, pumping more adrenaline into his veins as Marvin pleads for mercy and Wayne shuffles away, distancing himself from the pair.

"Now, Walt, it's—it's not like that." Marvin pulls at the snow, trying to crawl his way back, but Walter stomps down even harder.

"Then how is it?"

"I—I know what I did was wrong. There's no denying that. But, y-you gotta give me another chance here, bud, I—"

"You don't deserve a second chance!" The *click-clack* carries the tar and pine over his tongue, and the red and blue contorted mass drags itself between his legs, clawing at his knees for his attention. He holds his breath, sweat beading on his forehead, and he squeezes the trigger tighter, its cold metal searing his finger.

"Mmmmmhhhmhmmhm"

The ancient laugh lets out from all directions, its unsettling tone vibrating the earth beneath them. Dakota's eyes shoot open and the five men swivel as one, peering at the gravitational force hiding between the trees, the branches closing in around it.

"What's this?" it asks.

Walter's finger seizes on the trigger, and the sweat on his brow freezes solid.

"I thought I had my fill tonight," it whispers and yells somehow at once. "But I suppose there is always room for dessert." From the darkness, the thing's hand extrudes out from its sleeve and its fingers walk across the ground towards Wayne like an un-oiled marionette putting on a show.

"Get back, dumdum!" Eddie yells.

The arm snakes out and the custodian's frantic feet kick against the snow, unable to gain a foothold on the malleable surface as it stalks closer. Its long fingers wrap around his ankle, squeezing tight with a sudden snap that makes him scream out in anguish.

"Oh, Jesus! Help me, please! Take my hand!" he calls to Eddie.

Eddie starts forward, stopping as Dakota grabs hold of him and pulls him back.

"Please! Please!" Wayne scrambles, grabbing at the loose snow as he's dragged towards the black, rippling swell.

Walter raises his shotgun, and the blast kicks his shoulder, knocking the wind from his lungs as the buckshot lets loose, only to be swallowed by the void.

"Hmm… Very, *very* young indeed," it murmurs, reminding him of his opioid-driven stumble through the woods only minutes before.

Wayne's scream kicks into high gear as his legs vanish between the pines, bones snapping and torso twisting, inducing images of a woodchipper somewhere in the darkness rather than the snapping jaws of an ancient evil. The custodian's fearful face turns to one of sadness and his screams rise to an octave no longer audible as the four others watch on, their own howls resonating into a twisted harmony that masks Wayne's final words, never to be heard or passed along to his next of kin.

Marvin jumps to his feet, pushing Walter to the ground as he makes a break for the cabin. Walter turns, aiming the shotgun towards him and pulls the trigger, rattling the un-cocked firing pin within its seat. "Fuck!" He cocks it with a frustrated shout and fires off the next shell, shattering another window.

Marvin dives through the doorway and snatches the other gun from the table, then disappears into the dark caverns beyond.

"No!" Walter turns back to Dakota and Eddie watching the last of Wayne disappear into the shadows, his gurgled cries drowning in a mouth full of blood. "Boys, let's move!"

The pair break their hypnotic trances from the horror and they both get to their feet, joining Walter in seconds.

"Please, help me. Please!" Wayne calls out from between the pines. All three men stop, frozen in their tracks as he begs. "Somebody, please. It's gone. It left."

Eddie steps forward, transfixed by the voice, and Dakota shakes his head. "Don't listen to it. It's not him…"

A stillness emanates from the forest, its silence deafening as the wind dies down and the voice gives up its facade.

"Mmmmmhhhmhmmhm. Just a taste, come now. I haven't had dark meat in ages." The thing, draped in a mountain of mismatched pelts, spills out from its boreal cover like oil leaking from a burnt orange GMC and rises over them. A trickle of blood cascades from its hood, and it flashes a jagged smile past lips that have long been chewed away, then screams, "Ruuuuuun!"

The trio bolts for the mine and the thing bounds after them on all fours, letting out its terrible laugh that locks Walter's knees mid-stride. He stumbles and straightens out as they burst into the structure and all three grab at the door, swinging it closed.

The hulking thing slams against it, the impact jolting them forward and sending Eddie crashing into the table of cards and peaches. Walter coughs on the smoke left hanging in the room as he spins around and pulls the deadbolt shut. Another bash sends shock waves through them, and mortar rains down from the ceiling above.

"It's gonna tear this place to shreds!" Dakota screams.

"It's gonna tear *us* to shreds!" Eddie whimpers, and the windows explode inwards as the dead hands reach in, pulling away the frames with ease.

"Just a taste." Its rotten breath fills the room and makes them gag.

Walter stares into the dark cavern ahead, its faded sign reading *Deephold Mine - Workers Only.*

"We gotta go deeper!"

Dakota nods and grabs Eddie by the arm, thrusting him forward without a second of hesitation. "Let's go!"

They descend and a timeworn scream rattles Walter's vision as he holds his breath, withdrawing from the thing's never-ending hunger above, into the earth where Cold Keep's stones once lay below.

A DEVIL NONE
DIFFERENT

The shattering glass and tearing wood echoes down through the tunnels as the trio feel their way deeper into the mine.

"I can't see, Kota."

"Just a little further," Dakota says, unable to mask his anxiety.

The cool rocks caress Walter's fingers, and against his better judgment, he grips the shotgun's stock and uses it as a cane, feeling for any sudden drops. "Pull those matches out of your ass and get us some fire going, kid."

"It's not that simple, Old-timer."

"Well make it simple. We've got a twenty-foot-tall man-eater on our backs and an armed, Jesus-preaching sociopath to our fronts, so let's make happy with some light already!"

"Come on, Kota, just show him," Eddie argues.

"Show me what?"

"Just do it, Kota!"

"Fine, fuck! Okay!" Dakota barks. "Just... just remember, we don't have time for you to freak out, Jamestown."

"Freak out? Why would—"

A snap rings out and a brilliant flash of light fills the passage, stinging Walter's eyes as they adjust to the dancing flames suspended in Dakota's palm.

"What the hell is that!" Walter points, voice trembling like a man fearing the burning bush. "How—how are you doing that?"

Dakota takes off, leading their escape. "What, now you got time for stories?"

"Yeah, for ones like that!" Walter shouts, fighting the urge to smother Dakota's hand with his scarf.

"Tell him, Kota. It's a good one."

"Fine, Just keep moving; both of you." Dakota hurries them forward. "That tale I told you back in our cell, you remember it, Jamestown?"

"Who could forget?"

"Well...it wasn't the whole truth. There weren't any firemen in that burning orphanage like I said there was."

Walter gnaws on his cheek and swallows blood. "What's that got to do with... with that?" He points at the flames and stumbles over the metal tracks between his feet.

"Just listen. When the smoke got to me and I passed out, I didn't wake up in no hospital like I told you. Instead, I found myself on some kinda fairground."

"A fairground?"

"That's what I said, a fairground. Big top, cotton candy, and all that shit. And in the middle of it all was this man, skin as black as the witching hour, wearing this white dapper suit with a straw skimmer hat covering up his face. It was like he didn't wanna be seen or something. He strolled over and helped me up, greeting me with a nickname he had no right knowing, and as soon as I laid eyes on that long smile of his poking out from the brim of his hat, I realized it was the Devil himself come to drag me down for what I did to those poor kids; to my own boy."

"You were dreaming," Walter says, and Eddie jabs him in the ribs.

"I thought that, too, but as I stood there in death's doorway, he showed me something on the other side that dropped me to my knees and made me beg for my life. I hollered, cried, even kissed his feet, and that's when he flashed that great big grin and agreed to spare me, right then and right there."

"Just like that?"

"Sure, as long as I honored his name."

"Honor his name? Honor the devil?"

"That's right. Well… not *your* devil. We got our own. But a devil none different. I said 'no' at first, told him I wasn't selling my soul to save my own worthless skin. But he sweetened the deal."

"Your boy," Walter whispers.

"My boy… If I agreed to honor—no, worship him for as long as I lived, in return he would save my son from those fires, too."

"So you took the deal?"

"Hell yeah I took the deal. I'm standing here

right now, ain't I? I agreed, but he made me shake his hand, told me that consent was the currency with which you sell a soul. So I agreed without a second thought. Didn't need one because I would have done just about anything to undo what I did. Anything."

A scream lets loose from above and Walter grabs hold of the vibrating wall, stabilizing himself amidst the foul-smelling breeze.

"Only thing is," Dakota continues, "what that black man in that white suit failed to mention was that it was my body he would pluck from that fire, not my soul. That's his now, still burning with the rest of those innocent children I fried."

"That's some story, kid. But that doesn't answer *how* you're making those flames."

Dakota stares at Walter, his face hard as the stones around them. "You figure that out, and I'll start worshiping your name instead, Jamestown." The flames soak into his palm, its warm glow sinking beneath the surface of his flesh as it travels up and down his arm like some kind of marmot.

"So that's how you light the cigarettes."

"Yup... Come one, come all."

The earth shudders with another scream as the thing tears at the barricade above, pushing the men even further into the tunnels. Walter looks around, surveying the large blasted out passages and the wooden supports holding the earth's immense weight up. "So how does all of that"—he points to Dakota's flickering palm— "tie into your little deal?"

The flames climb back to the surface and cast shadows on Dakota's brow, making his eyes appear hollow and somewhere else entirely. "After that handshake, the bastard just left me outside Quebec. *Quebec* of all fucking places. So I walked, and I walked some more, but not long after, this burning started to build in my gut, and it got so bad I could barely stand upright. Then it pooled in my palms— warm at first, then hot and so unbearable they burst into flames. I panicked and rolled around in a nearby field trying to put 'em out. That's when the entire plot caught fire and the flames swallowed up some poor farmer's crops. But, as they burned, the pain stopped and my hands went out." A freezing gust of wind pushes them on, and Dakota continues, his blazing palm refusing to relinquish to the breeze. "A day later it came back and started frying up my insides again. I figured sparking up a bush or two would ease the pain like it did with the field."

"Did it work?"

"Nah, so I tried a tree next and that did the trick, but it was only after the thing was completely ablaze that I saw a nest with a couple fried eggs in the middle of it. That's when it occurred to me, that's when it started to make sense."

"You gotta hurt," Walter says.

"Hurt, maim and burn, baby."

"What about your boy?"

"Haven't seen him since the orphanage. A few days after the incident, I checked the newspapers and there he was, his face right next to the rest of the kids that perished in that fire I started. But I had to be sure that dark man was good on his word, so I dug up his grave, and you know what I found inside?"

"Nothing, Kota; it was empty," Eddie says.

Dakota nods. "That's right. No bones or ashes, no nothing. I guess the coroners must have assumed him dead when he hadn't come out from the fire. So I searched high and low, even with my face plastered on every most wanted poster from east to west. Those urges to hurt would always follow, though; they'd bubble back up like clockwork. As time went on baby birds turned to gophers, then neighborhood cats. It wasn't until I spotted a couple nuns coming out from St. Augustine's one day that I realized I had a serious problem that went far beyond critters and house pets. I was passing 'em by and something deep inside me said their habits would burn a beautiful yellow; and for some reason, I couldn't help but wanting to see it for myself. I even stalked 'em for a few blocks until I snapped out of it and decided enough was enough, and that I couldn't be part of the free world anymore. So I gave up on my boy, abandoned him and went straight to the closest station to turn myself in. One thing after another and I'm smack dab in the middle of Cold Keep. The end. That's all."

"What about your… urges? Did they stop after that?"

"Nah. You seen me rubbing my hands in the mornings, trying to soothe their ache. That's the burning creeping on back."

"So then how do you—"

"The cigarettes. I guess the lung cancer I dole out each morning is enough to please that dark man's hold on me; for the time being, at least. With each cigarette I light, the burning staves off little by little.

Not sure what unearthly strings had to be pulled, but one day the Boys-in-Blue just swept in and removed every lighter, match, and flint from Cold Keep without so much as an explanation. Just left me to deal out and light the death sticks to each man willing to suck on one. Since then, it's just been me and Eddie here against the world, stuck in Cold Keep while my son wanders somewhere out there without his daddy."

"What about his mother?"

A sadness washes over Dakota and he sighs. "One morning she just woke up, decided this world was too much for her, and made me cut her down from the rafters." Stones shift overhead and he points to the wooden supports above as they moan, threatening to collapse. "But you know what I fear the most, Jamestown?"

"What's that?"

"That my son is somewhere out there with the same burning in his belly as me, and the same way of keeping it from swallowing him whole."

"There!" Eddie screams.

A blast lets loose from Marvin's shotgun and the buckshot flies overhead as he vanishes deeper into the network of tunnels.

Walter takes off after him, but Dakota throws his free hand into his chest. "Are you crazy? He's armed and we got bigger fish to fry!"

Walter grabs him by the collar, pulling him nose to broken nose. "You and I had a fucking deal, kid! I bring you Eddie and you help me finish that piece of shit off!"

Dakota pauses, looking him deep in the eyes.

"What Marvin did to your son was a tragedy, but take it from me, this won't set things straight, Jamestown."

Walter shoves him back. "You wouldn't even know what straight is. I'm going to kill that man if it's the last thing I do, and considering that thing up there is set to bust in any moment, it might just be that. Now, are you a man of your word or not?" He lifts the gun, nudging Dakota forward, and he reluctantly proceeds.

"But, Kota," Eddie whimpers.

"Just stay in the back, Eddie. Sooner we get this over with, the sooner we can start looking for an escape from that *maji-manidoo*."

Walter takes his turn to pause and gives Dakota a quizzical look. "You know what that thing is? What it *really* is?"

Dakota nods, lifting the flames in his outstretched palm. "There were a lot of ghost stories told on the reserve when I was growing up. Ones of creatures hiding in reflections, of water dwelling beasts, and colossal spiders that would wear the meat of its prey like clothing. But there's one whose stories were only whispered after the snow had settled. A tale of an ancient, greed-stricken spirit who grew hungrier and taller with each innocent consumed."

Movement catches the corner of Walter's eye, and he whips the shotgun at an empty shadow, then breathes a sigh of relief and continues after Dakota.

"My generation wouldn't speak its name out of respect for the elders, but it was the elders who wouldn't speak its name out of fear. They would tell stories of the long winters that outlasted the reserves of dried meats and grain, of men and women eating their children and brothers to survive the season, only to turn into bloodthirsty creatures as punishment for their greed and gluttony. The victims would blame neighboring shamans for sending the spirit to their village. Spirits that would taunt the families in their homes for months on end, causing anger and scrutiny that would spill over into the summers and spark war amongst the tribes who once considered themselves friends. I never believed the tales as a child, not until I came to Cold Keep and started having these dreams… dreams of—"

"Food."

Dakota snaps Walter a look. "Have you eaten what it's offered?"

Walter shakes his head. "I… I don't think so... Maybe?"

A look of worry lingers on Dakota's face. "Never accept a meal from one of those things. Not in a dream, and especially not in real life. One bite is all it takes. Are you hungry now, Jamestown?"

A flash carries a deafening boom ahead, shattering a nearby deposit of ore, and Walter raises his gun, letting off a blind round in return. He cocks the firearm and looks down at the last shell begging to be fired. "Come on out, Marvin. The jig is up! Make this easy for both of us and I promise I'll end you quick."

A final crack of splitting wood surges through the mine from the world above and the clatter of rotten feet work their way down the tunnels with hideous whispers that fill the men's ears and empty their bowels. Its ancient words mix with another blast from Marvin's shotgun, and a slurry of fear bears down on Walter's remaining sanity, threatening to snap his mind in two.

"Move. Let's move!" Dakota yells, leading the charge.

"Come on, Marvin! Don't be yellow!" Walter screams, regaining some of his composure as Marvin screams back.

"I'd rather let that thing eat me alive before a pathetic piece of shit like you takes me out, Walter!"

Dakota angles his hand, illuminating the man in pursuit as he skitters around a corner, and Walter aims his barrel, pausing, refusing to use the shell until he has a better shot.

"Just a taste!" the thing screams, tilting the ground with every syllable spewed from its foul maw.

Stones of various sizes rain down around them, their thrumming joining in with Marvin's words.

"How many of those shells do you got left, Walter? Because I got myself a whole box here, and a —" His words cut short and curdle into a scream.

The trio turn the corner into the massive opening, flames filling the chamber littered with abandoned mine carts and tools; doors forking off in all directions, reminding Walter of Cold Keep's eight sided lobby.

"There!" Dakota points at Marvin trapped beneath the small mountain of rubble in the center of the room. He thrashes against the pile around him, uselessly digging at the rocks around his chest, then adjusts his oxygen tube and looks up at Walter with contempt.

"Is this what you wanted? Is this how you pictured it, Walter?" A string of spit dribbles down his chin and he lets out an anguished cough, reaching uselessly for the tank slung over his back.

Walter walks over, smiling down on him as the world goes quiet, and Marvin's face winces with smug pain, his true fear shining through.

"Go on then, do it!" Marvin barks. "I won't beg for my life. In fact—" His words die off and he stares into space, suddenly caught in a web of confusion.

"For your life?" Walter asks. "That's mine now, no choice in the matter." He raises the shotgun and pushes the cold barrel into Marvin's sideburn.

Marvin seizes wildly, his face spasming, the anger within melting away to an elderly confusion as he settles down and heaves against the rocks. "Edwards? What's going on? Why—why are—"

"Oh no you don't!" Walter pats him down, pulling the flask from his breast pocket. "Get back here!"

"What—what are you doing? Please, Edwards. Get me out of here!"

Walter grabs Marvin by the cheeks and tilts his head back, puckering his lips as the cap spins off, then he pours the entire thing into his open gullet, topping it off with a fist to the lips.

Marvin shakes free and tosses his head side to side, his eyes hardening once more as the gin drips down his chin and the killer's insolent smile returns.

"Almost lost me there for a second." He lets out a nauseating laugh, then spits.

Walter returns the smile, relieved. "You know how many ways I pictured ending your pathetic life, Marvin? I've stabbed, burned, poisoned, and bludgeoned you too many times to count in my mind over the years. But truly, if I had my way, I would run you over with that orange pickup of yours, put it in park, and listen to your skin sizzle against the hot tailpipe the exact same way you did to my boy."

He steadies the shotgun and closes his eyes, seeing Angie's kind smile, Lorrie's tiara, and Kevin's empty skull looking up from his leg, its mulched insides dripping out and leaking hot buckshot across his boots. A chill runs through him and he squeezes the trigger, ridding himself of Angie's warmth around his shoulder as the shotgun's metal curve shifts in its guard, evaporating Lorrie's curly hair between his fingers while the trigger creaks, leaving him with only Kevin's cold corpse to weigh him down. He cracks his tear-filled eyes and looks around at the men around him, truly seeing them for the first time.

Eddie: A man unaware of the guilt he does not understand.

Dakota: A man tormented by the guilt he cannot deny.

And Marvin: A man hated for the guilt he will not accept.

He lowers the gun with unsure hands and looks down at himself, seeing the man he has become: a man consumed by the guilt he does not, cannot, and will no longer accept for the death of his little boy. He drops it, taking one final deep breath of the tar and pine, savoring its parting bitterness, then lets it go, looking down on the man who truly deserves the weight of his boy's death. "Fuck you, Marvin. You're not even worth the bullet."

"Mmmmmmhhhmhmhm. Yeah… fuck you, Marvin."

The cold air in the cavern turns glacial, and frost spreads across the stones all around like parasitic mold, closing in as the ancient thing's whisper calls out.

Dakota moves into action, his flames rising higher as he ushers Walter and Eddie further into the stone temple, away from the thing's deep, cruel laugh.

"There you are," it whispers, its stink turning the air almost flammable as it crawls in from around the corner.

Walter points to the door in the back, and Eddie pulls the kettle from his hip, swinging it through the air as the thing turns its nose up at him and keeps its distance.

"Don't leave me, please!" Marvin cries after them.

They step through the frame and Walter pulls the door shut, watching Marvin through the gap, regretting not shooting him when he had the chance; not out of revenge, but to spare him from the evil spilling into the room.

"I can smell you. One, two, three and a half." Its flesh *clicks* against the uneven ground, fur robes swaying and hood rising, tilting to the crumbling ceiling above. It takes a step, its rotten stump coming down on the pile of debris and crushing Marvin beneath. His eyes bulge and his chest deflates, unable to pull in enough air to scream as a quartet of cracking ribs billow out and his torso shifts, then caves in completely.

"Jesus!" Walter gasps, managing to turn away.

"Ah... found one." It bends down, jaw unlatching from its skull as it plucks Marvin's carcass from the rubble like a horse lipping at a dandelion, jagged teeth finding resistance as they clatter against his oxygen tank and swallow it, and him whole.

Dakota's flames flare at the sound of the grinding flesh. "We gotta move!"

Walter nods and they turn, stopping dead at the collapsed tunnel that drains the last inkling of hope from all three of them at once.

"No!"

"No!"

"No!"

"Yes, yes, yes... Now, where is that dark meat?"

Dakota trembles, his flames glowing brighter as he bounces back and forth across the cavity looking for an exit that's not there.

"Kota," Eddie sheepishly calls.

"Keep cool, kid," Walter whispers. "Kill the lights, you're gonna give us away." He looks back, seeing the tidal robes crest nearer to the crack in the door.

"I—I can't," Dakota says, waving his hand

free from the flames, only to have them reappear in his other.

"Kota…"

"Take a breath. Get a hold of yourself."

The thing's reflective eyes lurch towards the light and it sings. "*In the big rock candy mountains, the jails are made of tin.*"

"Kota!"

"Howah!" Dakota turns on Eddie. "What!"

"Did that thing swallow up Marvin, Kota?"

"Yeah, Eddie, it did. We got bigger things to worry about right now!"

"Even that tank on his back?"

"*And you can walk right out again, as soon as you are in.*" It throws itself against the door and lets out a scream, showering stones as the boards bulge against its weight and hinges buckle inwards.

A geyser of flames leap from Dakota's hand and he holds it high, unable to control the spread. "Yes! Even his tank! What's that—" He pauses, eyes opening wide. "Yes! Yes, it did!" He grabs Eddie with his free arm and hugs him tight with a whisper in his ear.

Eddie pulls back and looks at him. "No! We all go, all of us!"

Dakota turns on his heels and grabs Walter by the shoulder. "Get Eddie out of here, Jamestown. Get him someplace safe until help comes, okay?"

"No, Kota! We all go. I just said we all go!"

"What? Why?" Walter asks. "What's going on, kid?"

Another assault buckles a second hinge inwards and spreads the crack wide open.

"You just get Eddie to safety, promise me."

"I don't—"

"Promise me!"

"Okay! I promise, I promise!"

Dakota works up a smile. "I told you you'd get me killed." He strips his belt and wraps it tight below his shoulder, forcing the flames into his free hand. "You go get your family back, Jamestown, and keep an ear out for my boy in the free world." He pulls both Walter and Eddie in for one more tight squeeze and cries. "Please be good, Eddie. You're a sweet boy."

"Kota, please, you're the only one that's nice to me." Eddie pulls his invisible hat off and places it on Dakota's head.

"Jamestown will be nice to you now. It will be okay."

"You take care, Dakota," Walter whispers in his ear.

"You too, Walter." He shoves them both back and plunges his arm through the hole in the door, holding it there for only a moment before his entire body jerks sideways and he screams.

Walter and Eddie grab him tight, dodging the flames in his free flailing hand, and their screams join in as he kicks wildly, his body thrashing against the thing on the other side.

"Pull!" Eddie screams.

"Not yet!" Dakota shouts. Another snap jerks him off his feet as the flames soak into his flesh, travel up his arm, across his shoulders, and pool at the belt cinched around his shoulder. "Now!" He pulls the leather strap free and the flames flow down his forearm and out the hole like a hit of opioids as he tears free and falls back.

Eddie reaches deep into his coat, brandishing his spoon like a noble swordsman and smiles. "Get back, Boogeyman!" He barges through the door, burying the utensil deep into the thing's hood, and it shrieks in pain with a cacophony of stolen voices, all mixing into layers of muddled evil as the warm glow runs down its throat and illuminates the horrible remains within its robes.

Dakota collapses in Walter's arms, and Eddie joins their side, pacing a wide loop around the writhing creature with the smoke spilling out from its tattered skin and rotted innards.

"We could use a little light here, kid!"

The thing whips its hood back, revealing what's left of its retched face and unhinges its jaw, calling to Walter with his son's helpless voice. "Should have checked the latch, Daddy! Should have checked the latch!"

Walter turns, and it lets out one final, deep laugh.

"Just—just feel for the tracks, Eddie. Stay between the tracks and—" His foot catches on the metal and the ground comes up hard, forcing the breath from all three men's lungs.

"Up, up, let's go!" Eddie screams.

Walter's airway kicks back on, and he pictures the flames chewing away at Marvin's tank deep within the thing's stomach. They get back on their feet with a combined heave and move.

"Between the tracks, New-boy. Just like you said!"

Walter gasps for air as they round another bend, revealing the moonlight shining in from the cave's mouth, its gentle hue gleaming off the tracks between their feet, lighting the way like a tarmac expecting a landing.

"Don't stop now, Eddie, almost there!" His ankle twists and brings him to his knees, but Eddie forces him up, giving him no time to feel the pain. They push forward, the mangled portal on the surface growing smaller as Walter's vision swirls with a mixture of pain, adrenaline, and relief.

An earth-shattering boom lets forth and the entire mine drops into a cockeyed slant, knocking them into a craggy wall. They recover and drag Dakota behind, his knees skipping off the sharp stones as the wooden supports collapse and give way overhead.

Rocks plummet down and a slab of shale collides with Walter's shoulder, another cracking Eddie on the back of the skull.

"Go, go, go!"

The earth closes in around them with one final contraction and they throw themselves into the night as a ball of flames rip past overhead, obliterating what's left of the small shack and showering the forest with rock and timber.

The deafening echo ripples across the valley's high walls, and after a moment it fades, leaving behind the distant wail of a dozen police sirens all working their way up Cold Keep's desolate winding roads.

Walter and Eddie throw Dakota aside, his face flushing with snow and jolting him awake.

"Huh! What? Did—did we make it?" He reaches out to the moon with both arms but sees only one. "Oh… yeah."

They laugh, and Walter grabs his empty stomach as his crooked nose, broken ribs, and black eyes ache, the pain no longer delivering its reprieve of guilt or rush of endorphins. And as the sweet smell of pine floods his lungs and washes away his need for reprisal, Walter closes his eyes and sees his son's face for the first time in years.

VISITATION

"Edwards, booth seven."

Walter steps into the small visitation room, massaging his jaw as it grinds away on a piece of tasteless gum.

"Kota, look, it's New-boy!" Eddie jumps from his seat and presses himself against the glass.

"Well, if it isn't crazy one and crazy two!" Walter laughs, joining Eddie and Dakota in their orange jumpsuits on the other side of the booth. "I like the new bachelor pad, boys. Sure beats the hell out of you-know-where."

Dakota chuckles. "One little prison riot and we got enough knots in enough panties you could use 'em as a rope to climb out of here." He adjusts his seat with his one arm and grunts.

Walter takes in their faces through the partition, wishing he could reach out and hug them. "Sure was lucky they kept you two lovebirds together after they shut Cold Keep's doors for good."

"No luck in it. Where else were they gonna put a couple of criminals with matching rap sheets but together?"

"Me and Kota stick together, New-boy. You should see him trying to put his pants on in the morning with that one arm of his, it's something else. Show him, Kota." Eddie pulls at Dakota's belt and he swats him away.

"Eddie here doesn't have much sympathy for the crippled if you couldn't tell, Jamestown."

Walter shakes his head and draws a thought-out breath. "I'm—I'm sorry I didn't come see you boys sooner, truly. After I got out, I—"

"Don't mention it. They had the whole joint locked down tighter than a nun's sock drawer once the big leagues got involved."

Walter looks around at the guards and leans in. "Tabloids only mentioned the riot and something about wolves or some shit, nothing about that demon locked in A-Block or the wake of destruction it left in its path."

Eddie's fingers rise to his mouth and Dakota rubs his back. "You surprised? Didn't take 'em long to make the whole story up. Wolves somehow picked a few locks in the process, too, but the papers conveniently failed to mention that."

"And people believed it?"

"Easier than getting them to buy that a fucking monster terrorized Cold Keep for three winters in a row while chewing up countless men, fathers, and guards in the process."

"Shoulda seen it, New-boy. After you got hauled off, the army started pouring in. Isn't that right, Kota?"

"That's right. The emergency response teams

took one look at A-Block and pulled out faster than a teenager without a condom. Within a day there were so many soldiers and government officials swarming the place that we all were crammed into B-Block. Some four to a cell."

"For years!" Eddie yells and punches the air.

"What the hell are you talking about, years? It was four months!"

"Oh… Well, it felt like years."

"What about that Boogeyman we locked in with the Assholes?" Walter asks, giving Eddie a guilty frown.

"Gone, New-boy! Tore its way out before anyone arrived. We must have scared that thing real good, though, cause it didn't come sniffing around no more after that."

"Nope." Dakota gives Eddie a proud smile. "After the cleanup they shut the whole place down and transferred everyone out, leaving Cold Keep to rot in that valley where it belongs."

Walter sighs. "Silver linings, I guess."

Dakota shifts in his seat and switches to a cheerier tone. "But we're pleased as punch in here, Jamestown. Some things are better, others worse. Sure beats the hell out of the old place, though. Plus, Eddie here doesn't try to get me killed every chance he gets, unlike my last cellmate." He smirks, and Walter's eyes fall to the floor.

"It sure is good to see you boys. I know we didn't have much time for closure, on the account of your arm needing patching up and all. And not to mention me being—"

"A cop?"

"Yeah… about that. I—"

"Save your breath. Eddie and I pieced it together pretty quick. Was only a matter of time before they sent someone in to poke around. Seems you went above and beyond with your extra credit assignments, though." Dakota laughs and Walter chuckles along.

"So, what became of Uncle Bill?"

"Bastard went back to running the show after the cleanup. But it was short lived once the inmate's stories started to gain traction with the higher-ups and paint his ugly portrait. Soon enough, some more bigwigs strode in and swept him away; right in the middle of one of his self-indulgent speeches, no less."

"You should have seen it, New-boy! He started crying in front of everyone when they came to drag him out. And you know what I did? Do you?"

"What did you do, Eddie?"

Eddie grins and pulls off his boots. "I took my boots off, like this, and I threw 'em right at his stupid face! The laces wrapped around his neck and everything!" He bursts out laughing, and Dakota claps him on the back.

"Not only Eddie, neither; all of us. One by one, boots started flying and he started kicking and screaming, threatening all of us like he still had an ounce of power left to his name. I even saw one knock the glasses right off his face!"

The trio laugh and slap their knees as Walter wipes away a tear. "I would have paid a good penny to have seen that, I'm not gonna lie." His eyes come into focus and land on Dakota's missing arm. "How uh… how are you getting along without the…"

"I got my days," he answers. "Eddie here has been doing all my heavy lifting, but the snake charges me two scoops of pudding every time he opens my tin. Can you believe that bullshit?"

"That's fair, Kota. You always say it's not fair, but it is!"

"Yeah, yeah." He nudges Eddie with his stump and Eddie shoves him back.

"No touching!" a guard shouts.

"Sorry, Boss-ma—" Dakota cuts himself off and sighs. "Seems we're still getting used to a real prison. They gotta be a lot stricter without a Boot to keep us in line."

"I can imagine."

"Better air, though, New-boy. No cigarettes in here." Eddie takes a deep breath and exhales.

"None?" Walter looks at Dakota's palm. "What about your… condition?"

Dakota lifts his hand and snaps, producing nothing but noise. "Seems my burning was left in the belly of the beast."

"So… no more urges to burn?"

"None so far. That thing down in Deephold mine was a pretty big kill after all. Worth every pound of flesh I paid."

"Good." Walter takes a deep breath and straightens himself up. "Listen, kid. I—I don't know how to tell you this, and I've thought long and hard if I even should, but it's your right to know, and if the tables were turned, I would want you to tell me. In fact, I didn't think that you could—"

Dakota rolls his eyes. "Get on with it, Old-timer."

The gum tumbles around in Walter's mouth and he bites down hard. "Right, well, not long after I made my way back west, I found myself scanning over some old files, searching for something I couldn't get my mind off of."

"Okay…"

"Records, reports of fires to be specific. I was just following a hunch, nothing more than a theory, but after a while, things, tidbits here and there started lining up, started making more and more sense."

"I don't follow, Jamestown. What are you saying?"

Walter takes another breath and squeezes his chair.

"I'm saying these fires I've been looking into all have one thing in common, a child. A boy recovered from each scene."

"A boy?" Dakota echoes.

"The same boy. Again and again. *Your* boy." He pulls out a newspaper clipping and presses it to the glass. "Is that him?" He points to a stoic child sitting on a curb, wrapped in a blanket as a building burns in the background.

Dakota's eyes scan the paper, reading the words aloud. "One rescued. Two dead in house fire."

Walter unfolds another scrap and holds it next to the other, pointing to the same boy's face huddled in a class picture. "Orphanage burned. Three perished, more injured."

"Jesus… Yeah, that's him," Dakota whispers, his voice heartbroken as he scans the page. "I—I don't. I—"

"There's more of them, too many to be a coincidence." Walter slides the clippings through the slit in the glass and Dakota tenderly tucks them into his pocket.

"I guess that answers my question."

"I'm sorry, kid. Maybe I shouldn't have—"

"No... no, I'm glad you did, thank you." Sadness wells up in his eyes and Eddie squeezes his hand. "Hey," he sucks back his tears and smiles, "your last letter said Angie was due to pop any day, so?"

"A boy," Walter says, unable to hold back a smile. He pulls a photo from his wallet, holding it up as Eddie touches the glass.

"Does he cry, New-boy?"

Walter pops a fresh piece of gum into his mouth and chews. "Only when he's hungry."

ARE YOU THE STILLHEARTS?

Robert barges into the room, carrying the sound of barking sled dogs that wakes Edith from her sleep. "Someone is here, my love!"

She tosses the quilt and drapes a gown over her body as she rushes downstairs, past the empty nursery. The chattering of hounds grow louder, and the couple steps into the brisk night air, meeting an exhausted-looking man coming off the back of his sled, carrying a fur-wrapped parcel.

"Are you the Stillhearts?" he asks.

"We are," Edith answers, leaning closer to her husband. "He's got something in his arms, Robert."

The man steps forward. "My name is Benjamin. We—I am here on behalf of the First Nations Ministry, the Church Missionary Society, but first and foremost as a representative of God."

Edith shifts from the doorway and pulls her gown tight across her body, giving her husband's hand a hopeful squeeze. "Do you think—"

"Best not to assume," Robert whispers, trying to stifle her expectations as his eyes calculate Benjamin's pale complexion. "Dear Lord, man, you are frozen through! Come inside."

"That is very kind, but"—Benjamin pauses, eyes shifting all around—"this is no social call; the nearest town is close by and I must be on my way."

"Then what is it?" Edith asks, trying to keep her eyes from the package in his arms.

"It is my understanding that you miscarried not long ago. Is that correct?"

Robert pulls on Edith's arm. "I don't see how that's any business of yours."

"I was told after complications, there was a stillbirth to a local couple that was left yearning for kin. Is that, or is that not you?" Benjamin asks more firmly.

Robert reaches for the knob. "You have some nerve coming—"

"That's right, that's us!" Edith stomps her foot in the frame and pins the door open. "Why?"

Benjamin steps onto the porch, unwrapping the infant nestled in his arms, and a gasp escapes Edith as she covers her mouth.

"It so happens we—I came across an unfit mother on *my* latest mission. She surrendered the child, and I'm informed you are the only woman fit to nurse within days of here. I believe God has brought us this gift to deliver unto you."

Edith squeals, throwing the door open as she rushes to Benjamin's side.

"Now wait a moment, dearest," Robert calls

after her, his voice drowned in his wife's cries as she scoops the babe and presses her lips against its soft scalp.

"So, you will accept this child of God as your own?"

"Yes. Oh God, yes! Thank you, thank you!"

Benjamin smiles. "Good. We will inform the church and process the certificates right away. I'm sorry, but I must be off."

"Wait!" Robert calls after him. "Just like that? Don't—"

Benjamin turns, exhausted. "If you would rather not take this child in, I would be obligated to bring her into town and seek adoption elsewhere, Mr. Stillheart." He reaches for the baby and Edith withdraws, maternal panic creeping in as she turns on her husband with fiery eyes.

"What is wrong with you? Why would you question what we have prayed so hard for? Don't you dare throw away our second chance! Please, I won't let you!"

Robert watches his wife clutch the babe in her arms, and he smiles at the missionary. "Let us at least feed you a warm meal. To show our gratitude."

"No!" Benjamin snaps. "I want nothing more to do with that…" He shakes his head, repressing something inside him. "I have—I just…" He gives up with a dismissive wave and steps onto his sled, then disappears into the night.

"Oh, bless you, God, for answering our prayers. Thank you!" Edith pushes into the house and gently pulls the fur away from the child's filth-covered body. "A girl, Robert, look!" She licks her thumb, attempting to wipe away some of the grime from around her daughter's mouth. "What have they done to you, my sweet girl? You are so thin!" She pulls her gown aside and massages her breast, stirring up the milk inside. "Can you believe it, Robert? Our prayers have been heard."

Robert peers out the window and watches Benjamin's lantern fade down their hill, the dogs' howls persisting on the wind. "A true blessing indeed." He nods at his wife and helps her sit as she lifts the baby to her breast.

"Oh, you are freezing cold, my little love!" She cries, holding her daughter to her warm chest as she latches on and suckles. "A second chance, husband. Can you—Ouch!" She yanks the babe away and it wails out with shifting, uncertain tones.

"What's wrong?" Robert asks, kneeling by Edith's side as she exposes the line of blood trickling from her breast.

"She bit me."

THE END.

NOW FOR A SNEAK-PEEK OF
COLD KEEP REQUITAL

Peace River

1970

The slew of televisions light up George's face as he watches the pair of convicts stick to the shadows, their jumpsuits an orange blur on the grainy screens.

He lifts the radio's receiver and holds the button down. "D-Block, you got some inmates out of their cells. Who did your rounds tonight?"

The speaker crackles and a voice calls back through the fuzzy band-waves. *Click.* "Relax, Officer Laundry, I'll give it a look. They aren't getting far."

"They're headed for the lobby."
Click. "I said relax, there's nowhere for them to go."

The escapees stop near the sealed exit at the end of the block and seemingly argue as one pushes against the door, the other pacing back and forth.

"Not sure where they think—"

An audible click somewhere on the dashboard of blinking lights and switches interjects and the door on screen pops open, flushing the monitor with the lobby's light pouring into the block. George lifts the receiver again. "D-Block, you idiots forgot to lock the damn door behind you! These goons are now in the lobby!

Click. "What are you smoking, Laundry? I sealed that door myself."

"Tell that to my CCTV, because I'm watching them head for shipping and receiving as we speak!"

Click. "Fuck me. I'm on my way. Just sit tight."

George scans the other screens, watching the guard climb down from his perch overlooking the block and descend the aluminum catwalks.

Click. "I'm a-comin'. No need to raise any alarms." He strolls past the escapee's empty cell and down the hall, coming to a halt as the door to the lobby slams in his face, sealing him in with the rest of the inmates. *Click.* "Hey! What's the big idea?"

"It wasn't me!" George flips the corresponding switch, toggling it on and off, the door refusing to yield to its command. Inches away, another flicks itself on, lighting up the small bulb labeled *Shipping & Receiving* above. "Oh for fuck's sake!" George flips it back, but the bulb stays lit. "What the hell is going on?" He looks up and adjusts the antenna on the television to the left, watching as the receiving door unlatches for the inmates and swings itself open. "Jesus. The system's gone haywire. Get in there!"

Click. "You're the one controlling the locks! Is this some kind of joke? It's not fucking funny!" The guard heaves on the door, trying desperately to break through after the men and George fumbles with the radio, turning its dial.

"We need backup in—" The needles jump on the band-wave display and the dial spins itself around, clicking through each channel, their static culminating into a sinister laugh. George hammers the box, desperate to silence the voice, then it dies all together. He looks back up at the screen to the left and follows the convicts to the next as they stop at the loading bay's overhead doors. A rattle pulls his attention back to the panel in front of him and another switch jiggles amongst the others, its red bulb flickering to life. "Oh no you don't!" He grabs it and squeezes, feeling it fight against his thumb. "I need backup in here!" he screams, knowing it will do little to alert anyone outside the stone room.

The switch digs into his flesh and forces itself into place with another click, releasing the door's hold on the other side of the prison, welcoming the convicts through. George runs to the intercom system hanging on the wall nearby and yells into it, flooding the entire complex with his voice as the men step out into the brisk night air. "You two, stop where you are!" He holds his breath, listening to his muffled voice peter out on the other side of the reinforced wall.

The inmates look up at the camera, their faces still too blurry to make out, then they wave goodbye and make for the gate.

"Bastards!" George clubs the wall with his fist, painting the stones red as he screams into the intercom. "Emergency. We've got—" A pop and shower of sparks explode from the box, throwing him to the ground. "Jesus!" He stands and runs from the room, falling down a set of stairs, tripping over himself twice and nearly dislocating his shoulder as he barges into the lobby, hot on their trail.

"George! Let me out of here!" the guard calls from behind D-block's door.

George fumbles with his mess of keys, but gives up, taking after the convicts through shipping and receiving, into the autumn night. "You there. Stop!" he shouts after the men as they step through the ajar front gate. He runs, drawing his club as sirens kick on and wash the courtyard with an anxious wail.

The watchtower's spotlights hum to life, but another electrical surge eviscerates their bulbs and douses the complex with an explosion of sparks, leaving nothing but darkness once more.

"Don't move. Stop!"

The gate groans and it begins to close inch by painful inch. "I said stop!" George slams into the riveted steel, nearly knocking himself unconscious as the only exit seals itself shut. He hammers the plates with his club, screaming out to the free men on the other side. "Get back here. Get back!" He collapses, breathlessly panting as the sirens take their turn to putter out and fail altogether. The complex falls into silence and George holds his breath, listening to the two men at large bicker on the other side.

"We should go back, Kota. See if he's okay."

"Are you insane? We gotta go, Eddie!"

Stay hungry for

COLD KEEP REQUITAL

JOIN THE NEWS-LETTER AT:
WWW.COLD-KEEP.COM

ACKNOWLEDGMENTS

I would like to thank all the wonderful people in my life that supported me throughout the making of Cold Keep Reprisal:

My loving wife for the countless nights of tolerating me being locked away in my office.

The Indigenous communities and its members surrounding my city for the words of encouragement and guidance when it came to crafting this story. The creatures in this story have been inaccurately depicted for too long in pop culture and Hollywood, and I wanted to do a small part in trying to set the legends straight.

The amazingly talented Kayla Kampbell for designing my cover. You have brought my book to the next level with your beautiful artwork.

The wonderful Danny Raye for editing my dumpster fire of a manuscript.

My amazing aunts, uncles, brother, and cousins whom the characters names and faces were based off of in this story.

Eddie, who I fondly remember from my childhood, but no longer know.

My beta readers, who made this book so much stronger than it could ever have been on my own: Claire, Ems, Darrell, Chelsea, Danny, Terra, Christie, and Elaine.

I thank Shawn C. Smallman for creating such an amazing resource in *Dangerous Spirits* that allowed me to accurately depict the antagonists of this book and write the legend right.

Harry McClintock for writing *In The Big Rock Candy Mountains.*

And last but not least, my loving father, mother, sister, brother, stepmother, Friends, and swath of animals I have running around my house.

Without each and every one of you, Cold Keep Reprisal would not have been possible. I love you all very much.

ABOUT THE AUTHOR

James Lurid is a Canadian born gentleman residing in Calgary, Alberta. When he is not writing he can be found rounding up his gaggle of pets, camping in his 1978 beast of a motor home, or relaxing with his wife while watching any-and-all things scary.
When the pandemic started, James decided the time was right to teach himself to write, and two years later out popped Cold Keep Reprisal.
His dream is what all writers want… to run away from the world and write in that coveted cabin in the woods! One day, cabin… One day…

Thank you so much for supporting me and my book, If you would like to help further, a review on Amazon goes a long way.